Kathy Little Bird

Titles by Benedict and Nancy Freedman

MRS. MIKE

THIS AND NO MORE

THE SPARK AND THE EXODUS

LOOTVILLE

TRESA

THE APPRENTICE BASTARD

CYCLONE OF SILENCE

THE SEARCH FOR JOYFUL

KATHY LITTLE BIRD

Titles by Nancy Freedman

JOSHUA SON OF NONE

THE IMMORTALS

PRIMA DONNA

THE SEVENTH STONE

SAPPHO THE TENTH MUSE

Kathy Little Bird

Benedict and Nancy Freedman

BERKLEY BOOKS, NEW YORK

THE BERKLEY PUBLISHING GROUP
Published by the Penguin Group
Penguin Group (USA) Inc.
375 Hudson Street, New York, New York 10014, USA
Penguin Group (Canada), 10 Alcorn Avenue, Toronto, Ontario M4V 3B2, Canada
(a division of Pearson Penguin Canada Inc.)
Penguin Books Ltd., 80 Strand, London WC2R 0RL, England
Penguin Group Ireland, 25 St. Stephen's Green, Dublin 2, Ireland (a division of Penguin Books Ltd.)
Penguin Group (Australia), 250 Camberwell Road, Camberwell, Victoria 3124, Australia
(a division of Pearson Australia Group Pty. Ltd.)
Penguin Books India Pvt. Ltd., 11 Community Centre, Panchsheel Park, New Delhi—110 017, India
Penguin Group (NZ), Cnr. Airborne and Rosedale Roads, Albany, Auckland 1310, New Zealand
(a division of Pearson New Zealand Ltd.)
Penguin Books (South Africa) (Pty.) Ltd., 24 Sturdee Avenue, Rosebank, Johannesburg 2196,
South Africa

Penguin Books Ltd., Registered Offices: 80 Strand, London WC2R 0RL, England

This book is an original publication of The Berkley Publishing Group.

Text design by Tiffany Estreicher.

First edition: December 2004

Library of Congress Cataloging-in-Publication Data

Freedman, Benedict.
Kathy Little Bird / Benedict and Nancy Freedman.—1st ed.
p. cm.
ISBN 0-425-20071-X
1. Cree Indians—Fiction. 2. Indian women—Fiction. 3. Women singers—Fiction. 4. Canada, Western—Fiction. I. Freedman, Nancy Mars. II. Title.
PS3511.R416K37 2004
813'.54—dc22 2004048997

PRINTED IN THE UNITED STATES OF AMERICA

10 9 8 7 6 5 4 3 2 1

To Johanna—who knew this book had to be written
To Deborah—who brought it the soul of music
To Michael—who writes in a language that encompasses all others
To Pat—a sister to us both

And our thanks to our editor, Susan Allison,
whose perception became part of the book.

And kudos for Claire, who brought
it all together.

PART ONE

Chapter One

I KICKED at the door. Every time Jason yelled I kicked. Every time Jellet's strap descended he yelled again, and I kicked again. I had worked myself up and began kicking in between times. Mum, from across the room, rushed over, took me by the arm and dragged me, still kicking, away from the door. She set me down on the kitchen stool, one restraining hand on my shoulder. "Stop that, Kathy. Your daddy will certainly hear you."

"I hate him." It came out in a flood of tears.

"Don't say that, Kathy. It isn't true."

"It is, it is. I hate him." I didn't see how this little room we were in could hold my hate, it wasn't big enough. The house wasn't big enough, or the world. Filled with my hate there wouldn't be room for anything else, not for people or cows or farms.

Mum was talking to me in that special voice she used to calm me down. "Jason has to be disciplined, Kathy. You know your daddy is a fair man."

"He isn't my daddy. And I'm glad he isn't."

"Shhh." Mum cast an anxious glance at the closed door from which the bellowing had somewhat subsided. She went on in a lowered tone. "All the more reason to be respectful. He took us in. Not many would do that. Every stitch we wear and every crumb we eat is his. You need to be grateful. And you need to get that temper of yours under control."

I looked at her defiantly a moment. But I was tired of the argument, and in an everyday, conversational voice said, "Okay. But I hate him."

The bathroom door opened and Jason came out, patterns of tears on his cheeks. He didn't catch anyone's eye, but slunk off to finish his breakfast in the kitchen. Daddy Jellet came out too. There was an air of satisfaction about him, a job-well-done kind of thing. Mum, who had argued against the beating, didn't seem angry with him, just resigned. I was the one who was angry, angry, angry.

I marshaled my other angers and lumped them in with this.

Why couldn't we play with other children and go to their houses? It had always been like that, but now that I was eight I asked why. At first Mum would only say we were different. We were Catholics but never went to church like other Catholics. We didn't speak to the Metis, although Mum was mixed blood, or the Anglicans, who considered themselves above us. And we certainly weren't like the Mennonites with their unpainted houses and benches pulled against the walls. They had nice flower boxes, always blooming, but I didn't like the way they dressed, the women in gray or black, with kerchiefs at their necks. The men were stiff and their whiskers were stiff. Even Mum referred to them as the "frozen chosen." They were big on shaking hands. They shook hands outside church and inside church, and they shook hands with whoever sat beside them in the pew. The thing they didn't do was smile, and they didn't laugh. They were formal and polite, and full of churchy customs. There were other families, outsiders like us, scattered around, but Jellet made no exceptions. "It isn't fair," I said in a loud voice, not looking at either grown-up.

"What's that?" Jellet's bushy eyebrows drew together and almost met.

"Run play," Mum said, and slid me off her lap. Even outside I could hear them. "I told you she'd be upset." That was Mum, and Daddy Jellet in an unpleasant hoarse rumble began blaming her for saddling him with so many kids that ate up every cent he brought home. I knew I was at the top of the list—Jellet was going on about my Austrian father, why hadn't she ever tapped him for child support? Mum didn't answer. She never answered this.

She'd told me the story though, many times. My father was interned as a prisoner of war. He was an officer on a German U-boat we'd sunk. He was fished out of the water, badly wounded. Mum was a nurse, and he was her patient. She nursed him back to health. They fell in love and married.

But, the way Mum tells it, they came from different worlds, and at war's end he went back to Europe. He never knew about me, never knew I was born. . . .

Why couldn't I have a real father in a real way? Why was I stuck with a word I hated—"adopted"? Mum told me over and over that "adopted" meant chosen. But I knew it meant I didn't belong.

"Daddy Jellet chose us, because he loved us."

I'd heard that all my life, but I didn't believe it. And I don't think she believed it either. That's why I'd get angry. Mum would take me on her lap then and whisper that she understood. She too was adopted.

Her face would soften in a gentle smile, and I'd hear once more the story of Mrs. Mike, Katherine Mary Flannigan, the person I, like my mum, was named for.

I walked along the road, kicking up dust. It had been sprayed with oil, but not recently, probably because it was the road to the res.

The First Nation Reserve was strictly off limits to me. They weren't "our kind" either, but a very particular friend of mine lived there. Elk Woman's government-built house was at the extreme edge of the compound. Outside it looked like all the others; inside there were herb bundles and bones hanging on the walls, and a large moose skull with dried tendons dangling from it. Elk Woman never closed the door and I could see the dark interior and Elk Woman herself, dimly. She had torn off a strand of tendon, which she used as thread. Her needle was a tin key saved from a can of beef and hammered out.

I stayed outside the door and announced myself by singing. Elk Woman liked it when I sang. She particularly liked the Mennonite song that was my favorite too. I threw back my head and sang into the room.

I am washed in the blood,
I am saved, saved, saved.

"Is it you, Skayo Little Bird?" She gave me a scrutinizing look as I entered, made her assessment and scowled. "Are you fighting with yourself again?"

"I guess so."

She pushed a ginger root toward me; there was a small pile of them on the table. She chewed on them for a while herself before spitting them out. I watched her work up a new supply of saliva and moisten the moose tendon again in preparation for rethreading. "What are you making?"

"I had this old horse blanket wasn't doing nobody any good, so I'm making a jacket out of it."

I nodded. Everyone made things out of other things. My dresses were stitched from pillowcases with holes in them, and an occasional flour sack in the same condition. "Waste not, want not" had been dinned into me since I was born.

Elk Woman yawned and put her sewing in a basket with an apron destined to become a dishtowel. She stretched, took out her cob pipe, and lit up. I watched as she puffed.

"Can I try?"

Without a word she handed the pipe across to me. It had a well-chewed stem. I went out on the porch to spit the last of the ginger root before placing the pipe between my teeth.

Elk Woman joined me, sitting on the step beside me, and nodded approval as I inhaled. For a while we passed the pipe back and forth in a companionable manner. "Now you tell me why you come, Little Bird. That stepfather of yours making problems again?"

"I hate him."

Elk Woman considered this, rocking back and forth communing with herself. Then she said, "Don't step on his shadow and he won't step on yours."

"I hate his shadow too."

"That's because you're at war with yourself. Don't be at war with yourself, Little Bird."

"I can't help it." I got up. How could I explain to her that I didn't want to be cured of hating him? I wanted to hate him, so I just said, "I got to be going." Then I remembered and sat down. Elk Woman looked at me, her question on her face.

"I was going to visit Abram, but I can't. I'm mad at him."

"Him too?"

"Yep."

"You need to make a study of shadows, Little Bird."

"Why? Are they magic?"

"Everything that is older than time is magic."

"What kinds of magic do the Cree have?"

"Let's see." She blew a smoke ring into space. We sat and watched, and then she blew another. "Well, there is singing.

Singing is older even than speaking. Before there were people, wind sang, thunder sang, grass whistled, owls called, wolves howled, and birds warbled just like you. Come to our ceremonies sometime, and you'll hear how we listen to the singing world, and sing back."

"Can anything be sung?"

"Anything."

"Anyone?"

"Anyone."

"Even a person?"

"Especially a person."

"Even me? Can you sing me?"

"I can sing you head to toe, and it will be a true singing. But because it's true you won't like it."

"I don't care. Sing it anyway."

I was so excited that I got up and sat on her lap so I could feel the breath of the song as it came out of her.

Elk Woman closed her eyes. She drummed with her fingers on the arms of the chair, at first softly and steadily, then in sudden bursts of hard raps. Her song lay far back in her throat, with lots of sobbing and a rolling, pounding beat. Spurts of angry notes got in the way of a pretty little tune, blocked it off at every turn.

"No, no," I cried. "That's not me." I took a giant breath and began to sing the tune the way it should go. I sang at the top of my voice so as to drown out the cries and shouts that were wrecking it. I took a giant breath.

Elk Woman's eyes brightened and she sang her version

stubbornly back at me. I jumped off her lap and faced her, so I could outsing her.

And I did. I sang her into the ground. Elk Woman became quiet, and my song rang out, pure and beautiful. It filled the room. That was me, that was the way I should be sung.

When I stopped, Elk Woman examined her pipe and relit it. "You're right, Little Bird, that's how you could be, how you were meant to be. But you're not there yet. Not by a long shot."

▼ ▲ ▼

I LEFT for choir practice. Officially it was choir practice for the Mennonites. But I had my own place outside the window by the soprano section. We practiced every Wednesday afternoon and Sunday mornings before the service and after Sunday school. That's how I met Abram. He was the P.K., preacher's kid. He liked to duck out and miss as many Bible lessons as he could.

By the time I got there, Pentateuch class was over and Early Prophets just begun, because there was Abram throwing his buck knife so the blade hit and shivered in the dirt. Nimety-peg, I was good at it too. "Can I have a turn?" I asked, coming up to him.

He squinted at me, blond hair in his eyes. "I thought you were mad at me."

"That was yesterday."

"Praise the Lord." He said that so many times he didn't know he was saying it.

"Elk Woman sang me today."

"She what?"

"You know, sang me. Sang how I am. I've got too many yells and ugly notes. But I can cure it with shadows."

"Shadows? That's crazy. You shouldn't put any faith in that stuff. My father says Indian beliefs are nothing but errant superstition."

"Not when they're Elk Woman's beliefs."

He scoffed at that. "You can't put an Indian up against an anointed preacher."

"You can if it's Elk Woman, she talks to the wind." I pulled the knife out of the dirt and threw it left-handed. It didn't stick, but fell over. I tried again, same deal. At home I got my knuckles slapped whenever I used my left hand. They were changing me into a right-handed person. I wondered who this person who didn't have a temper and who did everything with her right hand would be. I wondered if I'd like her. "Are those your books?" I asked. There were two of them lying on the ground. "Hymnbooks?" I picked them up and saw right away they weren't.

"They're Bibles. One is the regular Bible and the other is the version they hand out to us kids."

"What's the difference?"

"One's got all the juicy stuff deleted out of it. So I'm looking up those parts they left out."

"Is it worth going to all that trouble?"

"You better believe it."

"If you do things like that, Abram, how do you ever expect to receive the call?"

"I don't. I gave up on it." He said this in a blustery way,

but I could tell he was worried because he added an explanation. "Giving testimony, having everybody pray over me . . . no way I'm going to do that."

I considered this. "I suppose you have to be super good before you receive an altar call."

Abram nodded. "For a while I made an effort, but in one of my father's sermons it slipped out that holy scripture contains six hundred and thirteen commandments. That's when I gave up."

"Well, if you're not going to believe in the Mennonite way—try Elk Woman's and trade shadows with me."

He hesitated. "Do you know how to do it?"

"I know you have to believe."

"What exactly?"

"That's easy, that when our shadows blend together we are made one. Kind of like blood brothers, only we don't have to cut ourselves."

"So let's do it. My shadow is right here, stretched out on the pavement."

"Don't move!" In three hops I was beside him; hopping gave it more emphasis, more importance. "Watch this!" With a final leap I landed almost on top of him and our shadows merged. "Now SING!"

In the blood, blood, blood,
We are one, one, one!

"That isn't Indian," he objected, recognizing it.

"I haven't finished." I closed my eyes. "I call on the spirit of all things, flowers, plants, animals, mountains, and waters to witness." I peered through my lashes and lo and behold—a spinning world of dazzling colors, its brightness so intense it blinded me.

I seized Abram's arm. "Look at the sun with your eyes closed."

"Make up your mind, do I close my eyes or look at the sun?"

"Both. Quick, while the magic is jiggling around. Do you see it? A bright wheel of pure light and splashes of color. Do you, Abram?"

"Praise the Lord," he said.

The rapture increased and the brightness. The Great Manitou by this token acknowledged our two shadows as one. I began to dance, and Abram, throwing his arms wide, started singing psalms.

A deep, resonant strain of music flowed from the magic wheel, overpowering his voice. It was a second before I realized it came from the church.

The peal of the organ and the thunder of the choir reached us through the open window. I knew the routine by heart. The congregation knelt for the prayers and stood for the blessing. They were standing now.

Worship service was over and the girls were lining up on their side of the chapel. I stood straight and prepared to sing. Nothing could compare with singing, not even Abram, or trading shadows, or the scooter I saw in the hardware store window. Sounds came together in my head, wonderful, soaring, pulling me out of myself. The sound was often there even when I was quiet, and then I just listened to it. But it was best when I threw back my head and let the melody into the world, carrying me with it.

In the hour of pain and anguish,
In the hour when death is near,
Suffer not my soul to languish,
Suffer not my soul to fear.
I am washed in the blood,
I am saved, saved, saved.

I lived for this hour of choir practice twice weekly. It didn't matter to me that I stood outside. The only thing that mattered was the music.

Chapter Two

TIME collided, years of it, and the spring I was fifteen Mum wasn't well. The chores I had assisted at were now mainly my responsibility. Home schooling was pretty much a thing of the past, although we made a pretense of it. Mum still went over the papers I wrote, correcting spelling and punctuation. She claimed I was a wild speller. I put in all the letters, but not always in the right order. I was better at mathematics, but Mum was a whiz. She had been at the top of her class in nursing school. While she told me stories of the hospital, my hands were busy with mason jars, paraffin tops, and the wide rubber ring that went around the rims.

Sometimes it was fun. I liked straining blackberries though muslin. Once they were sugared, the boys couldn't wait for it to turn into preserves, but pestered me for a taste.

Jason at thirteen took after Mum; he always asked if he could have some. Morrie didn't ask, he took. If he was caught, he lied. If the lie was found out, he sulked.

Morrie was a Jellet. He got his handsome Cree looks from Mum, but he was mostly Jellet. He had some good traits, though. When he took things from the larder, he always shared with Jason. And when I was at my wits' end what to do about him, he'd bring me presents of stuff he'd pinched.

My work didn't end with straining blackberries. There was the wash to do and meals to help with. The wash was done on a waffle scrub board with lumps of homemade carbolic soap. The boys tended the goat and pulled weeds in the vegetable garden. Jellet slept all day and after supper went off to the pub. He kept telling Jason it would pass to him some day, just as Jellet himself had inherited it from his father. The Eight Bells gave him a chance to get away. I don't think he was fond of any of us, not even Mum, because, as he said over and over, she'd saddled him with us kids. The pub, that's where his life was.

The Eight Bells was strictly off limits. On the few occasions when I'd walked into town, I plastered my face against the glass and peered in. There was nothing to see, a lot of tables and upended chairs. Jellet didn't get home until one or two in the morning, and he slept in. The family was careful not to wake him. If that happened he'd come roaring out, and whichever boy he caught got a licking. Being nearly grown by now and a girl, I was immune.

Once the evening meal was over, Jellet consulted his watch, declared he was late, and left for the pub. Mum took the opportunity to lie down. I'm sure he had no idea there was anything wrong. She didn't want him to know and he didn't. She kept the door to her bedroom open so we could talk as I did the dishes.

Now that I was older Mum told me more about my real father. His name was Erich von Kerll. I'd known that. He was Austrian. I'd known that too, and even looked up Austria on the world map in the library.

The library was one of Abram's special places. It wasn't one of mine. By now I'm sure Abram had read every volume in the library. "Bookworm," I'd say under my breath. But then he'd tell me some interesting fact. One interesting fact was that Navajos were code-talkers in the signal corps during the war. The Germans never figured out what they were saying. They didn't know it was a language; they thought it was a new code.

When Abram took out books on World War II, I looked up *wolf pack, U-boat, enemy alien.* I worried about my father having been a Nazi, and asked Mum about it. She countered with what it meant to be an officer in the German navy. "He was never a Nazi. He was second in command of the U-186 when it crossed the Atlantic, raided the coast of Nova Scotia, and got all the way up the St. Lawrence to Montreal."

I looked at her in amazement; she sounded almost proud.

She caught my glance and flushed. "Anyway, eventually they were sunk by a British destroyer. I tell you this about your father, Kathy, so you'll know he was a brave man and a fine officer . . ."

"In Hitler's navy," I added.

"Austria itself was overrun and declared a province of the Third Reich. And he came from a naval family. You should have seen him, Kathy; tall, blond, and his eyes were gray."

"It's embarrassing that my father fought on the wrong side."

"Please be grown up about this, Kathy. It was that or a firing squad."

I plunged my hands deeper into the sudsy water. "I do want to know about him."

"He went to sea in forty-one. The U-boats owned the North Atlantic in those days. For months no Allied shipping got through their patrol. It extended all the way to Iceland. Then we started using convoys and there were tremendous sea battles. Your father was found floating in waves of oil, holding onto some wreckage. Six hours was the most they lasted in those waters. He was brought in suffering hypothermia and third-degree burns."

"And you fell in love," I said, wiping an already dry bowl.

"Not straight away. At first he was just a patient. In fact, I didn't want him assigned to me, being an enemy and all." Mum coughed and asked for a glass of water. As I handed it to her she motioned toward the old bureau in the corner of the bedroom. "Bottom drawer," she said hoarsely.

The bottom drawer was where she kept her Bible. I picked it up and brought it to her. A small scroll of paper had been tucked between the pages, along with several documents. "Our marriage certificate, your birth certificate, and . . . a copy of the annulment."

"What happened? Are you sure it wasn't because you got pregnant?"

"I've told you that he didn't know about you. But I think now he should. He belongs to an aristocratic family with wealth and influence. As a daughter you have a claim, it's your birthright."

"I don't want anything that's his."

"Don't be so quick to judge, Kathy. You already have one gift from him."

I looked at her questioningly.

"Your music. Music was part of him too. He had a sweet warm baritone. Many of the songs I sang when you were little—remember? 'Wenn i komm.' And 'Die Lorelei.' I learned them from Erich."

This shook me. But I wouldn't give up the resentment I felt. "If it wasn't me that made him leave, what was it?"

"I wouldn't go back to Austria with him. It was that simple."

"But why? Why wouldn't you?"

Mum turned this over in her mind before answering. "The war did strange things. It made you grab what life held out to you. And that's what I did without thinking too much about it. Then when peace came it brought a different reality. His family owned a chateau on the Bodensee. They entertained, held soirees, gave elaborate dinners. An Indian wife, Kathy?"

"Why not?"

She smiled. "Maybe now, in this generation. But I doubt

it. Europe is not as egalitarian as we are on this continent, and even here—"

"Maybe I will show up on his doorstep sometime. It might be fun." With my blond hair and fair complexion no one would suspect I was almost half Cree. I did have my Mum's eyes, though; they didn't go with my face, they were coal black and stormy. They held a hint. They told a tale.

▼ ▲ ▼

WHEN summer came Mum was better, and I wasn't needed around the house much. There was a stream by Abram's house, and we spent a lot of time on our bellies shooting at tin cans floating down. We took turns with Jellet's BB gun. He kept it in the hall closet and the pellets in the top drawer of the chiffonier. At first Abram regarded the gun with true Mennonite horror, but once he got used to the kick it gave your shoulder he broke as many bottles and pinged as many cans as I did.

But there were long stretches of time when nothing floated down the stream. And these were the times Abram brought to my attention the odd bits of knowledge he delighted in. For instance, the Sargasso Sea. I didn't know there was such a sea. "It's a body of water that lies like a huge lake in the middle of the Atlantic Ocean where the Gulf Stream flows into the colder waters coming from the north. It gets the name Sargasso from the grass that covers the surface of the water. But in spite of this kelplike covering, the area is a desert."

"How can water be a desert?" I objected.

"A desert is where life is extinguished. There are no fish, no seals, no crustacea, no birdlife."

"A desert of water," I marveled.

"Right. And this desert is seven miles deep."

"Seven miles of watery desert," I echoed, imagining seven miles of straight-down misery.

That very night Jellet was waylaid by a couple of toughs he had thrown out of his bar, and given a bad beating. He looked awful, like something from the bottom of the Sargasso. He asked Mum to manage the bar for one night. I went along in case she needed backup, and as a result soon had an exciting story to tell Abram.

The patrons were Eight Bells regulars, a rough-and-ready sort. Because they were regulars and knew I was the owner's daughter, they tended, after their first amazement at seeing females on the premises, to be respectful. Mum was Mrs. Jellet and I was Missy. They kept their raucous stories low key and their feet off the tables. There were First Nation guys too, but they sat by themselves, and were serious drinkers. Mum served at the bar and I brought orders to the tables.

It was a different experience for me, stepping into an all-male world of booming laughs and guttural curses I couldn't quite hear. It was an atmosphere of high good humor and companionship. Something a solitary girl like myself knew nothing of. One of the men stopped me as I went by his table. "Aren't you the kid that stands outside the Mennonite church singing?"

"Yes, sometimes." I was embarrassed to admit it.

"Well, how about you giving us a tune?"

"You mean now . . . here?" I was flustered, but my heart beat wildly at the prospect. I glanced at Mum; fortunately she was busy. So standing where I was, without any additional encouragement, I launched into:

I am washed in the blood,
I am saved, saved, saved.

Out of the corner of my eye I could see Mum's hands frozen midair. No one else moved either. The expressions on the faces turned toward me ranged from stupefaction to grins of pleasure. My voice soared with melody one second and reverberated with the soul's sin and suffering the next. A tear rolled down the cheek of one of the drunks at the bar. I had an audience. I'd never had one before. It was intoxicating. I was carried away.

They were carried away.

"Sing!" I called out as I came to the chorus.

Voices joined mine. "Saved, saved, saved," they sang.

It was glorious.

When the hymn was over there was foot-stomping applause, and cries for more. I was about to sing one of Elk Woman's chants, but Mum found a lot of things for me to do. She shoved a dishtowel into my hands and set me to wiping glasses. "Such an exhibition," she said under her breath, "I've never seen in my life."

"But didn't you think there was something wonderful about it too?"

"Kathy, Kathy, what am I going to do with you?"

"Let me sing another song?" I suggested.

"Certainly not."

As we walked back home that night with an escort of three, no two of which would trust the third, she said pointedly, "I wouldn't mention tonight's goings-on to your father."

▼ ▲ ▼

THE next day, Sunday, I stationed myself outside the little white church and waited impatiently for Bible class to be over. Abram had to hear of my debut and what a great success I was and how unfair Mum had been.

"She isn't going to take me with her tonight," I complained.

Abram said mildly that Mum was right. "That's a rough place, Kathy. You don't belong there."

Two things were wrong with this reply. One was his lecturing tone. The other, he wasn't as excited as he should have been about my singing. So I answered snappishly. "I belong wherever I want to belong. You're just a narrow, psalm-singing know-nothing, who has never put the purity of your precious soul in danger by going to a pub and having a pint. So what do you know about anything?" I made a long face at him and pulled down the corners of my eyes.

Instead of laughing as he usually did when I put on my Mennonite face, he was quiet and seemed full of hurt.

I was instantly ashamed of acting like a child. "What's wrong, Abram? You look low-hearted."

He didn't answer at once. When he did, it was to say, "The time came."

I thought a moment, "Does that mean . . . ?"

"Yes."

I nodded. Abram had just turned seventeen, the traditional time to come forward, kneel before the altar of God, and offer his soul in His service.

"They prayed for me, Kathy, the whole congregation. It was awful. I just sat there. I've humiliated my father, and Mother was crying. I've gone against their wishes, Kathy. They feel I've gone against God's as well. A preacher's son always receives the altar call."

"Couldn't you pretend?"

"About a thing like that?" His tone implied shock that I should suggest such a thing.

"You're right," I said hastily, "it's not worth risking hellfire for."

"One owes a certain integrity to oneself," he said with dignity, "to who you are."

I agreed with him, and put it as fairly as I could. "I think we've started to know ourselves, Abram. At least I know what I want to do. Ever since I sang at the Eight Bells, I've known. *Sing*. I want to sing, Abram. Sing to lots of people."

"That's crazy."

"Maybe. But it's what I want. And you want to ask questions and look for answers. We can't do that here in St. Alban's. Oh Abram, there's a world out there. That's where we belong."

"You're only fifteen," he said slowly.

"But I'm experienced at running away. I ran away all the time when I was a kid." I remember preparing for my escapades by making myself a large peanut butter and jelly sandwich. It didn't bother me that the grown-ups watched. I didn't try to conceal my intentions. I wrapped up my sandwich and put on my sun hat, and letting the screen door bang behind me, walked into the unknown with a light heart.

I never crossed Macdonald's field. I wasn't allowed to.

Whenever I ran away, I stuck to the road. It was easy to pick me up and take me home.

Mum reasoned with me. She told me it made her sad when I ran away from her.

"You can come too," I told her.

She laughed and hugged me.

Jellet didn't laugh. He got fed up with my running away, and buckled me into the backyard clothesline with a dog leash and padlock. That didn't stop me from stocking up with another peanut butter and jelly sandwich when the urge for freedom overcame me next.

I turned to Abram, who was revolving it all in his mind.

I knew Abram, and I knew he thought in large, slow arcs. To prompt him I demanded, "So, are you going to say it or am I?"

"You think we should run off? Go away?"

"Don't you?"

"We've no money. But it's something to work toward and plan for."

"By the time we have the money Mum will be well. We have to wait till then anyway."

"I think you should plan on finishing high school. That gives us a two-year time frame."

I knew he was right, but his acceptance of the situation infuriated me. I hate recognizing the inevitable, let alone bowing to it.

"Damn," I said. That got his attention. "You know what I wish, Abram? That sometime you'd just go for it and hang the consequences."

Again his smile held hurt. "I wish I would too."

"All right, let's practice."

"Practice what?"

"Practice *doing,* the heck with consequences. Are you game?"

"All right. Sure."

"Then come on."

I knew he was going to ask where, so I cut him off. "No questions. Just doing. Remember?"

He grinned.

Some people look worse when they grin—not Abram. He was especially cute-looking when he grinned. I took him to Jellet's pub. I'd discovered a window at the back in the storage shed that was open a crack. "Give me a boost."

He did and I made a grab for the ledge. I jimmied the window down farther and crawled through, then fumbled for a light.

Abram landed with a jar beside me. "Judas Priest!" That was his most outrageous curse. He had ripped the sleeve of his shirt on a nail.

"Why don't you just say 'damn' and get it over with?"

"I can't do that."

"What's the matter with 'damn'?"

"Well, if you think about it, you're damning whatever or whoever you're angry at to hell. You don't want to do that."

"But Abram, it was a nail."

"It could be the beginning of a habit. Next time it might be a creature or a person."

"Oh Abram," I said, although I knew it did no good, it was like talking to a wall. "Nobody takes these things literally. It's just a way of talking."

"What good is speech if it doesn't mean what it says?"

"Judas Priest, Abram, do you have to be so Judas Priest logical?"

He looked around. "What are we doing here anyway?"

The light was unhooded and revealed rows of Big Rock Lager and another stack of cans labeled Alberta Gold Beer. There was a keg of draft beer and something called Warthog. "We're going to get drunk," I announced.

Abram bit his lips over the protest that was forming. He crossed to the Alberta Gold and opened two cans. "Here goes nothing."

We clinked cans. After the first sip I asked, "Do you like it?"

He claimed he did, and after a while you didn't really care what it tasted like.

I made a stab at singing Abram. I'd tried for years. I'd get one part, only to have another part slip away. That's what happened this time.

"What are you singing?" Abram asked.

"None of your business."

When we finished the second can we couldn't get back out the window. I didn't mind. It was a nice storeroom, and Abram started confiding in me, telling me that his mind kept poking holes in his faith. "If I'd been in that rickety boat with Jesus and Thomas on the Dead Sea I couldn't have walked on water either. I'd know I was going to sink."

"That's because you've got good sense," I told him.

"No, it's the same thing that keeps me from accepting that God is calling me to the church. I don't know how to believe. I want to, but I can't. It's a failing in me."

He looked so miserable that I resisted an impulse to comfort him, and instead spoke briskly. "What about those who are called? Why are they so sure? Do they hear God's voice like you hear a person talking? Or maybe hear it in their own heads? I mean—how?"

"It's simple, fundamental. You know in your whole being."

Abram worried a lot about his differences with the believing church. He thought it might be traced to a man of his house and name who lived in Holland four hundred years ago. Dirk Willems was, along with the pastor of his church, accused of heresy. They fled over ice with their enemies at their heels. The ice grew thin under them and the pastor fell through. Dirk went back and pulled him out. As a consequence, he was captured and burned at the stake by the Inquisitors.

"You'd do exactly the same thing," I accused him. "You'd go back, pull the guy out of the ice, and be burned at the stake."

"You think so?" Pleasure that was almost bliss suffused his face.

"Because you're dumb, dumb, dumb!"

Abram laughed at this. "I have the feeling my father would like to see me burn in hellfire for the questions I ask. I can't accept without questions, Kathy."

"Well, there you are. It's just what I said. You've got to question, and I've got to sing." I told him again what it was like. "My singing held them like it was a spell I'd put on them, and on me too. It's magic, Abram. Elk Woman told me that years ago, and it's true."

Abram let go of his problem and considered mine. That was one of the things I liked about him. However, I didn't think much of his advice. People were always giving me advice, and I didn't think much of any of it.

"The singing part," he was saying, "is okay. But you know yourself, Kathy, a pub is no place for a girl like you. It's worldly and ungodly."

"Oh, go dunk yourself in the river. You might as well. You're holier than an old sock."

"If I were, I wouldn't be here drinking beer. Besides, like I said, singing in a choir, I can see that."

"Music connects with everything around you," I agreed dreamily.

Abram nodded, "Praise the Lord."

He didn't know he'd said it. It was like when you write a sentence you just naturally put a period to it and don't even notice.

A drifting kind of light-headedness came over me, and half-formed ideas began tumbling out. I didn't listen to them because . . .

Abram put his arm around me. He'd never done that before. Then he kissed me. I liked being kissed. I wished he'd do it again, but instead he went for the window and this time made it.

Chapter Three

I DIDN'T see Abram for a while because Mum was sicker than usual, and I was once again in charge of the house. That didn't prevent me from thinking about him. I had serious doubts as to whether he could make our plan happen. In spite of this decidedly major defect, Abram had a lot of things going for him. For one, he didn't think I should change from being a lefty. He thought a person should be what they were.

Abram was a big influence on me. I never let him know this. And I never tried to be like him either. I knew it was no use. It simply wasn't in me. But I respected his ways—with spiders, for instance. I never had any use for spiders. If I saw one I'd go out of my way to step on it or bash it. Abram felt differently. "They're one of God's creatures," he told me, as he carefully cupped a spider in a leaf or a handkerchief and carried it to some place he felt would be favorable to spiders. He did that with any bug or insect. I don't think his brethren in Christ taught him this. I think they squashed as many spiders as I did. No, it was Abram, it was the way he was.

Most of my information about the world came from him, and he got it from library books. Strictly speaking, he wasn't supposed to read anything but holy scripture because the elders told him that all knowledge was contained in the Good Book. Abram himself said that was probably true when God shaped the world, but a lot had happened and a lot of people had reshaped it since. Also, according to Abram, man hadn't interpreted God's word too well. Take lightning. It wasn't God's wrath emanating from the heavens as his father preached, because the St. Alban's public library stamp was on a volume that explained lightning as coming from the ground. Abram thought that was important to know. "You live in the world, and you should know how it works."

The rock upon which Mum founded her home schooling was partly that same library, partly her own background as a wartime nurse and the rigorous courses she'd taken at the Sisters of Charity, but even more the homespun wisdom of someone I'd heard about all my life, Mrs. Mike. She had taken my Mum in when she was a baby, and she and her sergeant husband raised her and imparted lots of good, old-fashioned ideas like—never give in to a man until you've got a preacher and a ring. It was things like this that got passed along to me.

Mum said it was more than Mrs. Mike's fundamental sense of goodness and fairness, it was the way she was—spunky and high-spirited, yet always instinctively on the side of the underdog. Why did she choose Oh Be Joyful from the mission in the first place? She was the one in trouble, an older girl sent to sit on a bench in punishment row along with the little kids. Oh Be Joyful, my Mum's mum, was the one who didn't fit in, the one they couldn't control. It was typical of Mrs. Mike to stand up for her.

"That's the way she was, and that's why I'm 'Kathy' and you're 'Kathy.' It's a proud name, and you must try to live up to it. You see, when you live in Alberta as we do, there's a lot to contend with. But think how it was in those days—no trains penetrated this far, there were only dogsleds, and the telegraph lines were always down. As for paved highways, forget it. The Indians used to say, 'It's a good land for men and dogs, but hard on women and horses.' It was hard for Mrs. Mike, but it held all the important things."

"And what are they?" I'd ask.

"They're different for different people. You've got to discover yours for yourself, Kathy."

I took that as a challenge to grow up.

But I didn't think I would grow up until Abram and I ran away. That's when I'd start to live my life.

An uneasy feeling nagged at me, however. I felt as if I were becalmed in the Sargasso Sea. Nothing moved or was likely to move. I was entangled in seaweed, mosses, and kelp beds, helpless, drifting, going nowhere.

I attempted to fight this feeling, but it persisted, and one day when Abram and I were stretched out by the stream, leaning on our elbows and taking aim along our jawline with Jellet's BB gun, I came out with it.

"Abram," I said, putting the gun down, "I've got to know. How much money have you saved? Please, tell me it's a lot."

Abram looked uncomfortable. "I raked leaves for Mrs. Pringle, but she didn't pay hardly anything. Then I helped out in the drugstore when Mr. Stalling's wife was sick. But she got better. . . ."

"I don't want to hear your biography. Just tell me the dollar amount."

"Thirty-five bucks."

"Oh, Abram." His words were confirmation of my fears. "That's nothing. We could eat maybe for three days, but what about sleeping? We'd have to hide in barns and be on the lookout for dogs." I jumped up, wrapped the gun in the pieces of flannel it was kept in, and hid it in the bowl of the old oak so I wouldn't have to bother with it for a while.

We started to walk, past farmland, through fields, into woods where the sun filtering through branches created patterns of light.

"I'm sorry, Kathy."

I saw that he was. I saw that he had disappointed himself too.

"I haven't been able to put anything by either." We walked on in silence. "I can't go anyway," I said suddenly.

He stopped where he was. "But—"

"I know. It was never practical. It was a dream, a Cree dream, and we believed it for a while."

Abram thrust out his chin, the way he did when he was determined. "I can make it happen."

"I don't think so. It's Mum. She isn't well."

"I'm glad you told me. I'll pray for her."

I squeezed his hand. Abram would pray for her with a wonderful purity of purpose, but it wouldn't do away with the small, hard kernel of fear in me.

▼ ▲ ▼

WINTER came and deepened. Snow piled into drifts and on sunny days there was the sound of icicles dripping from the eaves and porch rails. I took on more and more of Mum's tasks. Mum *now* and my memory of Mum didn't blend easily. When I looked at her I saw her as she had been, always moving, doing things that nobody noticed or thanked her for, but that made the house run. The house itself had the clean smell of soap when she was in charge of things. Now that it was up to me I began to see what she had done, and to wonder how she found time to teach us into the bargain. While Jason, Morrie, and I did sums and essays, she supervised with mending in her lap, or her hands might be busy canning, pickling, and preserving.

I knew this was not going to be my life. Yet I only remember Mum as happy.

"Not happy," she would correct me, "joyful."

Joyful was her Cree name. And she lived up to it. She

laughed, made little jokes, told stories, all the while keeping an eye on us. Then one by one she gave up things that only months ago she had done without effort.

To escape thinking about it, I took to singing everyone. Mum was a slender, crisp melody, with little runs for the joy she put into things. Jason was a boisterous refrain, light and good-hearted. Morrie of course was a hop, skip, and a jump up and down the scale. And Jellet a lot of bombast.

It was Abram I had trouble with. I did him as a kind of gospel hymn, but that was only part of Abram. Anyway, it got me through the winter. I also tried slipping into the old dreams about my Austrian father. When I was little I'd imagined him as living in a castle on top of a hill, with hunting dogs at his feet. He'd come for me of course, and the castle would belong to me then, and the dogs. As I grew older that dream faded from its unlikeliness.

Spring went by too fast and summer was brief, as it always is here. I'd counted on warm days to get Mum well. They were here but didn't seem to help. I was as housebound as in the winter with the Sargasso Sea closing about me. It was almost impossible for me to get away, because if I didn't do the chores, Mum would. So I stayed close, only seeing Abram once or twice. We laughed about the plans we'd had and said what children we had been. I think he felt shy with me, and for some reason I did with him.

I hated to see fall come that year. I had no dreams to pull around me, and I was afraid of another long white silence. Cabin fever, Mum called it. But it was on account of her that

I dreaded it. She slept a lot during the day and coughed most of the night. Her movements slowed, so that one felt her think about doing something before asking it of her body. I didn't want to sing her anymore because the little runs and trills weren't there.

There was no holding back Alberta's climate. Housebound most of the time, there was nothing for it but to resurrect the old fantasy world. The one I liked to relive was when my father came back. He got lonesome for Mum and wanted to be with her again.

And there was I, a daughter he didn't know he had. In some of these daydreams I rushed into his arms and he hugged and kissed me, and said he would never go away again. Sometimes he'd pack us up, Mum and me, and take us back to Austria. Just for a visit of course. It wasn't a castle anymore, but a nice snug house. He taught me to sail on the Bodensee. We hiked forest trails and searched for sprigs of edelweiss. He loved me so much that he wanted me to stay with him forever.

Observing me, Mum would frequently say, "You're so quiet, Kathy. What are you thinking?"

I'd laugh and shake my head—out loud it would sound stupid.

Snow gusted against the house, blown high by wind. Wolves howled. In mockery I sang back at them. I sang the quiet, I sang the storms. I didn't sing Abram anymore. I didn't know him as well as I had. When I was fifteen I had known him. When I was eight I'd known him best of all. Now that I was seventeen I didn't know him at all.

Warm winds, springtime chinook. I began to think it would be all right, that the family had made it through another year.

With the thaw came comforting buds, light new foliage, and Elk Woman. Saskatoon berry jam, freshly baked bread, stalks of wild asparagus. She took to coming by with these and other gifts produced from her voluminous skirt. She would look around for the pail in which she made tea, start the water boiling, draw up a chair, and sit with Mum. They were old friends. They had gone to school together, and she had given my Mum a wolf tail to remind her she belonged to the First Nation people. Elk Woman always slipped a small packet of herbs under Mum's pillow. "Good medicine." Mum would smile and say she thought the last one had helped her. I thought that was good of Mum, being a nurse, to pretend so outrageously for Elk Woman.

One day, a bright, sunny, blue-sky day, Elk Woman motioned me to the porch. "You're a strong girl, Kathy. And you've strength in you that you don't know about yet."

I had an intimation that I wouldn't like this conversation. I didn't want to hear what Elk Woman was about to say.

"Mum feels better today. She sat up in the rocker for a while. Now that the weather has changed . . ."

"My little bird, Loki the Trickster has made up this dream for you. I, your friend, tell you your mother makes the long canoe trip."

The top of my head was blown off, as though Jellet had aimed his shotgun at me and pressed the trigger. "Get off this porch," I spoke quite steadily, looking Elk Woman in the eye. "My dad's asleep in the back bedroom. He doesn't allow Indians on our porch. I'll wake him up and he'll run you off."

"Oh little bird," Elk Woman said sadly, "don't pull away from your friends in bad times."

I threw my arms around her. She was a power woman, a wind shifter. "God won't let her die, will He?"

"When you come to the end of your life, you got to die."

"But she's not at the end."

"The best you can do for her, Little Bird, is to let her know you'll be all right. It's you she's worried about."

I looked at her hard, trying to see into her. "Why should she worry about me?" I asked. "I'm grown up."

She returned my glance speculatively, as though testing the validity of my statement, then said, "Have you talked to your brother?"

"To Jas? No. I can't. I can't talk to him, not about Mum."

"You should. More important than giving him dinner, is to set his soul right."

"I can't do it."

"There's no one else," Elk Woman said practically. "Now go in and see does your mother need you."

I looked at Mum with Elk Woman's eyes and saw an emaciated woman, her usually glowing copper skin a faded yellow, her face dominated by eyes. The circles under them were like the frame of a picture setting them apart, making them alive.

Mum must have heard me come in, because she asked, "Has Elk Woman been talking to you?"

I nodded.

"Jas is almost grown. A big boy. Jas will fall on his feet, like a cat. Jas will be all right. And Morrie won't remember—" The word *me* trembled her lips, but she didn't utter it. Her voice faltered like a toy that's overwound and starts up again. "And you, Kathy, music. Music is what you're about." She had tired herself, and signed that she couldn't talk any more.

I sat and rocked and waited. After a while her voice came again. "I've been saving up, Kathy. A present. Jas has the money for it. It was to be a surprise for your birthday. But I want to see you with it. It's at the pawnshop, a guitar. Go with Jason into town and get it."

A guitar. How thrilled I would have been even yesterday. Now it was an inheritance, like the reading of a will. But Mum was smiling, anticipating my pleasure. I managed a smile too and went to find Jas.

He was out back checking his polliwogs, waiting for them to become frogs. One thing I liked about Jas, eventually he returned the creatures to where he found them. I think he picked that up from Abram. Not that Abram ever preached to anyone. But Jas noticed the way he did things, and did them that way too.

"Mum wants us to get the guitar."

"Okay." He disappeared to retrieve the money from some secret place. The bills were pretty dirty, but still legal tender, as they say. "How come you get to have it now?" he asked. "It's not your birthday yet."

"She wants me to have it now."

"Because she's dying, right?"

"Jas, if you cry I'll never forgive you."

"Who's crying?"

I reached out and took his hand. I know I shouldn't have favorites, but he was my favorite brother. Morrie played tearing-around games and practiced for the minor leagues in the backyard. He'd miss Mum, but she was right, he'd forget.

Jas made a big effort. "I bet you're happy about the guitar."

"I hate it."

"Yeah," he said. He understood.

When we finally stood before the pawnshop, there it was in the window. In spite of myself, I was excited. A name was scrolled on it in gold print—Martin. I let Jas negotiate the business, and reaching through the back of the window, picked it up and plucked the strings. It wasn't tuned, but the sound was mellow and sweet. I sat down in a dusty corner and cradled it, working the frets, tightening, plucking again, bending my ear close.

That was it.

My guitar and I spoke with one voice, my voice, but enhanced, reverberating, it was like singing in chords.

I hurried back to sing to Mum, but softly, so as not to wake Jellet. Austrian folk songs, that's what I sang. The ones my father taught her, and she taught me.

"You have a knack of carrying a person right into the music," she said.

Elk Woman stole in soundlessly to listen. Jason stood in the doorway.

Mum murmured, “You have a wonderful gift, Kathy.”

Elk Woman grunted. “See that it doesn’t ruin your life.”

Mum looked at her reprovingly. “How could anything so lovely do that?”

“Loki the Trickster sees to it.” She added matter of factly, “It’s his job.”

▾ ▴ ▾

MUM lived more and more in the past. She would tell me things about my Austrian father as though they happened yesterday. But more and more it was someone else she talked about. Someone called Crazy Dancer.

She married Crazy Dancer first, before she fell in love with my father. But it was a Mohawk ceremony, and before they could do it again in church he was shipped off to Europe. The troopship was torpedoed and went down with all hands. Only Crazy Dancer wasn’t on that ship. He came back at the end of the war to find Mum married to my father.

It was hard for Mum to explain two loves. “The war destroyed so much. What was left, we destroyed. None of us knew how to pick up the pieces.”

When she told me, “Your father and I were happy,” I believed her. Then in the next breath, “I’d try to wake myself out of dreams, because it was Crazy Dancer standing by the bed, looking at me. Sometimes he would be sitting in a chair, fixing something, he liked to fix things. He especially liked motors, carburetors, housings, and fittings of all kinds. We usually had an old car or motorcycle but no transportation, because it would be in pieces on the sidewalk, and Crazy Dancer would be joyously greasing or filing away at some part. Very few of these parts belonged to the original engine but were swapped, traded, and on rare occasions bought from the owner of another vehicle, never from a store.

"You were a year old when he came back. The first thing he did, before saying 'hello' or 'I love you,' was help carry the buggy with you in it up two flights of stairs. He was the old Crazy Dancer, full of high jinks and wild imagination. But, though he tried to conceal it, his health was gone."

As a nurse, Mum knew the signs: chronic bronchitis, then emphysema. She saw that he got proper medical attention. It was too late. Too much scarred lung tissue, too few active cilia, too frequent respiratory infections.

"Double pneumonia," Mum said, reliving her last desperate effort to save Crazy Dancer. With a paring knife, she performed what she called a "lay tracheotomy."

"I didn't do it as skillfully as a surgeon would, but there's a place under a man's Adam's apple where the membrane is thin. With a paring knife and a drinking straw I was able to keep him alive. I got him in the car, threw you in the backseat, and drove to the hospital. He held the straw in place himself and tried not to pass out. And you know what that crazy Indian did? He patted me on the knee to show he approved of my driving. He'd taught me, you see. And . . ."

Her lips still moved, but I could no longer make out the words. I folded the story away with that of the young Austrian officer in Hitler's navy who had gray eyes. And the one about a girl who married a Mountie and passed her name on to me. These were the tales I recounted to myself. Like the castle in the Austrian Alps, dream and daydream, their fabric was a lost reality in which I could no longer hide.

Chapter Four

Two nights later I had to accept another reality; with Jellet at the pub, Morrie tumbling around in the living room, me singing, Elk Woman sitting unblinkingly beside her, and Jas lolling against the wall, Mum died. She died without a word, without a sound.

I didn't know. I was still singing when Elk Woman took crushed rosemary leaves from her pocket and began sprinkling them over the bed.

I put down the guitar. "What are you doing?" It was a question I didn't need to ask.

"She had an easy passing, just slipped the moorings."

I stared at my mother, a slight figure who was no longer there.

"Where is she now, Elk Woman?"

"There aren't words, little one. She is weaving herself into the great design."

"Then she hasn't just ended?"

Elk Woman smiled, "She has just begun."

With a great cry Jason threw himself at the bed and, grabbing Mum by the shoulders, tried to shake her alive.

▾ ▴ ▾

ELK Woman went to the Eight Bells and told Jellet. He closed the pub and brought a couple of cronies home for moral support: Hubert, who weighed three hundred pounds all muscle but wouldn't hurt a fly, and Black Douglas, the only cardsharp our little community could support.

They brought two bottles of Irish whiskey. At the house Hubert made a great fuss about adding it to coffee. Getting out the percolator and putting water on to boil was as far as he got before flopping down at the kitchen table to catch up with the other two.

Jellet was going on about losing a loving and loyal companion in the prime of life—how disgusting, how maudlin. But as he talked I realized he truly was grieving. He just didn't know how to do it except with other people's words. His buddies kept assuring him they would stand by him, ready to help any way they could. Of course they didn't have specific suggestions. I sat in a corner listening to them.

I'd put Morrie to bed and left the light on in the hall. This was strictly forbidden. I think Jellet noticed, but he decided not to say anything. Black Douglas laid out a hand of clock solitaire. He was waiting for me to turn in before suggesting poker, and in the meantime probing Jellet as to how he had come to marry an Indian girl, pretty though she was.

A change came over Jellet's face. His usual sour expression vanished. I'd seen him happy only a few times in my life, and then when he was roaring drunk. This was a different kind of happiness, simple, faraway. He didn't smile, but his mouth softened with remembering.

They'd met in the Italian campaign of World War II. He had been assigned as a replacement driver for the New Zealand general, Tuker. Tuker's penchant for poking his nose into every corner of the front lines at Monte Cassino sent half a dozen drivers to the hospital. When he ran out of New Zealanders, he borrowed Jellet from the neighboring Canadian corps. Tuker disagreed with the Fifth Army plan to destroy the Monte Cassino fortress monastery by air power. He was convinced he could take it by ground action. He asked General Mark Clark's headquarters in Naples to supply him with blueprints of the buildings and topographic maps of the environs. Intelligence claimed no such information was available. Tuker blew his top, rousted out Jellet, and set off for Naples, where he intended to research the monastery himself at the public library.

"He stops a war to go to the library?" Hubert asked.

"Did he have his library card with him?" Black Douglas, a few sheets to windward, snickered at his witticism.

Jellet, ignoring this, tried to picture for them the steep rut at the side of the road, and how it was the jeep turned over, breaking his arm. Tuker himself had to drive back to the casualty clearing station, where Mum, a surgical nurse, set Jellet's arm and gave him a shot of penicillin against infection. Then a shot of morphine. He thought she was the most beautiful girl he'd ever set eyes on, and the kindest, and the gentlest—the only person in his life who had treated him with any consideration.

Here Jellet launched into a bitter tirade against his parents, his family, his father's administration of justice. Whenever an infraction occurred, his father took out his appointment book, set a date, a time, and an estimate of the requisite number of canings. "Saturday, before breakfast, 6:40 A.M., here in the study, eleven strokes—" The boy had plenty of time to think it over. When World War II broke out, he traded home for the Italian front. You got shot at, but you didn't have to make an appointment.

At war's end Jellet came back to Canada to learn that his parents had died. Most of the estate went to other relatives, but he inherited a small piece of property in a little town near Lesser Slave Lake, which his father had foreclosed on. Formerly an elegant pub, it had rapidly deteriorated into a hangout for bums, Indians, and riffraff in general. The family urged him to sell it and go to work in their law firm.

"In other words," Jellet said, folding his hands, "take orders from them. No way. I told them all what they could do, moved here, cleaned up the bar, and hung out a sign, OPEN FOR BUSINESS."

It struck him that he'd heard the name of this town in Italy. The beautiful nurse at the Cassino front who'd sat with him, eased his pain, talked to him, smiled—she was from here.

It was a sign from God. He had his own business free and

clear. With a wife and children and a cellar full of beer, he could build a good life. The Eight Bells became a going concern, but the muse he had built his fantasies around now lived in Montreal. He tracked her through the Sisters of Charity Hospital. It was a bit of a shock, however, to find that in the meantime she'd married and had a baby, particularly that the father was German. Also, Mum was quite open about Crazy Dancer.

Jellet decided to go slow. He wasn't so sure this was the right woman for him after all, twice married and Indian. The war was over, and people who had gotten used to seeing Indians in uniform or mentioned in the casualty lists reverted to old habits and treated them like the invisible minority they'd always been.

On her part, Mum was puzzled by the sudden appearance of a ghost from the war, and too wrapped up in her own problems to pay him much attention.

"Maybe I should have packed it in then and come home," Jellet said mournfully. Black Douglas performed a cascading shuffle; they polished off the whiskey and started to look for a bottle of vodka Jellet claimed to have hidden on top of some cupboard or other.

When it was found, Jellet resumed. Yes, it was the war that brought them together. Both had lived through experiences no civilian wanted to hear about. They found things to shudder at, to shed tears at, and they laughed over the fact that it was she who ended up driving General Tuker to the public library in bombed-out Naples. "You missed a fantastic dinner," and she told him of the meal the general had treated her to. Jellet's memory was of the shot of morphine and her touch.

They made a deal. "The baby," Jellet said, "needed a father. She needed a home. I needed a wife. We were married."

Now the vodka was gone. While they were looking under sinks and behind furniture for a replacement, I stole out. I knew the rest. Jellet's family and friends took one look at Mum and cut them off, socially, economically, permanently. Jellet responded by withdrawing completely from society. He had no truck with anyone from the town. No church, no school, nothing. The Eight Bells and our falling-down house . . . and a tiny strip of birchbark from Mum's old life. She planned one day to make it into a toy canoe. That was all. We lived as hermits.

▼ ▲ ▼

As I stood graveside, a spasm went through me to see Mum lowered into the ground, joining all the yesterdays since the world began. It was awful to see dirt shoveled in, until I remembered she liked to sift through the soil with her fingers for earthworms, which she prized. She liked the smell of loam, the good, rich earth smell. Cree songs told of these things and this is what I sang standing there on that desolate, windy plain.

Afterward I ran off to Abram. He came out of his house and walked with me, and these were his words. "You husk the body off," he said, "so the soul can be free."

I thought about it. It seemed sensible. "Why can't we know these things?"

"I guess because we're human beings."

"And sinful?" I asked.

"No, I don't think so. It's just that we can't comprehend great things yet."

"But it's my Mum, Abram."

The tears I couldn't shed gathered in his eyes. He would have felt better if I'd been able to storm and cry and carry on in my usual fashion. He could have comforted me then. Only, I couldn't do it. I felt detached from myself and from the world, alienated and alone. For once Abram couldn't help.

▼ ▲ ▼

I RETURNED to the house to find a bouquet of wild flowers and a rabbit left on our porch. There was a note signed by the Mennonite community offering sympathy and prayers. Away to the side was a single wild lobelia. No need to tell me. Abram. Jellet almost stepped on it, but I snatched it up.

Jellet was watching me; he had things to say. "Now that your mother's gone you'll have to step into her place, try to fill it. That will mean being a mother to the boys."

"Then they'll have to go to school," I snapped. "I can't teach them."

"That's for me to decide," he said.

I ignored this and went on. "I'll need help in the house too. A Mennonite girl for a few hours a day."

"What do you think I am, a bank?"

"It won't cost much. I'll talk to them."

"You'll do no such thing."

I was amazed to hear myself stand up to him. "You're not going to make a workhorse out of me."

"Your mother not cold in her grave, and back talk from you already?"

"I don't mean it as back talk. There's a limit to what I can do."

"What you're *willing* to do," he blustered.

"Yes." I had stood up to him, but had I won concessions? The first test would be Monday.

I walked the boys to school, talked to the teacher, and got them properly registered. On the way back I hummed to keep up my resolve. Jellet would be furious. But done is done.

▾ ▴ ▾

ELK Woman slipped in the back door. She hadn't been at the funeral. Jellet and his buddies would have run her off and enjoyed it. But she was Mum's only friend, and she had nursed her to the end. Her herb medicines had soothed Mum's cough, and her other potions, who knows, perhaps dulled the pain.

Elk Woman told me that she had known the day Mum would die. Mum had known too. The voices of the Grandmothers always came to a Cree, and that's what my mother was, a Cree, born of a Cree mother and a Metis father.

Elk Woman had come to take me to the res. "Your grandfather, Jonathan Forquet, is here. He is an old man, a sick old man, but he walked across Alberta to be here."

Mum hardly ever spoke of Jonathan Forquet, and then not as her father but as a wise man who had helped her through a difficult time. I remembered her saying, "I was his daughter, but he was never my parent. He chose to be a parent to the Indian nations from Nunavut to the Yukon."

"Why didn't he come in time . . . to be with her?"

"It's not necessary," Elk Woman said. "He'll be with her on the other side. What is necessary is to walk beside her a little way on her journey."

Jonathan Forquet.

I squeezed my eyes closed trying to remember. As a young man he'd been a hunter and trapper. Then he heard of the teachings of the prophet Handsome Lake and for him the words of Manitou and Christ blended. From this time forward he was called to officiate at longhouse rituals. And now he'd come to hold the ceremony that closed his daughter's life.

▾ ▴ ▾

I WAS amazed to see the entire res assembled to honor my Mum.

Elk Woman, in her ratty coat out at the elbows and holes in her shoes, had tied a wind-band across her forehead and seemed to command large shadowy forces, reaching from the mystical Grandmothers themselves to the shaman around whom they gathered.

My grandfather.

He leaned on a cane, and the hand that held it trembled. His hair was white and very fine. It fell to his shoulders. But it was the eyes that held me. They burned with a mystic charge. He stretched out a thin, almost transparent hand. "Child of my child. I am your mother's father. Let us sit and talk a moment."

He crouched down where he was, and I did the same.

He sat quietly, staring into space. Just when I thought he had forgotten about me, he began to speak.

"Among the Cree, grandparents have a large responsibility in rearing children. I wasn't able to be that kind of grandfather to you. But I come now from across Canada, all the way from Quebec province so you would know my face, and I yours."

"So we could trade shadows." The old words were reborn in me, and I said them.

"Ayiii!" He brought me to his breast and held me there. His breath brushed my cheek. "Elk Woman tells me you will be a singer. But first you must be a person. You must breathe, walk, love, suffer, hope—and mostly you must dream. We are a people of dreams. Your mother will be with you in dreams."

My grandfather might appear fragile, but his voice was strong, deep, and resonant. I felt he knew unknowable things.

"Is my mother's soul . . . somewhere?"

He released me to look deeply into my eyes. "It is in the sun breaking through clouds. It is in the swaying of treetop nests and the call of the loon. You will find it in our music. Listen, it starts."

A piercing shriek. Rattles, drums, dancers whirling in the dirt, jumping, leaping, the dancers another instrument treading out rhythm. The chant was a Cree prayer, calling to the four points of the compass, calling life. A chant punctuated by persistent wailing that stole into my soul.

Elk Woman muttered in my ear, "The people sing of a Cree child given to Mrs. Mike and the White world. She grew up to nurse the wounded, fix automobiles, fight for Canada, take care of three husbands, bring up three children, live a life, and now returns to the ancestral dream."

The singing died away. There was no climax; it simply ended and everybody started to eat. Children played about our feet, women breast-fed infants. Life started up again. I realized I wanted to sing Cree music. If I could get inside the rhythm I could sing the universe.

▼ ▲ ▼

ELK Woman shook me awake. It was dawn, and my grandfather wanted to see me. I'd slept snug and warm on wonderful soft furs, which had been heaped over me as well.

Elk Woman poured water into a large basin. Washing was evidently important, apparently breakfast was not. We skipped that, and Elk Woman hurried me along to my grandfather's tent. The old man preferred sleeping on the ground; a patched lean-to suited him better than a back room in a government-built house.

He was finishing his own wash-up and greeted me with a look that claimed me, as did a single word. "Granddaughter."

Then, "We came for her sake, your mother's sake—and found each other. Now we go back to our lives, but so you won't forget, I have a present for you." His eyes twinkled. "You want to see it?"

"Yes."

"You can't." That was his joke, and he enjoyed it. "It's invisible."

"Invisible?"

"Yes. You can't see it, touch it, hold it. You can't smell it or taste it."

"But I can hear it?" I was beginning to enjoy this.

"Yes, certainly. You can certainly hear it."

"It's music. A song? An instrument? A flute?"

"Nothing like that. I said you can't hold it."

He let me go on guessing. Finally we were both silent. I started to make another guess, but he held up a finger.

We waited, saying nothing. We didn't move. We barely breathed. All was quiet.

He lowered his hand. "That's it." His lips silently formed the words.

What was it? What were we listening to?

All at once I knew.

It was the world breathing. It was the pulse of the universe. It was the sound behind silence.

To hear it you had to stop all motion, be absolutely still. Only then could you sense it, the song that goes on forever. The song that never ends.

▾ ▴ ▾

JELLET refrained from mentioning my absence. The boys, however, deviled me for a full account, and wanted to know if the chiefs wore war bonnets. I drew out the description into bedtime. "Cree songs are part of us," I told them, hoping to infuse them with the pride I felt. "They're in our blood."

When Jellet found out about the boys being in school, he raged as I knew he would. But there was not much he could do. His only recourse was to go on about it to the four walls. Loyalty, duty, and disobedient daughters bounced off them. Eventually he tired of it and the household settled down.

I tried at first being a mother to the boys, but they'd rather I was their sister. Morrie was too big to take on my lap; he wanted me to run and climb and intercept balls. Jason, now that he had started school, stayed late at the playground for the sports he'd missed all his life. I didn't see anyone until dinner.

You feel numb at first, and that gets you through. It's afterward, when things return to normal and you pick up the old routines, that's when you feel the loss, the emptiness.

Jellet never acted on my request for a girl to help in the house, but threw his dirty clothes in the hamper as always. When he had no clean shirt to wear to the pub, perhaps then he would open negotiations.

It was a standoff. Jellet kept changing his clothes, shirt, underwear, socks, even his cap, and tossing them into the hamper, making sure I saw him—then stomped off to work.

Jas and Morrie cheered me on. They even offered to help me do nothing. Kids can be wonderful.

As I passed the hamper I slammed down the lid. It was time to start the stew for dinner. I cut up onions and potatoes, but was short on carrots. I substituted celery and sliced bell pepper.

I brought it to a boil and turned down the gas. What next? Usually this was the time I did the wash, so I could keep an eye on the dinner. I peeked into the hamper. Of course I wouldn't do his stuff, but the boys deserved clean shirts. I fished out their clothes. There were a couple of towels at the bottom. One was his, leave it. Also, his handkerchief.

Actually, Jellet's stuff wasn't enough for a separate wash. I might as well do the whole thing rather than spend time sorting it out. It would save a lot of arguing and yelling. Maybe he would appreciate it and—

Whoa! What was I doing?

I was giving in.

I slammed the hamper shut.

▾ ▴ ▾

THE upshot was, Maggie Toland, thirteen, came twice a week after school to help with the house. But I didn't have Mum. I didn't have her to talk to or sing to.

How little I had known her. She had been a nurse. And she'd gone overseas to Cassino. She'd been in that battle. But she didn't talk about it, and I didn't know what it meant in her life. I wish I'd asked more. I'd never know her now as a woman.

I had to see Abram. I'd die if I didn't.

I found him sitting on the bottom step of his porch, whittling. I sat down beside him, put my arms around him, and kissed him.

He didn't seem surprised, but kissed me back. At first his

kissing was a bit hit-or-miss. But it improved. So did mine. We made it last a long time. I felt surrounded by him, absorbed into him, part of the healthy, clean young male smell of him.

When he finally let go of me we looked at each other differently.

I tried to look behind his eyes to get at his thoughts. "You wouldn't think less of me if I was in love with you, would you, Abram?"

Abram wasn't the boy I'd met for years outside the Mennonite church; he was a man, known and yet unknowable. He kissed me in a different way, a way that made me dizzy, in a way that made me want to hold him. I ran my fingers through that thick shock of blond hair. Our breath mingled, our body warmth was shared. I felt as though I couldn't breathe.

Abram pulled back. I could see he was as shaken as I was. He told me I should go home now.

I nodded. I respected him for this. On the instant I knew I'd be safe with Abram all my life long.

Chapter Five

It's odd how you can go along day after day and things stay the same, then some incident occurs, perhaps trivial, perhaps unimportant, even ridiculous, that changes your life. With me it happened over a head of lettuce, July 1963.

I'd been marketing and was on my way home with a loaded shopping bag. A car backfired and suddenly I was conscious of ordinary time jamming together. A horse that had been tied into traces reared, pawing the air. It broke loose and plunged down the street. Rolling bloodshot eyes, frothing mouth, laid-back ears, nostrils that snorted and flared as he dashed at me.

I pressed into a doorway. The animal's breath scorched my face as it charged past. I stayed as I was, unable to move, hardly daring to believe I had escaped being trampled.

In a numb state I watched as the horse was coralled by its owner and led docilely back to the wagon, where it was properly hitched into the team. I managed a few deep breaths. I was even able to assess the situation. My grocery bag had split its seams; canned goods and vegetables strewed the street. A large lettuce was rolling toward the drain and I dived for it.

So did someone else, the person who owned the horse. We reached for it, trying to stop its progress, and nearly bumped heads. The owner of the horse stood up, lettuce in hand. "Sorry. So terribly sorry. Are you all right? Shaken up, I suppose? Anyone would be. Oh, here is your lettuce, and don't worry, I'll retrieve the rest of your purchases."

I let him pick up celery, parsnips, lard, and a loaf of bread. There was nothing to be done about a smashed bottle of vinegar.

He was standing in front of me, arms full. "I have a flour sack in the wagon. I'll just put these things in it."

I followed him to the wagon. He was still talking. "I hope you'll forgive me for frightening you to death. Although actually, I find it hard to forgive myself."

I thought he was being a bit dramatic. "It's all right. It was an accident. No harm done."

"That's very generous of you, Miss, eh . . . ?"

"My name is Kathy."

He removed his cap, revealing a mop of curly carrot-red hair. "Jack Sullivan at your service."

I had to smile at the grand manner he assumed.

"I know I'm presuming on a very short acquaintance, but

as proof of your forgiveness, would you perhaps have a soda with me?"

"A soda?" That was a rare treat indeed.

We didn't sit at the counter, but at one of the small round marble-topped tables. The chairs were wire-backed with cushions of red and white stripes. Sitting across from him, I had an opportunity to size up Jack Sullivan. He wasn't in overalls like the Mennonite boys and men, or the farmers. That set him apart. That and the red hair. His sleeves were rolled up and there was a sprinkling of light red fuzz on his arms. He was freckled and his eyes a sort of dancing green with laughing lights in them.

He described himself as an entrepreneur, travelling between Canada and the States, selling the ponies he raised here for American dollars across the border.

"I've never been in the States." Then I found myself saying, "But I'm planning on going."

"You'll like it. Americans are free and easy, not formal and tied in knots. And the cities—big-time, glittering, exciting. You'd fit right in."

"I would?"

"A girl with your looks? I'll say. It doesn't seem right to waste it on the cows. When are you thinking of going?"

"Well, I'd like to go soon."

He peered at me intently, and his eyes were not all one color, but many. His face too was never in repose for long at a time. Ideas, thoughts, schemes chased across it. Smiling broadly, he said, "Just remember, I've room for one more in my wagon."

I laughed too. And that was the end of it. At least I thought that was the end of it.

Jack talked about the Big Apple and Chi. I didn't realize at first they were New York and Chicago. You had to know them pretty well to call them by their nicknames. The Loop, that was downtown Chicago, right on Lake Michigan, with a zoo and fancy hotels, and apartments with doormen, and glamorous restaurants.

In the next breath—Broadway. "They have human signs walking up and down the street."

"No," I said in amazement.

"I kid you not. Those old Bowery bums are paid maybe fifty cents to walk around advertising Coca-Cola and Philip Morris."

"But that's awful. It takes a person's dignity away to be a signboard."

"It means a bowl of soup, a cup of coffee, or more likely a spot of gin."

Of all the places he'd seen, Broadway made the biggest impression. The names of stars were outlined in bulbs that flashed on at night and lit up the world of entertainment. Cabs came and went, disgorging theater parties. "Talk about handsome couples. But most of those sophisticated women couldn't hold a candle to you."

I didn't know how to handle compliments. I felt exhilarated, as though I wasn't me, but the exotic beauty he seemed to think I was. Odd how it had apparently escaped everyone's observation but his. I wished I had worn my best dress. But one doesn't wear a best dress to the store. Besides, how could

I have known I'd meet this attractive, well-traveled gentleman?

It wasn't his polish alone that intrigued me; it was an unexpected quality about him. Other people, at least the ones I knew, were dull by comparison. You more or less knew how they'd react and what they'd say. But Jack's mind darted nimbly from subject to subject. One minute I saw the lights of Broadway and the next rubbed shoulders with crowds in the subway.

The only time I had been in a crowd was when Abram took me to the Mennonite Easter party. There were tables set up behind the church and people greeted one another joyously with, "He is risen." The response: "He is indeed risen." With this accomplished they were free to inquire after absent relatives, exchange recipes, eat crumble cake, and wander toward the improvised stage where children recited poems and the fourth grade had prepared an elocution exercise.

There was a wonderful display of painted eggs. Abram, whispering they symbolized life, bought one for me, with a blue and gold lily emblazoned on it. I felt a shiver of excitement like when we exchanged shadows. I remembered capering around the edge of his. He'd stood before mine with outflung arms reciting psalms. It was impressive.

Of course the Mennonite Easter wasn't to be compared with Jack Sullivan's Times Square on New Year's Eve. "You wouldn't believe the crowd, people jam-packed against you, you couldn't get your hand to your face. There was some clown blowing one of those party favors at my neck and I couldn't free my hand to brush it aside."

I was so fascinated by these tales of a wider world that it somewhat belatedly occurred to me how long I had sat over the sarsaparilla soda. I should have been back an hour ago. I should be in the middle of dinner preparation and here I was, listening to snatches of big-city life. "I have to be going," I said, jumping up.

Jack Sullivan in his turn, got to his feet. "But not like this, so fast. I have to see you again. Can it be this evening? There's a barn dance . . ."

"No, I couldn't possibly. Perhaps another time."

"Time," he lamented, "is what I don't have much of."

"Maybe tomorrow, for a few minutes. A short walk?"

"I'll be there, wherever 'there' is."

"It would be better if you didn't come to the house. My stepfather is very strict. How about here—seven-thirty?"

"I'll reserve the table," he laughed.

We shook hands on it and his fingers didn't want to let mine go. As soon as I was out of earshot I began to sing him. I sang his red hair. I sang the places he'd been. I even sang his eyes, disparate, with many colors. Jack Sullivan was fun to sing. A wild Irish ballad was what I devised, a cross between "The Kerry Dancing" and "Kathleen Mavourneen."

I'd never known anyone like Jack Sullivan. He was such an alert, alive person. I wasn't sure if he was good-looking. His features were a tad too sharp, but he had a dimple in his chin, his eyes danced with fun, and he was brimming over with wonderful tales. And he thought I was pretty. On that splendid note I brought my song to a loud crescendo.

One of the things I would do when I got home would be

to look at my face in the mirror and try to see what Jack Sullivan saw. I'd wear my other dress tomorrow. I remembered Mum letting the hem down. And I'd brush my hair out.

When I got home there were the dishes I'd left from lunch piled in the sink. Mum would never start a meal until her kitchen was spotless, but I worked around the mess, putting away the things from the flour sack. I cut thick slices of brown bread and cheese, put the vegetables on the stove, rinsed the lettuce and tore it into a salad. I recommenced the singing, only now it was in my head.

The next day it seemed to me time was out of kilter, slow and draggy, then unexpectedly speeding up. It was that way with everything. I'd been singing Jack Sullivan in my head, when abruptly it changed to a song of freedom. I kept humming it, picturing myself on the road. Was that Abram by my side? The song said yes, but red curly hair and green eyes kept intruding. I decided Jack Sullivan *was* good-looking, and that I had exaggerated the sharpness of his features.

I'd been wise not to let Jack come to the house. Jellet left for the pub, but Morrie was sure to tell tales, and then, as Mum used to say, "the fat's in the fire."

I waited until the boys were outside shooting baskets before changing into my best dress. It was a warm evening, but I prudently put my coat on over it. Before leaving the house I scrutinized my face in the bathoom mirror. If I'd been designing it I would have done it differently. The nose could be straighter, the lower lip not so full and pouty, the hair would look better with a wave. And the dark eyes, just like Mum's, were disturbingly at odds with the rest of my face.

Oh well. I slipped a small hand mirror into my pocket and took out the lipstick hidden behind an empty aspirin bottle and never used. I'd have to apply it well out of sight of my brothers. I ran down the porch steps and called to them that I was going for a walk. They paid no attention. But they would have if they'd seen me in my best dress.

Safely around the bend by the mailbox, I got out the mirror and lipstick, and followed the curve of my mouth. The mirror was too small for an overall effect, but judged piecemeal it looked fine. I took off my coat and laid it over the rural mailbox for picking up on my way back.

▼ ▲ ▼

I HAD never stolen out to meet a boy in my life. I didn't count Abram; there was nothing illicit about meeting Abram, nothing exciting. It was generally during the day, dusting off our plans for breaking free. But now I was meeting a stranger. And my heart skipped a few beats.

I knew perfectly well that I was not behaving as Mum would have wanted. This was definitely not what a proper, well-brought-up young lady would do. Jellet kept me in a straitjacket, and I was busting out. After all, Mum, by my count, had been married three times: a Mohawk with the crazy name of Crazy Dancer, my father von Kerll, and Jellet.

She'd married Jellet on account of me. And if she were here, she'd know I had to go my own way, be my own person.

Jack Sullivan, who are you? Will you be important in my life? At the moment I couldn't recall exactly what he looked like, except for the hair. I liked red hair, and it would be nice to have someone in my life who didn't wear overalls.

When I reached the drugstore, Jack Sullivan was waiting for me at the same table. He got up when he saw me, just as in the movies.

"Hi," he said, "I'm glad to see you. I was afraid you wouldn't come."

"I said I would, didn't I?"

"I thought maybe you'd change your mind."

I sat down and looked over the menu, although I had made up my mind to order a chocolate malt.

Jack Sullivan told me I was looking very pretty. Again, just like the movies.

"You know," he added, "you brought me luck. I sold two of my ponies this afternoon."

"You did?"

"Yep, I bought me a car and exchanged the wagon for a horse trailer."

"You work fast, don't you?"

"It was you. You brought me luck."

"Do you really think that?"

"I do. We Irish believe in luck, especially good luck. One horse I might have expected to sell, but two of them—that's luck, pure and simple."

When we finished our malts he took me out front and there was the car, a maroon Ford. I walked around it, with him pointing out its best features. "I checked the motor, it runs quiet. And the upholstery's in good condition, no tears."

He opened the door, and I leaned in and ran my hand across the back of the front seat. "Hop in," he said.

"Where's the horse trailer?"

"That's what I'm going to show you."

I got in.

Never go with a stranger.

Jack Sullivan was a stranger. I shivered slightly. I was dipping a toe into the world. Soon I would breast the full current, taste it completely. I was alive with a sense that freedom was at my fingertips.

Nothing was impossible. I was Kathy von Kerll, who was strong and young and vibrant, and Jack Sullivan knew it. That is, he knew as much as a stranger can know something like that.

I listened to the sound of his voice without listening to the words. I liked his voice: fluent, pleasant, full of wit and laughter, rushing on and on. How that man could talk! I was used to silent men. Jellet never spoke, except to criticize or invent some new chore. Even Abram was rather silent. In his case it came from the difficulty of putting thoughts into words. He was particular about this; he liked them to fit exactly. But Jack used words to beguile you into seeing his particular slice of world. This consisted of his car, his horse trailer, the deal he had just pulled off, and his two remaining horses. And all these good things, he concluded, were the result of him being Jack Sullivan and meeting me.

He explained the route to financial success, generating a picture of a man of prospects. "It's predicated on the capital at your disposal, your stake. Take me, for instance, I started with nothing and parlayed it into something. Now that I have something, watch my dust!"

I liked the way he drove. He kicked up a lot of dust here too. One arm on the steering wheel, the other around me. He was daring a cow to wander from a break in the fence and appear in front of us, or for a gully in the road to break an axle. I knew these things wouldn't happen, because he led a charmed life. A daring, ambitious life. "All I have to do is whistle for things, and they come to me," he said, and I believed him.

Suddenly he swerved off the road and stopped on a dime. We were in a field, a field that was different from the surrounding fields in that it held a horse trailer. He jumped out of the car to show me. Old and rusty, the paint chipped and scratched. I had to repress my disappointment.

Jack saw it as the quintessence of horse trailers and the shaggy ponies tethered beside it as narrow-in-the-forelock, high-stepping, sleek thoroughbreds with fortunes riding on them. He'd had the better of the bargain, and his enthusiasm was infectious.

"Where will you be going?" I asked.

"I'll cross into Montana, hit the small towns. I did good business in Minnesota. I'll definitely take in Wisconsin and Illinois, work my way over to upper New York State. I'll hit Broadway again in the fall."

He lifted me to the rear of the trailer, where I sat with my legs dangling. When he swung up beside me, the ponies raised their heads to look. They whinnied a sad, plaintive tone. Their big bulging eyes regarded us softly. The horses wanted to get going.

Jack was sitting close, almost on top of me. And he positioned me in his arms for a long kiss. It was different from the kind Abram and I had experimented with. This kiss was wetter because Jack used his tongue. I didn't like it as well as Abram's kissing. But I suppose this was the way it was done in the Big Apple and in Chi.

Jack Sullivan had roving hands. Abram never tried the things he tried. I knew I had to allow Jack certain familiarities because I saw he expected it. When he moved on a girl it was with a practiced technique. There were no hesitations; he knew how to cup my breasts and stroke and get me in the mood.

But I wasn't going to go all the way with a stranger in a horse trailer, even though he told me my eyes were black as coal and the most beautiful he'd ever seen. I pulled myself from his embrace and slid to the ground.

"Hey," he said in protest, "what's the idea?"

"I have to get back."

He lifted himself down and stood beside me. "Don't be a tease," he whispered.

"Let me make myself plain, Jack. I will never go any further without a preacher and a ring."

"Wow! What makes you think you'll get that out of me?"

"I don't think any such thing. I'm just telling you what the table stakes are."

Table stakes was Jack's phrase. "Damn," he said. "I talk too much. It's my worst fault."

"Oh, I don't know." I flashed him a smile and gave him a wisp of a kiss on his cheek just in passing as I got back into the car.

"So it's home, James?"

"It is." And I slammed the door.

"You'll never see me again," Jack said. "I don't like to waste my time."

"That's a shame," I replied, feeling sure I would see him again.

"A preacher and a ring. Whoever heard of such a thing?"

I didn't say a word and he started up again. "Getting hitched, settling down, raising a family. That's where that kind of thing leads."

"That can't be right, because I've no intention of settling down. I want to travel and see the things you talk about just as much as you do."

"I wouldn't mind you traveling with me," he conceded.

"But I couldn't do it without a preacher and a ring."

"Well, then, it looks to me that you're going to be stuck in this little backwater forever."

"It does look that way," I agreed cheerily.

He drove in silence with both hands on the steering wheel, and stopped in front of the drugstore, which was now closed. He didn't get out, or go around, or open the door for me. He just sat there.

I peered into his face. It was hard to read his expression in the dark. "We needn't go out again, Jack, since you feel you're wasting your time. But I'd like to bring the ponies sugar lumps. They'd like that, wouldn't they?"

"Hmm. I guess . . ."

"So maybe tomorrow you'd just drive me there?"

"Okay," he said grudgingly, "if nothing else comes up."

"Same time," I said, letting myself out.

I ran a good part of the way back, retrieved my coat from the mailbox, and put it on over my dress. "Do you know what you're doing?" I kept asking myself. Suppose I got Jack Sullivan to the point of actually marrying me? Was that what I wanted? I always thought I'd marry Abram, and we'd go away together. Abram thought so too. The trouble was we weren't any closer to doing it than we were last year or the year before, or when we were ten years old for that matter. Abram didn't know how to make things happen, and Jack did. At the moment he was my only avenue out of here.

Abram held no surprises for me. I knew him. I'd grown up with him. Although he wasn't a good Mennonite, he was a good person. I could trust him and count on him. Oh, and I'd left out a very important item: He loved me.

And I kind of loved him, although I got exasperated with him.

When I got home, Jason asked if I was thinking of entering the Olympics in long-distance walking. I knew he was curious about where I'd been, and I'd have to be careful.

The next night too I went for a walk, again with my best dress under my coat. The coat I left again on the stanchion of the mailbox, and walked into town, not pausing until the drugstore.

A car tooted its horn. A redheaded driver leaned out and grinned. "Got any sugar?"

I delved into my pockets and came up with a handful of sugar cubes pilfered from our table.

"The horses will be happy," he said. "Get in."

I did.

Jack was in a good mood. He had forgotten he was mad at me. He resumed his one-arm driving. "So tell me about yourself, Kathy."

He hadn't bothered to ask me about myself before. I took it as a good sign. "I'm a singer," I said.

He gave a low whistle. "Now that's surprising, a singer out here in the sticks. Where do you sing, in church?" And he roared at his own humor.

"I sing in clubs," I responded haughtily, recalling a short bio of Patsy Cline I'd found in a magazine in one of the trash bins behind the market.

The remark intrigued Jack. "What clubs?"

Here I was on more sure ground. "The Eight Bells."

"Well, what do you know." Jack's whistle again demonstrated how impressed he was. "Sing something."

I had quite a large repertoire. As part of my housekeeping I'd taken our radio into town and had it fixed. I ran through a number of songs in my head, looking for something he'd go for, then launched into a pop number, snapping my fingers to find the rhythm.

When I finished there was another whistle from Jack, quite different from the others. This one was long and appreciative. "You're good."

"I know."

He laughed. "You know, do you?"

"Yes."

"You're a queer one, Kathy. I don't think I've ever met anyone like you."

We sped into the night with a sliver of moon hanging over our heads. The horses were tethered as they had been last night. I proffered my sugar cubes with a flat palm so their soft nuzzling mouths wouldn't accidentally nip. Abram had taught me that.

Jack was watching, taking this in. "I see you know your way around horses, too."

I didn't really, but I let this stand. I wanted him to think I was accomplished, with many facets to my nature. After I'd fed and patted the ponies and decided the dappled-gray silver was my favorite, we sat at the back of the horse trailer and dangled our feet.

Jack confided his plans, marvelous plans that on the instant had grown to include me. He would lay New York City at my feet. With my talent, he'd promote me onto the charts. I'd be doing recordings, singing on radio—all my daydreams spilled out of his grinning Irish mouth. "I've got to be moving on," he told me. "And you're coming with me. That's right, isn't it?"

I laughed at him, pretending I didn't want it more than anything in the world.

"You're the one thing that's keeping me in this godforsaken place." He shook his head as he said this, as though arguing with himself.

Chapter Six

JAS was waiting by the mailbox for me.

"What are you doing here?" I snapped. Attack worked best with Jas.

"I knew you were up to something. I saw you get into a car with that redheaded guy. . . ."

I thought fast and decided to make him a co-conspirator. I spun out a romance and swore him to secrecy. He was old enough now and was caught up in the adventure. I exaggerated a bit, especially as to being in love. I wasn't sure I was in love. When I was with Jack, I was. When I wasn't, I hardly thought of him.

I knew in my bones that the way to find out how I felt was to visit Abram. I hadn't seen Abram this past week; now I had to see him.

The next afternoon I went directly to Mr. Renfall's lumber company, where Abram was at work stacking crates and boxes. I knew, because he told me, that the money he made was divided into three piles: one for his parents, one for the church, and one he held out. That was for us, our running-away money.

He pulled me into a back corner of the storage shed and kissed me.

It was Abram kissing, not Jack. Abram kissed in a way that brought me to my toes. I felt his love and his commitment. And for some reason felt sad to be loved like this.

"Oh, Abram," and I stroked his face, his good, strong face.

▾ ▴ ▾

My third date with Jack, things took a different turn. I was fighting not only Sullivan but myself. He had an exciting way of scooping me up in his arms, making me feel not only that I was a woman but that I was his woman. His hands were never still; they petted and stroked, sometimes gently, almost lazily, sometimes brazenly. Until now I had kept him in check, and if I felt we were being swept along, I would say, "Watch it, Jack—that's a preacher and ring move." After a while I curtailed it simply to "That's a p.r."

He took it pretty well, usually modifying his behavior. The trouble was I wanted this earthy, aggressive lover as much as he wanted me. It would have been easy to relax into his embrace totally. But I knew if I did, he'd be gone in the morning, and with him my chance of ever getting out of here.

"P.r.," I said breathlessly, sitting up and fastening my bra. "Things can't go on like this. We both know it. You're too much for me, Jack, too much a man. I can't fight you off any more." I took a deep breath, risking everything. "So the only thing to do is let you go your way."

"There's one more choice open to us. We could get married." The words ripped out of him like an explosion. He seemed as surprised by them as I was. "There, I said it, a preacher and a ring. What do you say?"

This time it was I who threw my arms about him.

▾ ▴ ▾

I GOT home late and with a gesture to be quiet pulled Jas from his bed into my room.

"You won't have to cover for me any more, Jas. Guess what? I'm getting married."

His mouth opened and forgot to close. "Who to?"

"Jack Sullivan, of course."

"What about Abram?"

My enthusiasm for my marriage fell abruptly away. I stared at my brother. "He doesn't have a horse trailer."

I was well aware that I was being stupid. But I dug my heels in harder and pursued my course even more recklessly. I could hear Elk Woman down the years: "Stop fighting with yourself, Little Bird."

▾ ▴ ▾

JACK always said I put some sort of spell on him, and I think I did. He definitely was marriage shy. The preacher in St. Alban's was a doddering old fellow who knew Jellet. So Jack arranged for us to be married in the next town. I wondered if he would show up, but he was waiting for me at the drugstore and we drove the thirty miles with hardly a word between us. I stole a couple of glances at him. He looked especially fine. His shirt was starched and he wore an ascot at his throat, neatly tucked into his collar. I was marrying a gentleman who knew the right way to do things. He even had a bouquet of store-bought flowers for me.

I remember the preacher's house. I don't remember the ceremony. I was afraid the whole time that Jas had told my stepfather, and that Jellet would burst in and stop the proceedings.

I do remember it didn't take long. I was surprised how quickly something as important as wedding vows could be over and still make a difference to the rest of our lives. Jack fished in his pocket and came up with one of those Cracker Jack box prizes, a ring so soft you could push it into different shapes. "Just for now," he whispered. His kiss in front of the preacher and his wife was rather tepid. I hoped he wasn't sorry already. We walked out into the sun, and there was Abram pedaling up, with Jas panting and quite a way behind.

When Abram reached me, his face distorted, he gasped, "You haven't—?"

"I have. I got married." And I waved my finger in his face. "It's just a cheap ring that I can bend, but later Jack will get me a proper one."

Jack stepped up beside me. "I'm Sullivan," and he extended his hand.

Abram didn't take it. I don't think he saw it. He was as upset as I'd ever seen him. "You've done it then." This was said half under his breath. Then to me, "It's all right, Kathy, you can have it annulled."

"Annulled?" Jack spoke up. "What the devil are you talking about?"

Abram placed a hand against Jack's chest and sent him reeling backward, but didn't bother to look at him. I was the one he saw. "You thought I'd never get the money. But I've got two hundred dollars, and I can manage the rest. I can and I will."

"Abram, Jack's my husband, and I'm going away with him."

"But you don't know him. Kathy, for your sake, for both our sakes, listen to me—"

Sullivan came up with a strutting swagger. "Hey, what do you mean, trying to bust us up?" Then to me, "Who is this dude anyway, Kathy?"

"A friend," I said, looking at Abram.

"That's what I am to you?" Abram said. "A friend?"

I turned away from the look in his eyes, then whirled around and lashed out. "You were my ticket out of here. But you were a pretty slow boat, and an express came along."

I linked my arm in Jack's.

Abram continued to look with a hard, scrutinizing gaze into my face. "I don't believe you, Kathy."

"Well, that's your problem, isn't it? You'd better go pray about it."

"I will," he said, simply.

"Come on, Jack," I said, smiling at him, "we've got a lot of traveling to do."

Jack smiled back, but there was a wild gleam in his green-gray-blue eyes. "How about I take just a second to teach this neighbor lad a lesson?"

"I'm not your enemy," Abram said.

"Ha!" Jack said gleefully. "Afraid of getting your pretty face messed up?"

For the first time Abram assessed Jack and made a sincere effort to explain things to him. "This is as wrong for you as it is for Kathy. I've known her since we were children. She's headstrong. She won't admit it now because it doesn't fall in with her plans, but she's in love with me."

Jack snorted at this calm assertion. "So much in love with you that she marries me!"

"Praise the Lord, you understand."

"I understand you are a raving lunatic."

Sweat broke on Abram's forehead; a desperate note crept into his voice. He said to me, "Before God it's true that we love each other, and you know it's true. Now, while the marriage has not yet been consummated and there's still hope of annulling it—tell him, Kathy."

"Save your breath for your prayers, Abram."

"Consummated?" Jack Sullivan roared. "For your information, my man, it will be consummated before the hour's out." And giving me a tug, he pulled me toward the car.

"Kathy," Abram called.

That final plea was too much for Jack. He spun around and socked Abram square in the face. Abram saw the blow coming but made no effort to avoid it or raise his hands to fend it off.

He stood there and took it. A thin red stream curled from a nostril. He didn't seem to notice because he didn't bother to wipe it away. This indifference infuriated Jack. He danced around him, looking like an angry hornet. As he struck attitudes, pantomiming feints with his fists in front of him, I saw that he was a small man.

And I saw something else. I saw that he looked foolish with his fancy footwork, jabbing at Abram. Abram stood like a rock, taking the punishment. It was as though he didn't feel it, as though he was unconscious of it. His eyes never left me.

His eyes said, "You know I'm right. Come back, you can still come back."

His eyes said, "I love you."

He was probably right. He generally was. One fourth of July a firecracker didn't go off. I wanted to investigate, but he held me back. I was so mad I screamed and hollered. Then the thing went off in a stream of flame. Yes, Abram had been consistently right all down the years I'd known him. He was probably right now.

I probably did love him. But that had nothing to do with anything. I was a married lady. I was Mrs. Jack Sullivan. And Abram would have to get used to the idea.

I kissed Jas good-bye, but he was mad at me for not marrying Abram, and he wiped my kiss off. I got in beside Jack, and we started up. We went slowly, as we were pulling the trailer and two horses. I stuck my head out the window to wave good-bye to Abram. He was standing in exactly the same position. I waved, but he didn't wave back. I leaned out farther and blew kisses to show them how happy I was.

I turned on the radio and, with my head against Jack's chest, began to hum along. I felt close to tears, but just then I found a really neat station. They were playing a Patsy Cline single. It was just last March she died in that terrible plane crash, and they dedicated a lot of programs to her and played her most famous songs: "I Fall to Pieces," "Crazy," and "Walkin' after Midnight." The music put me back on high as it always did.

Patsy Cline! There was a lady who could sing!

But I had some thoughts as to how she could maybe come on differently, and sing with more contrast. I always saw exactly how a piece should go.

Jack didn't want to spend sixteen or twenty bucks for a motel, and he didn't want to wait either. So it happened in the car. He just pulled off to the side of the road and parked.

It went too fast for me. Before I was really into it, it was over. It was one of those experiences, I decided, that was overrated. In my opinion, too much was made of sex. Besides, I hadn't realized it was going to hurt.

However, more important things were happening. We had by now gone farther from St. Alban's than I had ever been. There were streams I had never seen, and metal bridges that clattered as we passed over them. The car chewed up the miles. Sometimes we were in patches of forest, then it was farmland, with rape and wheat, and machinery moving in the rows. It was exciting not to recognize anything.

Late in the afternoon the narrow road joined the Trans-Alaskan Highway, four lanes running straight as far as the eye could see. "This is more like it," Jack said. "From now on we'll really make time." He told me the Americans built this highway during the war.

The ascot had gotten mussed up during our brief acrobatics in the backseat, so I took it off and kissed the place in his throat where his shirt opened. He was pleased at this and asked me how I liked being Mrs. Jack Sullivan.

"I like it fine. There's a different sky over us, Jack. It's as though I'd been kept in a box, you came along and took off the lid."

He laughed at my analogy. Jack liked to laugh. He liked to be happy. He was a fun-loving guy, boisterous and carefree. Not as tall as some. Not as good-looking. But his resilient nature exuded through his pores. I had picked right, after all. He was just the kind of person to go through life with.

I wondered briefly what Mum would have thought of him. But I knew she'd prefer Abram. She'd had a soft spot for Abram. "He's dependable," she told me more than once, "and there's a kernel in him that's going to sprout into something fine." But he hadn't the keen, flashing wit, the ability to see the fun in everything. Jack looked on the bright side, and I liked the picture of our lives he spun for me.

He was enthusiastic about my becoming a big singing

star. He'd help me, open doors for me, swing some of his contacts my way. First, he'd showcase me in the clubs, then he'd wangle a recording contract.

"With a voice like that, you need a manager. Me."

I was only too happy to turn my future over to him.

And it looked very rosy as we tooled along, dragging our horse trailer.

We stopped for sandwiches and coffee, and drove on until we hit a town large enough to boast a motel. It was lovely to stretch out on a bed. Jack had to make love again, after watering the ponies, of course. This time it went better. I could see I was getting to like it. I closed my eyes and pretended it was Abram. Except he wouldn't go about it like this. He'd be slower and more intense, because that's the way he did everything.

▼ ▲ ▼

WHILE Jack went to find the Coke machine, I took a shower. There was plenty of hot water. What a luxury! At home, by the time the boys got through, mine was downright cold. I slipped between the sheets in a shirt I took out of Jack's suitcase. The only thing I had brought with me was my guitar; that and the papers from the bottom of Mum's old dresser—her marriage certificate and annulment along with my birth registration were the only proof that I was me. As for letdown skirts and patched sweaters, I would wear new ones or none at all.

Jack came back with the Cokes, and we were sitting up in

bed drinking them when there came a sudden hammering at the door. We were both stark naked again—Jack had seen to that—but he threw a towel around himself and let in our company.

It was my stepfather. He had his drinking buddies with him. Hubert politely removed his hat, but Jellet made straight for me, and Black Douglas was right behind him. Then, suspecting I was naked as a jaybird under the covers, Jellet stopped in confusion. I pulled the blanket around my ears. The room seemed full of men.

Jack, who had never set eyes on my stepfather, was asking who the devil he was and what they wanted. Jellet found his voice and denounced me as a whore and a harlot.

"Are you through?" Jack jumped to my defense. "Because if you are I call on God himself to witness that you broke in here full of threats and verbal abuse and . . ."

"Hold on, hold on," Jellet spluttered.

"No, you hold on." Jack's voice rose to a tenor. "Your stepdaughter and I were married this morning by Preacher Bartlett."

"Married?" Jellet fell back a step.

"That never occurred to you?" I asked sweetly. "Jason didn't tell you? I suppose you were whaling him too hard and he omitted that little piece of information."

Jack slapped his thigh and almost lost his towel. "Talk about a wild goose chase!"

"But she just ran off," Jellet was telling his pals. "Didn't have my parental consent or anything like it."

"You're not my parent and never were."

"How old is she?" Black Douglas put in, with the air of a judge on the bench.

"Seventeen," replied Jellet. This came as a shock to Jack, as I could see out of the corner of my eye.

"You're within your rights, Jellet," Douglas intoned gravely. "But give it a thought, my friend, give it a thought. This here Irishman married her fair and square. He's got a couple of pretty classy suits hanging in the wardrobe, not to speak of a car and a horse trailer."

"Sure," Hubert chimed in. "Here's someone's who's pretty well fixed come along and took her off your hands."

Jellet turned on them angrily, demanding to know whose side they were on. But I could see he was thinking things over, weighing them in the balance, so to speak, and I signed Jack to repress the urge for a wisecrack and let things work themselves out.

Black Douglas left to return with more Cokes, and a treaty of peace was concluded. Jellet even went so far as to shake hands with Jack.

When they finally departed with handshakes all around, Jack let loose with a war whoop. No way would Jack Sullivan have given up his bride. He had spent the entire time that our marriage was being toasted figuring how to take all three of them on. "The big guy is out of condition. A couple of jabs in the gut would put him away. Your stepfather is the kind that needs a weapon; he's no good bare hands. Only the dude in the black hat worried me. But the one thing on his mind was how to fortify his Coke from the flask in his pocket without sharing."

▼ ▲ ▼

I WOKE up thinking I was sick to my stomach. But that wasn't it. My head didn't ache, my throat wasn't sore, but I felt terrible. It took me a while to realize it was Abram. The hole I felt was not where a tooth was missing or tonsils taken out. It was because I had left Abram.

I looked at the man still asleep in the rumpled bed. A red-headed man with red fuzz on his arms and on his chest. I had traded Abram for him, and I didn't even know him. I didn't know who he was. It was as though the roof fell in on me, burying me under the rubble of what I had done.

I had made a choice that was responsible for the fact that I was sitting in an unheated room in the middle of the night. It had gotten me out of bed and made me look at myself.

I had made a choice, and it got me up in the night and made me think I was dying. It was cold sitting in a chair, but I didn't put my sweater on. I didn't get back under the covers, and I didn't get dressed. I wanted to be cold. A stillness came over me, the stillness I had known on the res when I stood with my grandfather and felt the world breathe. I began to hum the world in a chant I'd learned from Elk Woman. The Cree music made me strong. I had to be strong enough to forget the past, which was Abram, and focus on the future, which was Jack.

When Jack woke up, I asked him, "What do you think? Is it possible to feel bad about the right choice, and pretty good about the wrong one?"

"What are you talking about?"

"It's just a philosophical question. I thought you might know."

Of course he didn't.

▼ ▲ ▼

JACK and I stepped from one quagmire into another, from explosive scene to chaotic happening. Many times we sneaked out of a place because we couldn't pay the bill. Out back doors, down fire escapes. In a coffee shop I'd pick the bread basket clean and squirrel away the little butter, jam, and honey pats. Even a salt cellar was swept into my purse, which already had broken crackers in the bottom. Jack made a lark of it. It was called "getting your money's worth."

Many times we couldn't afford dinner. We'd go into a store for bread, cheese, and cookies, and eat in the car. We'd pick up those little packets of dried soup, where you just add hot water. The tap water in motels usually wasn't very hot, but we managed.

We had to sell the ponies for less than Jack had hoped. I discovered that in all deals he was vastly optimistic and projected profits that were rarely realized. Without horses there was no reason to keep the trailer, so that went as well. After a transaction Jack always celebrated with a couple or three drinks. The worse he came off, the more he drank.

When a deal collapsed completely, we still had to have a party. He called this "celebrating bad news." "That's when you need it," he said. "When things go right you're happy anyway."

I noticed, however, that he celebrated then too.

Unfortunately, the celebrations themselves were what got him down. The morning after, his high good spirits deserted him. He became morose and ugly, a side of him I'd not seen before.

I had to get used to bar talk too. I saw why Mum never let me near the Eight Bells; the men sprinkled their conversation with words I had been taught to avoid. However, I soon learned that nobody heard them. Like Abram's "Praise the Lord," it was simply a way of underlining what was said.

I learned that ponies were far from Jack's only source of livelihood. He had peddled everything from Fuller brushes to insurance to a product that ostensibly removed stains on anything from blouses to saddles. It took the stain off—and the material as well. I've known it to bite through the trim of a car.

But Jack had a natural flair. The gift of gab, he called it. And we didn't starve.

In the beginning it was fun, kind of a game, the two of us outwitting everybody else. Stealing out of bed before sunup, rolling the car fifty yards down the road before starting it. It was generally a house, as motels had a nasty habit of demanding payment in advance.

I wasn't listening to the radio as much. I was listening inside myself, remembering the songs Elk Woman sang as she kneaded bread, as we searched for berries, as she lit her pipe. Some of the notes didn't land squarely on the frets of my guitar, and when I tried them on a bar piano, they seemed to hide in the cracks between the white and black keys. But they fit perfectly into their own melodies and produced strange tonalities that echoed the sounds and cries of nature. They flowed like the streams I'd played in, shone silver like the mud-banks I'd slid down. The notes were elusive, dew caught on leaves, tiny transparent prisms of sound, chords that spoke of rain and earth. And pounding moccasin feet dancing my mother on the long journey. Celebrating. Cree songs were full of celebration, of life and death in an eternal round.

Elk Woman used to explain it to me as we sat and smoked. Now, driving these long stretches with Jack, I tried to put it into words. I couldn't, but I put it into sound. I got excited and sang out loud.

Jack didn't like it. "What's that outlandish screeching? Are you singing or yelling?"

"I'm feeling the earth breathe."

▾ ▴ ▾

THEY say you remember first times, a first kiss, a first love. I remember the first time I was paid for singing. It was an elegant place with a piano, a big midwestern square piano in a corner by the bar. I rushed over to it and saw that it had been degutted, the strings torn out. Nevertheless I ran my hands over it. It was dusty and the finish marred by beer bottle rings. Still, the place was an improvement on most of the dives Jack had taken me to. It had fancy toothpicks in little cellophane packets. That seemed to me quite a cut above having them lie around in a cup.

We were pretty much on our uppers because Jack had taken to making bar bets, and the last couple of times he lost. This particular time he left me eating a Salisbury steak with a side order of fried onions. After a week of chicken salad sandwiches with the chicken mostly absent, this tasted like heaven.

I was wolfing my food, barely conscious of what Jack was up to. He'd gone to the bar to cadge a free drink, and I saw that he was pulling one of his favorite cons. It was a number game he called Double or Nothing.

Jack would soften them up with tales of the great gambling capitals of the world: Monte Carlo, Las Vegas, Montreal. How on the train to Windsor Station a dedicated bettor would stake hundreds of dollars on the raindrops crawling down the windows or the timing of the next thunderclap.

Double or Nothing. He'd learned this fantastic game of chance from a man who pitched pennies with silver dollars. Each time you won, you could collect or let your bet stand, shooting for double. All you needed was a cocktail napkin to keep score on.

There was always someone curious enough to ask for details.

Jack would oblige. "You bet against the house. No checks, no credit, no rings or watches, cash on the line. You run out of cash, you got to fold. Each time it's double your stake or quit."

So someone slaps down a buck, and the bartender produces a paper napkin. Jack invites the mark to pick a number from ten to a hundred at random.

"Seventy-six," says the mark.

Jack writes it down for all to see.

76

"Now write it backward and add." Jack does the arithmetic.

$$\begin{array}{r} 76 \\ +\ 67 \\ \hline 143 \end{array}$$

Jack says. "Doesn't win. Not a palindrome. If you quit now, you get your money back. If you want to go on, you got to double your bet. That's the game—Double or Nothing."

The mark puts down another dollar, and Jack goes on.

"Do it again. Write it down backward and add."

The mark writes

$$\begin{array}{r} 143 \\ +\ 341 \\ \hline 484 \end{array}$$

"Aha!" Jack shouts. "You did it! That's a palindrome. It reads the same way forward and backward. See, 484. And backward, 484. In this game a palindrome wins. You doubled your bet to two dollars. You got a palindrome. So you win two dollars."

The mark holds out his hand for his winnings, but Jack smiles and shakes his head. "No, friend, you didn't actually bet, so you didn't win anything. That was just a demonstration. I was explaining the game."

He goes on to another subject, but now three or four onlookers want to try the game. Jack protests he can't bankroll a table full of players; they should go to Vegas or Montreal. They plead with him, all they want is to learn the game, what's a dollar or two. One big spender calls for drinks all around, and Jack finally agrees.

The con was usually good for fifty bucks. The mark quickly figured out small numbers got you nowhere and would gingerly try something bigger, like 78. Wow! Eight-to-one profit. 79. Hallelujah! Thirty-two to one. Then he gets greedy. He goes for the biggest, 98 or what comes to the same thing, 89. But this baby goes on and on and on, each time forcing the mark to double his bet. Since it's strictly cash, no credit, no checks, they usually quit at $64 or $128, netting Jack a fifty.

The trouble tonight was that the bartender got his hands on it first and put it against Jack's tab. There wasn't enough left to pay for our breakfast and my Salisbury steak.

I continued to sit in front of it. The manager came up and waved a hand in the general direction of the food. "Your boyfriend didn't pay for this, miss."

"He's not my boyfriend, he's my husband." And I waggled my wedding band at him.

"It's still not paid for."

"I tell you what, throw in another cup of coffee and I'll sing."

"You'll what?"

He looked so comically incredulous that I laughed. "Just one song. If you want more you'll have to pay. Fifty dollars and I'll sing till you close."

"Well now, I doubt we'll have to worry about that. But go ahead. Sing one song, and I'll not only give you a refill on the coffee, we'll make it dessert too."

I went out to the car and brought back my guitar, then surveyed the room for the best spot, where I'd be facing the most tables and could still be seen from the bar. I chose a surefire number and tuned my guitar, speaking to it silently as I always did. "Sing with me," I invited. I could tell that it was a little out of sorts from banging around in the trunk of the car. But I hoisted myself onto the old piano and from the first chord I struck, it was with me. We were a team. It seemed to know what I wanted before I touched the strings. I soared, it soared. I whispered, it whispered. Together we cried and exploded in raw uncooked energy.

The men at the bar didn't touch their drinks. The people at the tables stopped eating. They'd never heard anything like what burst from me and my old guitar. I'd never heard myself sing like this either. The notes came out exactly the way I wanted, full and round, soft and dreamy, breaking into harsh cries of pain.

The audience was with me. I could do no wrong. Or rather, all my wrongs were right, and anyone could tell I'd been born left-handed. Sure, they'd changed me over, but I wouldn't let them change a note of the music. It came out just right.

When I finished there was no applause. For a count of five, that is; then the storm broke. They clapped, they stamped, they banged on the varnished bar top. They whistled, they cheered.

The manager somewhat hesitantly let me know he couldn't quite get fifty dollars together. So a collection was taken up. Nearly a hundred dollars was in the plate. I sang until closing.

My last number I screwed up the courage to tie a shoelace around my forehead and started with a whoop. It was the Cree way of saying, "This is me, here in the midst of creation. I'm one with it, with you."

But the gang at the bar didn't get it. The couples at the tables resumed talking. They weren't listening anymore.

"What's the idea?" Jack demanded later. "You had them eating out of your hand. Then you start with that no-tune Indian stuff."

"You think it has no tune?"

"And no rhythm. To get right down to it, it's not music. It sounds like wolves howling in the night."

"Yes, yes! That's part of it, the wolves. But also the trees bending in the wind. And someone crying, far far away—"

"It's not music, and that's that. You want to kill your career before it gets started?"

I didn't argue, but I was beginning not to pay much attention to what Jack said.

The hundred bucks in his pocket put him in a good mood, and he didn't stay mad. We splurged and went to a class motel. There was perfumed soap, shampoo, and a hair dryer on the wall. We lay between clean sheets and Jack renewed his plans for my career. Suddenly I seemed a better bet than ponies.

"Did you ever wow them. We'll make a million on you. Two million. Maybe more. We'll invest it too."

I let him talk. And there's no one who could come through in that department like Jack Sullivan. He spoke of how I would climb on the charts. He spoke of the Grammys, of the Grand Ole Opry. There would be recordings in my future, contracts, deejays—maybe movies.

I listened until he fell asleep. But I couldn't sleep. I relived every note I'd sung that evening, going over the phrasing, changing the chords, adding a run, holding a final note. It had been like the evening at the Eight Bells, until I improvised the wind-band. I felt them slip away then, stiffen up, resist the alien modulations and the old, old way of looking at the world. They didn't like to be reminded that there once was a world without trailers and jet planes and TV, a world that still existed on the Canadian prairies, and that would outlast their supersonic age.

Why couldn't they hear the wonder in the Cree songs? Why did they stand outside and refuse to enter? Was it because they'd never scuffed their feet in the dust of the road leading to the res, hadn't sat and smoked with Elk Woman, hadn't looked into the eyes of an old shaman who was my grandfather?

This is what I had to give them, that no one else could. Only I could bring them a breathing world.

Chapter Seven

As we junketed east Jack kept the car radio tuned to music stations, insisting I memorize the Peggy Lee repertoire. But in the long stretches between towns there was nothing but static. That's when I went inside myself, recalling that many times I'd been able to call Mum out of her illness with the Cree songs. There'd been interest in her face as her hands pressed the intricate rhythms into the bedclothes. Being Cree, she had them in her blood. Abram was Mennonite through and through, yet when I sang them to him he said, "It comes at you unexpected and sort of grabs you."

That proved anyone could like the music. Anyone but Jack and the people in the bar. Somewhere there was an audience for it, there had to be. Jack had his way in most things, but when it came to music I wouldn't give in. I decided to try it again when I got a chance.

By this time Jack thought we could cross to the American side. He avoided the traffic of the main route through Winnipeg and chose a small station with a single Mountie reading the Sunday supplement, who glanced at our papers and turned to Sports. The U.S. border patrol was more efficient. They asked us to open our bags and rummaged through them for about thirty seconds. Presto! we were in the States. You couldn't tell the difference except that the roads were better. Jack told me Americans pronounce *out* like *ow.*

We headed for Grand Forks and Fargo. Our routine was for Jack to park somewhere and leave me in the car while he went into the establishments and struck a deal. I could honestly say that I was a hit on both sides of the border.

Jack claimed it wasn't so much my singing as me. I knew what he meant; there was a magnetism between me and the audience, a connection that snapped, crackled, and popped.

For the first time we had money, ate regular, and I was able to buy myself a pair of shoes. An eyelet blouse, I decided, was in my future, and a tight-fitting pair of jeans. We had reached a new plateau, and I think it was a plateau for Jack too. In fact he'd never had it so good. I was better than ponies. Motels and all that went with them—showers, soaps, shampoos, perfumes, hair dryers, and coffee in the room—were now our way of life.

It was interesting how quickly we adjusted to the new lifestyle. The only trouble was Jack was able to drink more, and he did. I was the one who generally drove back to the motel with a morose and disoriented husband beside me. His gambling was more serious now, the stakes higher, the bets more outrageous. I thought of Loki the Trickster more than once.

One thing that fascinated Jack was my name, von Kerll. He claimed that a *von* before any Kraut name, German or Austrian, was like the English *sir.* It's the mark of the aristocracy.

Jack was full of questions about my father, and got me to tell him all I knew of him.

"He grew up at his grandmother's place, a beautiful old home on the Bodensee."

"A beautiful old home," he repeated musingly. "Could it be a castle?"

"Could be," I said, remembering my childhood fantasies.

"But don't you want to know? Aren't you curious?"

"Why should I be? He deserted my Mum and me, why should I care about him?"

"He may be rich."

"So what if he's rich. I don't want anything from him."

"But if your parents were legally married . . ."

"Oh, they were. I have the license."

Jack pulled over, stopped the car, and made me dig it out then and there. He read it carefully, word for word. When he looked up it was with a triumphant expression. "Don't you see, you could be entitled to something. We could have hit on a sweet grubstake."

"You're dreaming, Jack," I said sharply. That's one thing

I disliked about him; he was always looking out for number one.

Of course there were things I liked about him. If we passed a sign, even a hand-lettered one, advertising a rodeo, barn dance, outdoor concert, or county fair, he'd immediately scrap our plans to be somewhere or other by dinner, turn off, and drive a hundred miles out of our way. That's what made it an adventure being married to him.

I saw it first and exclaimed, "Look, a fair!"

"How many miles?" he asked, but he really didn't care; he turned off.

It was a lovely fair, tents and a band with plenty of brass. There were rides and sideshows, a two-headed cow and the body of an alien in a large jar. The body was green and reminded me of the bloated carcass of a pig. We rode the water chute and slid to a splash landing. We flew an airplane in circles. We lay on a wheel that turned upside down and whirled around until sparks flew. We felt our way through the house of mirrors, flattening our grotesque faces as we bumped into ourselves. We laughed the whole time and I got a stitch in my side. "I have to catch my breath," I said, and felt in my purse for Kleenex.

That's when I discovered our money was gone. All of it.

"Pickpockets!" Jack wailed. "They work every crowd. I should have kept the money. I don't know what we'll do."

I knew. I undid my shoelace, tied it across my forehead and started to sing. Instead of *moon, toon, spoon* . . . a wild Indian railing preceded the first note. It was the chance I'd been looking for.

It caught their attention all right. But when I launched into the body of the song, the crowds walked past us, sometimes dropping a dime into my open guitar case.

"What the hell's come over you? Give them what they want."

But I continued the dissonant Cree invocation. After an hour there was enough change for gas, so I stopped and looked around for Jack. He'd gone off to a corner bench to sulk.

During the drive back he lectured me about sticking to what I did well and forgetting that weird Indian business. The longer he talked, the more determined I became. That's when he guessed. "Have you got Indian blood, or what?"

"My mum."

"Damn," he said, "that's just like you, Austrian royalty on one side and a redskin on the other." Then after a pause, "Well, all the more reason not to sing those outlandish, heathen songs. Do you want the whole world to know you're an Indian?"

"Yes."

We weren't close after that.

▼ ▲ ▼

THEN came an evening when I started to actively dislike my husband. It was closing time at one of those honkytonks, and the crowd spilled outside but were milling around, still talking, when an argument broke out. It was over a debt that one guy owed another. Before anyone knew what was happening, a knife was palmed and the next minute stuck in this fellow's ribs. He crumpled up on the sidewalk.

There was a lot of blood. Someone said he was dead. An old tramp who was shuffling by was the only one to get down on his knees and try to help. The old man put his fingertips on the wounded man's carotid and bent to listen to his chest.

At this point police and ambulance arrived. I felt Jack's fingers dig into my arm. "Come on," he mouthed, and started to back me out of there.

An officer was going through the crowd, notebook in hand, taking names and addresses. As I watched, they placed the vagrant under arrest.

"Wait," I said to Jack. "He didn't do it."

"Shut up." Jack increased his pressure on my arm.

"Take your hands off me, Jack Sullivan."

Instead he hauled me backward toward the car.

"All right, all right," I said, giving up and going with him.

On the way back to the motel I started to think of Abram. Abram would have given his name to the officer. Abram would testify for the old man who had no one to stand up for him, no one in that crowd anyway. They were pals of the guy who had done the murder—because I was pretty sure the guy on the ground was dead.

"Why didn't you want me to give my name to the police?" I asked Jack.

"Honey, you *never* give your name to the police."

"But they'll pin it on that poor old man who had nothing to do with it."

"And that's not your concern, now is it?"

I didn't say anything, but again I compared him with

Abram, and I knew for a hard fact that I should have stayed in Alberta and waited for Abram.

"What are you so quiet about?" Jack asked.

"Nothing."

I told Jack I had a headache and spent that night on the far side of the bed. I didn't sleep; I kept thinking of the old man, and of Abram.

The next day, as we drove along, my mind kept reverting to the incident—that's what Jack called it, an incident. I called it murder.

"What will they do to him?"

"What?"

"The vagrant? Will they execute him?"

"Will you stop it with that guy? He'll go to prison, and have three squares a day, which is more than he has now."

"It isn't right," I muttered.

"Kathy, will you for Pete's sake leave it lay?"

"I always thought the guilty were punished, and the innocent went free. That's the way it's supposed to be."

Jack pursed up his mouth. He looked mean. I didn't like him much anymore. I twiddled dials hunting for a country music station and began to sing along with Loretta Lynn, but my heart wasn't in it.

We stopped for hamburgers and an order of fries.

"How many minutes does it take to electrocute a person?'

"Oh for God's sake!" He clapped money down on the table and got up.

"I'm not finished."

"Put it in a doggie bag. Wrap it in a napkin. I'm out of here."

I continued chewing.

"Well," he said, leaning over me, "are you coming?"

I continued chewing.

"All right, let's have it. What's going on with you? And don't tell me it's that damn bum."

"Abram always said you do what you have to do to live with yourself."

"Abram? Who the devil is Abram?"

"You know, my friend—who saw us off."

"What's he got to do with it?"

"He always said—"

"Yeah. Okay. I know what he said. So what?"

"So I'm going back to the police station."

"Now see here, Kathy—"

"I'm going back," I repeated.

"Well, I'm not."

"That's okay. I'll take the bus."

"I'm not giving you money for the bus."

"You don't need to, I've got my own money."

"You been holding out on me?"

"They're tips. I figured the tips were mine."

"Now see here, Kathy—"

"I don't want to hear any lectures."

"No lectures. I'm giving you a last chance to be reasonable. We don't even know for sure the guy was dead."

"He was dead."

"How do you know?"

"I could tell."

Jack rolled his eyes heavenward, only there was a ceiling in the way. He wrote a number on a matchbook. "That's where I'll be. Call me when you come to your senses."

I watched through the window as he got in the car, slammed the door, backed out, and—I waited to see if he would drive off.

He did.

My spirits suddenly rebounded and I inquired when the next bus was due. There was time for a giant Coke and to play the jukebox.

On the way back I sat behind the driver. The bus made some rural stops. People got in who he knew and called by their first names.

"What is Martha like?" I asked, inching forward.

"She's a good sort. On her way to see her daughter four stops on. Now that young woman is no better than she should be. She's got a kid too. Martha tries to be there when the little girl gets home from school. There's lots of trouble in this world, missy."

"I know. You can let me off at the stop closest to the police station."

I walked down the main street, entered the building, and went up to the officer on duty. I gave my name and stated I was a witness to the stabbing on Hope Street.

"Is the man dead?" I asked.

"He's dead all right."

"I thought he was."

I was brought in to see the sergeant, who was warming a pot of coffee. He offered me a cup and we sat with the desk between us, drinking the hot dark brew.

The sergeant looked at me curiously. "How come you want to testify?"

"I didn't see anyone telling it as it was. They're all friends of the guy who did the stabbing."

"Yeah." Then drawled, "He's got friends everywhere."

Did he mean here on the police force? I looked at him for confirmation, and he smiled over the rim of his Styrofoam cup.

"Of course," he went on, "all you need say to get the old bum off is that he just happened along."

"That's how it was," I assured him.

"In that case . . ." He rummaged in a drawer and brought out a printed form. "Fill this out, sign it, and we'll turn him loose right now."

I brought my hands together. "Oh, could we?" Then I attended to the affidavit. The sergeant looked it over, nodded, and led the way through a back room and down a short corridor with cells on either side. "There he is. Hardly worth bothering your pretty head about." My man was stretched out snoring lustily under a thin gray blanket. He started at our approach, opened his eyes, and looked at us in alarm.

"It's all right," the sergeant said. "I'm letting you go. This young lady was present at the brawl. I have her sworn statement that you just happened along."

"Did you have to wake me out of a beauty sleep to tell me something I already know?" the old man grumbled.

"This young lady did you a big favor, friend."

"Hmmm," was the response.

No one thanked me, especially not the old tramp, but I felt good and started humming a Cree victory song.

When we got back to the front office there was Jack, breezy as ever. "Hi, sweetie," he said casually as I came in. "Ready to go?"

"The man was dead," I said to him.

"Kind of thought he was. Leastways, he wasn't looking too healthy."

I don't know if I'd expected Jack to be there. Or what I would have done if he wasn't.

▼ ▲ ▼

IT was back to the good life.

That's what Jack called it. And for him I guess it was. I was pulling down a couple of hundred weekly singing what he wanted me to sing and what the audience wanted to hear. And he was drinking it up.

Don't get me wrong. I loved performing, and singing three or four nights a week was great experience. The first time a drunk followed me on stage and started caterwauling into the mike, I didn't know what to do. But I learned under fire, incorporating him into the act and setting him the task of beating time. The audience went for this and even liked the fact that he couldn't get it right. It added a comedic touch to my number.

No, I never tired of performing. But it looked as though Jack was right about the Indian songs; they just didn't go over, even as encores. I put them aside. Later, I told myself, because I still believed there was an audience out there. At the same time I knew instinctively that singing other people's songs and copying their styles would get me nowhere. If there was a route up, it certainly wasn't this.

Nevertheless, while my husband was lapping it up or busy conning a mark, my voice was growing stronger, louder, better. But there weren't contacts to be made in these out of the way spots. No one of importance heard me. I'd be stuck in two-bit hole-in-the-wall places forever. My career was stalled.

The closest I came to the big time was Minneapolis, where the owner applauded with the audience and signed me for the following year. But as we drove south through Wisconsin and the places got bigger and better, we started hearing, "Booked up . . . ," which meant, "Never heard of her."

Chicago seemed more distant than ever. If we were lucky, we'd make Madison.

We were having breakfast, coffee heated in the motel and rolls out of a doggie bag, when . . . Jack let out a whoop and a holler and waved the daily paper in my face. "Look at this and tell me what you see."

I looked and handed the paper back. "I don't see anything except unpronounceable Vietnamese names."

"No, no, here—the bit about the UN. Here it is. Erich von Kerll. It's got to be him, the newly appointed trade commissioner from Austria."

"Von Kerll?" I snatched the paper back. "You think it's my father?"

"It's got to be. It's your father, all right, and we're in the chips."

"Wait a minute, Jack. None of your wild schemes. If it is my father, so what?"

Jack looked at me dumbfounded. "What do you mean—so what? So he's the trade commissioner, with his name in the paper. He could open doors for you."

"We don't even know it's him."

"Of course it's him. I told you that *von* meant something." He settled down to read the article, and I read over his shoulder. There was a confirming sentence. ". . . left his home on the Bodensee to fill the post recently vacated by . . ." I stopped reading.

My father was here in this country. And he was someone important—but what was I? A struggling nobody, just another girl singer . . . Someday, when I'd made it, I could see myself dining with him at the Waldorf, or one of the other posh spots Jack told me of.

Not now. I didn't want to meet him with my hand out for favors, introductions, acceptance, money. That wasn't how I'd pictured it. In none of the Cree dreams where I'd so often met my father had it been like this.

Jack chose to disregard my reaction. He was off and running. "Think what he could do for you."

I was unresponsive to these fantasies. "I'm sure that's the first thing that would come to his mind."

He didn't hear me. "First off, we attend to your wardrobe—" He broke in on himself to exclaim, "This is the chance of a lifetime."

"What would we do? Just show up? He must have a whole staff of people. They'd throw us out on our ear."

"Why should they do that? A beautiful, gifted daughter. He'd be delighted. Any man would. Besides, didn't you always tell me it's what your mother wanted—for you to meet your father?"

When he brought Mum into it that changed things. "But he's in New York," I said feebly.

"You stopped reading after they mentioned Bodensee. The article goes on to say . . . See, right here—he's part of a team of experts visiting agribusiness centers to study the latest advances in farm machinery. Anyway, at the moment he's in Milwaukee, just hours from here." Jack grabbed both my hands and dragged me reluctantly into a wild conga. My feet found the rhythm and we whirled and pranced and whirled some more until he fell into a chair with me on top of him.

"I won't just barge in on him," I said after I had caught my breath.

I did agree to write.

It seemed odd. I was suddenly projected into the dream of meeting him. Only in my dream Jack Sullivan didn't stand over me as I wrote. What would von Kerll think? How would he react? Someone turns up claiming to be his daughter, a daughter he didn't know he had. Would he even believe me? I tried to picture the man who would open this letter. The second-in-command of U-boat 186. Tall, blond, with gray eyes that Mum had fallen in love with. Stories of him rushed through my head . . . a little boy in a sailor suit who lived by the Bodensee and had his leg amputated in the war, who married his nurse, and then left her. What would we think of each other?

Would he despise me as a fortune hunter? A gold-digging opportunist? Because that's what I was. I hated myself for writing.

Jack told me to say he should reply care of the local post office. I objected, "Wouldn't that look odd to him? No permanent address, no home?"

"The man's not going to worry about details like that. He is being told that he has a daughter."

In my letter I added nothing of myself or Mum. He hadn't the right to know anything. Unlike Jack, I didn't expect him to rush to embrace an errant daughter, lavish riches on me, incorporate me into his life. I no longer made up fairy tales.

Apparently even an answer was too much. Jack and I went to the post office every day for a week. "I can't believe it," Jack kept reiterating. "How can any man be so coldhearted as not to want to meet his own daughter?"

I didn't say anything. I didn't want Jack to see how much it hurt. Erich von Kerll had shared winters with me and Mum. I'd wasted a lot of dreams on that man.

Then finally a reply, sort of. The letter came back. Insufficient postage. I was glad he'd never received it. I knew in my heart it should not have been written in the first place. So I hid it and let Jack think what he would about Erich von Kerll.

Chapter Eight

It was a routine evening. I went on, did my first set, and got a big hand. Guys crowded around. Out of the corner of my eye I could see Jack at the bar, pretty far gone. In this half-inebriated condition he wasn't as sharp as he thought he was, and was squandering our money. I would have made a scene; after all it was really not *our* money, it was *my* money he was losing. But an uneasy possibility kept me quiet. A day or two might prove me wrong.

A day or two proved the opposite. I was pregnant.

I hated finding this out in an ordinary motel room. What I was experiencing was so extraordinary, so unusual. It was like a miracle had happened to me—in this everyday kind of place with ugly flowered wallpaper.

Such a large event had never happened in my life before

and I wanted to talk it over with Mum. I wanted her to tell me what it was like to grow a baby in your body, to have a new life to nurture and take care of and see that she became a really good person.

Kathy.

Another Kathy.

I needed to be by myself to think it through.

It was hard to get away from Jack, but I couldn't think about it properly with him constantly at my side talking his Irish banter.

As luck would have it, he ran out of beer, and I offered to go to the corner for a six-pack. The fresh air was bracing, and I ran a whole block just for the joy of being out and away and by myself for a few minutes. The wind was in my hair and I felt elated. I had life in me, and running was a celebration. It was then I was sent an omen—wild geese passed overhead, their flight an arrow in the sky. They were heading for home. I didn't know until that moment that I missed the Canadian prairies that I had opened my eyes to every morning for eighteen years.

I took a side street, and another, and wound up by docks, cranes, tramp steamers, bales, and boxes of cargo. They were being off-loaded.

I liked the tangy smell of oil, fish, and salt. It stung my nostrils in an exciting way. I sat down on a coil of rope off to the side, pretty much out of sight, and watched men haul and lift, swear and laugh. I liked their arms, powerful, hairy, muscled.

Jack's arms weren't much bigger than mine, only with orange fuzz. Yet he had made me pregnant, and it was this I had to think about, and the gypsy life we led. How could a baby be part of it? I'd read magazine stories where an infant slept in a bureau drawer, or the drawer of a wardrobe trunk. But that was not the way Mum raised us.

I wasn't feeling deliriously happy any longer. Jack was going to be furious that I'd gotten myself into this pickle. He liked things as they were. Why not? I was a meal ticket, with relatively little upkeep and hardly any overhead. It occurred to me that I'd gotten myself into another box.

I decided to delay telling him. Once he knew, he would have the upper hand, and the baby and I would be dependent on him and his whims.

"Well," I said to the little package inside me, "your timing is not the greatest. But don't worry, we'll manage."

▾ ▴ ▾

"YOU were gone an hour after that six-pack."

"I took a walk." Spoken demurely, sweetly, so he wouldn't dump us when he found out. Some people are naturally kind and sweet-natured, my Mum for instance. But it's wearing on me to even pretend. I dreamed of being rescued by a big-time record producer. He'd hear me, the bucks would roll in, and I'd get a nanny for Kathy. Because of course the baby was Kathy, she couldn't be anything else. One of those big blond Swedish girls would be perfect. We'd live in a penthouse in New York City or maybe a horse ranch in Nashville while I sang ethnic songs at the Grand Ole Opry. And I'd thought of a beautiful Cree lullaby to sing to Kathy.

"So now what's taking so long?" This from the couch where he sprawled watching the tube.

"I can't find the bottle opener."

"It's in plain sight on the counter."

I was careful to pour the beer so it ran down the inside of the tilted glass. Jack didn't like a head. I brought it and curled up beside him on the couch.

It was hard when he was in one of his losing spells not to say anything. Hard to laugh at jokes I'd heard before. Hard to be all sweetness and light. Hardest of all was repressing a desire to tell everyone about my baby. Jas and Morrie were uncles. Imagine. How surprised they'd be. And Elk Woman should know so she could sing Cree prayers for Kathy. Elk Woman was able to dream the Grandmothers, who would protect and guide her. My thoughts, like the wild geese, flew in formation back to Alberta. Back to . . . but I choked on his name. I'd taken a different path. I'd left him standing alone before the preacher's house.

There was something else I had to repress—my music. That's the way I had come to think of the Cree chanting that filled my head. I let it out only under my breath, and only in the bathroom. The power was in Jack's hands. I couldn't alienate him and I couldn't lose jobs. We needed all the money we could pile up.

I was almost six months along when I told him, and by then anyone with half an eye could see. It was New Year's Eve and I'd pulled off an unexpected gig, subbing for a group stuck in a blizzard. The roadhouse gave me a bonus. I figured Jack would be in a good mood, and the time was as right as it would ever be.

I'd nerved myself up to it once before, but then JFK was assassinated and Jack was upset, blaming LBJ, blaming Hoover, the New York underworld, even Castro. No one could come near him for days. Now he was a little high on champagne. I seized the opportunity, and with a big grin, which I plastered over a scared, sinking sensation, suggested we drink a toast to the baby.

Rage, fury, accusations pelted me. I stood my ground. I wanted to say I hadn't done it by myself, that he should try to be happy about it. But he had the power, and ended by saying, "We'll have to attend to this."

I smiled my most ingratiating smile. "Too late."

That precipitated another eruption. He accused. He calculated. Then in case he'd made a mistake, calculated again. He pleaded and threatened by turns. I went into the place in my head where I keep my music, and stayed there until he stormed himself out. When I saw he had simmered down sufficiently, I told him my plan. "I feel fine. I never have morning sickness. Sometimes I'm a bit on the queasy side when I turn in, but a cracker to nibble on fixes that. Anyway, since I feel good I'll be able to sing right up to the end."

"No one's going to pay money for a pregnant broad to get up on stage."

"I'm carrying it well. You didn't even know. I had to tell you."

"Six months is not nine months."

"I've got it worked out. I'll wear one of those caftans that hang loose, and I'll have a flowing scarf. I'll be a bit on the heavy side, but they won't know."

"Well," he considered, "I guess there's nothing for it but to take things a day at a time."

"I wonder," I asked the room in general, "if she'll have red hair."

Jack glared at me. "She better have." Then, "Wait a minute, why *she?* Boys run in my family."

"Girls run in mine."

My life with Jack hadn't been what I'd imagined. I'd known for some time that the road map I'd drawn from Mum's kitchen straight to stardom had been unrealistic. Things got in the way. People got in the way. Life got in the way, especially babies.

I put my hands flat against my hard, smooth belly. I felt that each job now would be my last. This week or next or the week after I'd be given the boot. There are limits to what a caftan can conceal, no matter how voluminous. I'm sure most everybody guessed, but no one had said anything . . . yet.

I prepared for the inevitable by saving whatever I could, watching out for sales, and forgetting the beer when I could get away with it, claiming I'd run out of money. Fortunately, Jack never knew for sure if I was holding out on him. He suspected though, and he was surly.

We weren't doing too well in Wisconsin, so Jack got on the phone to Minneapolis, where I'd gone over so big. On the phone Jack was the greatest. To hear him tell it, our passage through Wisconsin was like a prairie fire. The biggest clubs in Chicago were clamoring for me, but there was a chance we could squeeze in a return appearance, being friends and all. They bit.

Minneapolis–St. Paul. That's where I'd look for a nice rooming house with nice people, a place I could bring a baby to.

Jack Sullivan wouldn't make much of a father. I wished it had been someone like Abram. Someone kind like him, reliable like him. In the past, whenever I had to go through something, Abram had been there. Like Mum's dying; I never could have gotten through that if not for Abram. And life, I reasoned, was as important as death. In a way they were twin happenings.

Sometimes I got scared about having a baby and about our future. I will say for Jack that he did try to comfort me, but it was a puffy cotton-candy kind of comfort. It consisted of spinning another tale; the trouble was I had stopped believing in them. I don't know exactly when that happened, probably it was back in some fleabag rooming house where there was no hot water, or one of those nights we had to skip without paying. Somewhere along the way I couldn't force myself to it. It was a game I could no longer play.

A flat-handed pounding on the bathroom door. "How long are you going to hold the can down?"

That very night was the night I was fired. The owner was actually rather sweet about it; he slipped me an extra twenty. What I hadn't anticipated was Jack's reaction. He grew very quiet. I had never seen him quiet. He kept looking at me in a speculative way. I felt I was being evaluated and coming up short. The biblical term occurred to me . . . weighed and found wanting.

What did he see? A woman swollen with pregnancy, about to have a baby. A career nipped in the bud, an asset turned liability. Domesticity foisted on a carefree spirit. How unattractive that must all seem.

I knew in my bones he was figuring the angles. What if he left me? From his point of view that was a fairly good option. Shucking off me and the kid meant his old freedom, and I knew he was considering it. The cold I felt traveled to my heart.

He slept in mornings, and I house-hunted, taking the car, checking out ads in the paper. The place I liked was a big countrified house on Oakdale Street, and the people were friendly. It was a couple, Mr. and Mrs. Mason. The wife was especially nice, offering me lemonade and a slice of pie, homemade lemon meringue like Mum's. I felt two fat tears on my face and wiped them away fast. But I think she'd seen them. The price she quoted for the large back bedroom where the sun flooded in was quite reasonable. It was just the kind of room to bring a baby to, bright and cheerful, with chintz curtains and a bedspread that matched. If I ever have a home of my own, that's what I'd have—flowered chintz.

The windows opened onto a large yard with trees. To a child it would look woodsy. I would tell her about real woods, I would tell her about Alberta. "I love it," I said.

Jack had often warned me never to praise anything I was negotiating for, but that slipped out. Mrs. Mason seemed genuinely pleased, and I don't think she put the price up. In fact, when we were in the kitchen and I was finishing the pie, she looked across at her husband as though asking his approval and then mentioned a lower figure.

"We could do it for that if you and your husband and the baby were to stay a while."

"Oh yes, we'd want to stay."

She beamed at that.

Jack and I moved in. It didn't take Mrs. Mason long to figure out that he had no job and wasn't looking for one. In a lot of ways she reminded me of Mum. For one thing she disapproved of Jack sleeping till noon, and about eight-thirty started up the vacuum.

"Does she have to run that thing at this ungodly hour?" Jack protested to me.

From then on I intercepted Mrs. Mason, and we had coffee together. She confided that they had always wanted a family. She herself came from a large family, second generation in this country, originally Swedish. "From Uppsala," she said. "But George and I haven't been blessed with children. When you don't have them, it seems like such a privilege."

"Ours wasn't planned," I said. "It just happened."

"What do you want?" she asked. "A boy or a girl?"

"Oh, it's a girl. She's already named—Kathy."

"Like you?'

"Yes, and my Mum. It's a tradition in our family." And I told her about Mrs. Mike. "That's why the girls are always Kathy."

"I've a great respect for tradition. It links the generations." She got up to fill our mugs. When she came back she told me that her husband owned his own business. "It's small, a bicycle shop. But it's ours. He buys, trades, repairs, and sells them. Both the used and the brand new. By the way, I've been meaning to ask. What is it your husband does?" She refrained from finishing the sentence with "when he works."

"Jack? Oh, he's my manager. You see, I'm a singer."

It was plain that Mrs. Mason had never expected that a singer and her manager would be boarders in her back bedroom, so I gave her time to digest this information.

"Where do you sing?" she asked.

"That's Jack's department. He does my bookings."

"I was wondering, because my husband is a Moose, and the lodge has a monthly get-together . . ."

That night, lying in bed beside Jack, I mentioned the Moose and the Shriners as a possibility for additional bookings. But a series of prickings across my abdomen stopped me, letting me know the baby was preparing its move. I panicked. I needed to talk to Mum. I needed someone who had been through it to tell me what it was like, to say I'd do well and have a fine, healthy little girl.

I needed it, but I didn't have it. All I had was Jack, and he had gone to sleep without answering me. Would he ever be there when I needed him? Suppose when I went to the hospital Jack simply decamped? What would I do? I hadn't worked in three weeks and our savings were running low. Even my secret hoard would not stretch much further.

I reached out my hand to Jack, an inert lump on the far side of the bed. "Do you love me, Jack?"

"Sure, honey," and he turned over.

The pains started several hours later.

I shook Jack awake. He inquired drowsily if they were regular.

"Go back to sleep," he said, when I admitted they came when they wanted to.

By morning it was a different story. The pains were strong, and they clocked.

Now it was Jack who was in a hurry. He bundled me into the car. Mrs. Mason ran out in a robe, her hair in curlers, to give me a hug and a kiss.

I'd never been in a hospital. How stark it was, how impersonal. It stank of cleanliness. They put me in a short, stiff, white muslin gown, slit up the back, and came in to shave me. They pulled and tugged, and for a while it took my mind from the labor pains.

Not for long. They grew in intensity. They grew until they enveloped me. I became the pain. And I realized a terrible thing . . . this child could not get born. It was stuck inside me, battering to get out. But it couldn't, it would tear me apart trying, but it couldn't.

When my insides finally expelled their burden, I felt degutted, as though I'd been turned inside out, and was as weak as water.

They put the baby in my arms. I smiled. She had red hair.

▾ ▴ ▾

I WAS speaking to Jas. He sounded just the same. The same boy I confided in, who was angry at me for not marrying Abram.

"Jas," I said, "it's me, Kathy."

"Who?"

"Kathy, your sister. How many sisters do you have?"

"Kathy?"

"I called to tell you, you're an uncle. You and Morrie. I just had a baby. Her name's Kathy. And she has red hair. How are things with you, Jas? And how's Abram?" Abram had moved away.

You think you're insulated and then a possibility like this jars you, displacing the comforting pictures in your head. The one I liked best was Abram sitting on the steps of his house whittling. I wanted him right there where he'd kissed me and knew he loved me. I was devastated that he had moved.

"Moved where?" But I didn't wait for an answer. "He didn't go and get married, did he?"

Jas only laughed.

▾ ▴ ▾

I WAS wakened by the nurse.

She put Kathy in my arms.

My heart pounded. I held her against me, afraid to move.

The nurse laughed. "No, no, give her the breast. Your milk won't have come in yet, but sucking encourages lactation and strengthens the baby's ability to feed."

I transferred the precious bundle, held her in the crook of one arm, and with the other hand put her little face against my breast. My nipple sprung hard as her tiny mouth closed over it. What a strange and marvelous sensation to give suckle from your own body, to nourish your child. It wakens such floods of love.

I looked into the little face. She was all eyes. Big, dark, beautiful eyes, and that fringe of red hair. "Oh you blessed thing," I crooned at her. "You blessed thing."

She resumed her effort at nursing, and I began to speak to her seriously. I realized that in this first meeting with my daughter we should get to know each other. "To begin with I'll tell you what's important in this world. I wish you could do the same. Before you started getting born, did you see the plan of all possibilities laid out? Did you pick me? By the way you look at me I know you're trying to tell me. But by the time you can talk, you won't remember. And I suppose that's the way it's meant to be.

"Since you can't tell me about your world, I'll tell you about mine, this one you've come into."

I touched her little cheek with my finger, it was so soft. "The most important thing is that you're Kathy. Like me and my Mum, right back to Katherine Mary Flannigan. You see, the namer and the named are bound together by closest ties. That is why I am so lucky to be both mother and namer to you, Kathy."

Closing my eyes and travelling inward, I called. The Grandmothers came, and my own mother, and Oh Be Joyful and Mrs. Mike—"Know this new Kathy," I begged, "be with her, watch over her steps and her heart."

The nurse came back. She reached to take Kathy.

"Oh no, let me have her a moment more. We're just getting acquainted."

"There'll be plenty of time for that." She gave me my night medication in the forrm of a pill to swallow. "This will give you a good night's sleep. You need to get your strength back, you know."

She lifted Kathy from my arms. I tried to explain I still had important things to tell her, especially about Mum. "Oh, Kathy, how she would have adored you. It doesn't seem right that you won't know each other, that you'll never know her except what I can think of to tell you.

"She was a woman of two worlds. I don't think she was at home in either. She was Cree. She looked Cree, and she married a First Nation person. I think that was one side of it. The other, she was adopted by Katherine Mary, the first Kathy, and raised white. She graduated from nursing school at the top of her class and went to war, a white man's war. And she married a second time—white.

"All that is buried somewhere deep inside me and you. It's called DNA, and it makes you up, part of you, like fingernails. Kathy, the thing I want to tell you about that other Kathy—she lived. I want you to live. She loved—and I want you to love. Because she never held back, but gave herself completely, she became Oh Be Joyful's Daughter. That was her Indian name and that was her heritage. All her life she brought others joy and finally . . . finally . . ."

I was being shaken awake. I thought Jack was part of the dream. He wasn't. He had my clothes laid out on top of me.

"We're blowing this place."

"What?" I asked, still groggy, still asleep.

"Come on, baby, we're getting you out of here."

I nodded. That was okay with me.

"Let me help you into these," and he started to dress me.

"Does anyone know? The doctors? The nurses?"

"That we're getting you out? Of course not."

Jack cranked the bed up until I was sitting leaning against it, dressed except for my shoes, which he was fitting to my feet.

"Where's the baby?" I asked.

"I'll tell you about that in the car. . . . Oh, she's all right," he hastened to add. "She's fine."

"But where is she?"

"Now, lean on me and we'll get you down the hall."

"I can't stand up, Jack. I feel as if my insides will spill on the floor."

He captured a wheelchair from the hall and helped me into it. I was dizzy and felt strange sitting up straight. I may have fainted. I'm not sure.

In the car I asked, "Where's Kathy?"

"Don't you worry about Kathy. She's better off than we are."

"I want my baby!"

"Of course you do. But just for now Mrs. Mason will look after her."

"No."

"Just till you get your strength back, and we get on our feet. Believe me, it's best for the baby."

"But, but—"

He quelled my fears, stopped my questions with sensible answers.

We put up at a motel, and I was so glad to be helped into bed that I let everything slide until morning.

It took two or three days for my strength to return. I used the breast pump Jack foresightedly provided. I had plenty of milk, but no baby.

"When we're able to get her," I said, "it would be nice to go back to Alberta. Just for a visit. We could stay at Jellet's, it wouldn't cost much. And I'd get to see Jas." I said Jas, but I meant Abram. "Jas is a good kid, you know. I miss him." I knew who it was I missed. "I miss Morrie too—after all, they're uncles now and don't know it." And I told him about the Canadian geese I'd seen winging their way back.

"That's not us, honey. We aren't going back." Then he told me if we attempted to reenter Canada we'd be arrested.

"What!" But I stopped the protest that rose in me and waited to hear what he had done.

"That's why we had to find that out-of-the-way border crossing into North Dakota. You remember, we were pretty much on our uppers. I was flat broke. Didn't have a cent to give you for the shopping."

I nodded numbly, waiting for the blow to fall.

"We had to eat. So I left the market without paying. I figured, they're a company, they're insured against loss. It didn't mean anything to them. . . ."

"So you shoplifted?"

"It's a misdemeanor. Not worth extraditing a person, but they'd pick us up at the border."

"You, maybe. I didn't take anything."

"You were with me. You drove the car, ate the food."

I didn't say anything. What was the use? A heavy hopelessness descended. I couldn't go home. I couldn't take my baby home.

Jack's plan for little Kathy left not only my breasts but the rest of me aching.

Apparently he'd talked the Masons into taking Kathy until I was able to work. This seemed monstrous to me. Jack talked and talked and convinced me it was for the best. But deep inside I knew it was monstrous. I had to have my baby. My breasts called for her, my womb ached, my arms were empty. They laid her against me in the hospital. I felt a little warm being, knew an overwhelming content, felt love. I looked into her face. We communicated.

Jack said we had to move on. There was the matter of the hospital bill, and we had run out of money. I remembered the suggestion Mrs. Mason had made about the Moose lodge. It was a different lodge; this was in Illinois. Jack also checked out the American Legion and the Veterans of Foreign Wars. I was a hit at their events, and at a Masonic Temple dance.

Jack made dates with clubs too.

"Don't you think we can pick Kathy up pretty soon?" Each time I asked this, Jack stalled. He always had a reason why it couldn't be done—we had a lot of debts, doctors, hospital, anesthesia—until we broke even. Then, when we broke even, it was the moving around. Constantly changing surroundings was unhealthy for a baby, we had to get our feet under us, there was a great opportunity in the next town, a real gig, two solid weeks . . .

Finally, reality struck. He never intended that we should

raise our daughter. I had to sit down; the blow paralyzed me. I think I'd known. I think I'd known from the first, but I'd cowered in dark corners and pretended on bright stages, unable, utterly unable to face that Kathy was lost to me.

"It's better this way, hon," he said when I charged him with it. "She's got a stable home. A kid needs that. And she's got all the love she can handle from two decent God-fearing people."

"And a room with chintz curtains and a chintz bedspread."

"What's that?"

"Nothing."

Often my eyes would fill with tears. I'd go into the bathroom, lock the door, sit on the stool, and cry. I tried to recall what it was like to hold her. She was put in my arms; I held her, talked to her, looked into her little face. We had a conversation. I told her about her name—and naming. She wanted to tell me about the other side, where she came from. I couldn't lose her.

I wouldn't accept that I had lost her, I couldn't. I wanted my baby, I had to have her.

If I wanted her, I would have to go get her. The only way to do it was to run out on Jack. I got up while he was still snoring. I thought of taking the car. After all, we paid for it with money I'd earned. But this was something Jack would never forgive. He could do without me, but not without the car.

So I caught the first bus out of town, telling myself with every turn of the wheels I was closer to my little girl. When the bus finally pulled into the terminal I realized there was another connection to be made. I had missed it and had an hour to wait.

I sat on a hard bench, my eyes closed, trying to picture it, imagining how it would be. I'd talk to Mrs. Mason first, of course. She'd be upset. She must be very attached to her by now. Attached! What a word. She loved her.

Well, I loved her too, and she was mine.

I couldn't wait to get my arms around her. How would it feel finally to hold her again?

The bus rolled up, its brakes screeching to a stop. I boarded. This was the last leg of the trip; at the other end was a little redheaded daughter. She couldn't understand when I talked to her, but I could sing to her—the Cree ballads no one wanted to hear, and that wonderful lullaby. That she would understand.

Telegraph poles whizzed by. We passed a lot full of old tires, not the best part of town. We were slowing down. I looked out the window and there was Jack waiting for me.

He smiled and waved. I rubbed the window with the arm of my sweater, hoping it was a mirage, that he would go away. But he was still there, still smiling.

A smile is simply a distorted face, the lips spread open. I don't know why people think it kindly and jolly—I didn't. I didn't like Jack's smile.

I wasn't getting out of the bus. He had to come in and get me.

"Honey," he said, "I'm not mad. I don't blame you. You just want to see your baby. Don't you think that's what I want? She's mine too, you know. I want her just as much as you do. But I want to do it right, Kathy. I want us to make a real home for her. I want to be able to take care of her properly. A little girl like that, she'll want piano lessons and maybe ballet. And we'll be able to give her those things. Just not yet." He got me into the parking lot and walked me to the car.

He opened the door.

I stood there. I didn't get in.

"The Masons understand this, honey. They know it's just a temporary arrangement while we get our feet under us."

We stood facing each other by the open car door. "All right," he said in a change of tactic, "I'll take you to the Masons. We'll go right now. We'll say hello, get acquainted. What do you say?"

I got into the car.

"Take me back, Jack."

Chapter Nine

MY voice was fuller these days; maybe it was from having a baby. I don't know why, but I was able to throw a note into the air and sustain it in a way I had heard no other singer do. Wherever I sang, people loved it and wanted more. My breasts no longer ached and I didn't use the pump, but my mind was always on Kathy.

"You still send the Masons money, don't you?"

"Of course."

"A hundred dollars every month, right?"

"Right."

"That's good."

"They'll be able to get the kid anything she wants."

"No. I know them. They'll save it."

At the moment things were pretty bumpy with us. These

days Jack lost as much as he won, maybe more. He claimed stud poker was his game, but as we moved into bigger towns and classier joints, it became obvious that he was overmatched.

I had a talk with him, and he promised to stay away from bar bets and football handicapping. Poker, on the other hand, he didn't consider gambling. It was, he insisted, a science.

Gambling was in his blood; he was like a drunk hiding bottles in the chandelier.

I wasn't angry. He didn't tell me deliberate lies, he meant what he said. But it was discouraging to watch the money disappear. I needed things; my shoes were run down at the heels. And I wanted a dress I'd seen in a store window.

On the other hand, you couldn't be gloomy long around Jack. He was always good for a laugh. He whipped up a story for every occasion. Life to him was one big party, and if you were light on your feet and quick enough, you could keep ahead of the bad parts.

▼ ▲ ▼

I GOT into the habit at night, before I slept, of asking Abram what I should do. Should I ditch Jack and get my baby?

Then what? Could I earn a living? I needed Jack to get dates. Maybe I could take little Kathy back to Canada. I grinned, imagining how pleased Jellet would be. Abram, you've got to tell me. It's like I fell down a well and can't climb out. Or maybe I was at the bottom of the Sargasso Sea.

I knew what Abram would say. "Later, when you've made

a success, you can make a decision about Kathy. It will work out. You'll be together. Have faith."

I gave up on daydreams; they were scarier than the nightmares.

Worse than the scary ones were the ordinary everyday dreams. I'd be bathing her in a little plastic thingamajig that floated in the tub. She lay on her back and dabbled her hands in sudsy water. I had bath toys for her, a rubber duck that she chewed on happily.

I baby-oiled her on the counter. Mrs. Mason supplied me with talcum powder and urged me to use it freely. But I'd read that it wasn't good for infants to inhale talcum, which proved I was a better mother than Mrs. Mason. . . .

I put Kathy in a pink silk bassinet with flounces of lace next to my bed and sang her to sleep over the disruptive noise of Mrs. Mason's vacuum. . . .

Jack shook me awake because I was crying.

▾ ▴ ▾

NOTHING changed, it just went on until a particular Saturday night almost two years later. Saturdays were big, with more of everything, more audience, more money coming in, and, as usual, more going out. A fellow at the bar named Mac steered Jack to wagers he lost heavily on.

Mac was a short, broad man, but powerful, built like a wrestler—and older, late thirties or forty. He gave a good account of himself, though. If you believed him, he was a freelance promoter. However, I had come not to trust characters that were too ready to reel off their vitas.

Jack ferreted out the full story. Mac had made a very decent thing out of promoting music—records, demos, the usual. He had contacts, hung with the right people, was on a first-name basis with one of the performers at the Grand Ole Opry, developed quite a client list. Then what happens? He takes promoting one step further and cuts himself a bigger slice than he's legally entitled to. Of course it all fell in on him. He got jail time. And when he got out he's a has-been. No one would have anything to do with him, his calls weren't returned, doors closed in his face. He wound up scrounging for a living, another Jack, but smoother, more sophisticated, which he proved by taking Jack to the cleaners.

After one of my sets, he came up to me. I somehow knew he would.

"Hey, Kathy," he said, breezily, "I like your style."

"Thank you," I replied frostily. I might have added, "And I'm on to yours," but I didn't.

"You know, I just might be able to do something for you."

"Oh?" This kind of propositioning was standard, but I listened.

"I'm in the music business myself. And I must tell you, a voice like yours doesn't happen every day. It isn't just the voice. It's the whole package, the way you come across."

"Could you get me an audition with a record company?"

He was more knowledgeable about these things than Jack. "First, cut a demo, and we'll try to get the deejays to play it. That's the usual route."

"You're the first person I've met who talks my language."

"Oh, I'll do more than talk."

Would he? Could he?

If he really knew how to go about it, we might hook up with him. I'd cut a demo and be heard by the right people. The rest would follow; the world was there to be conquered.

When I was famous, I'd get my baby. Kathy would be proud of me. I'd raise her like a princess.

When I was up again I sang my first number directly to Mac. I tried a top note I'd been angling for. It came out round and gold and sexy. It had been there all the time; now it spilled into the room.

Mac applauded loudly.

Jack noticed. Back in our motel room he said, "I don't like the way you came on to Mac. What's the idea making up to him, shaking yourself at him?"

I laughed. "That was part of the act."

Jack accepted this. He knew by now I couldn't stand still when I sang. I was all over the place. Still moody and irascible, he said, "I want you to sign a contract with me."

"What?" I was dumbfounded.

"It's the only way to protect you from guys like him, guys that want to muscle in."

I was even more amazed when he pulled the papers out of his pocket. He had it all drawn up; it was even typed. Actually it made me feel important, like a star. He called the night manager in to witness my signature. Then, from the same pocket he produced a miniature bottle of rum, the kind they give you on airplanes. He'd won it from some mark who'd run out of cash. We both had a drink, more like a sip, and Jack brandished the contract.

"This will be worth gold some day."

I climbed up on a chair and began to sing.

Next door they pounded on the wall for quiet.

▾ ▴ ▾

THREE nights out of four Mac would show up. Between them, they kept me off balance. I wanted Mac to become familiar with my various routines, but Jack's sour mood persisted, I didn't know whether over me or the money he was losing. By now he was into gin rummy, which he also analyzed thoroughly. "The trick is to keep a close watch on your opponent's discards. That, and the way he arranges his hand, gives a good picture of what he's holding."

The problem was Mac never sorted his cards. He'd pick them up, glance at them, and play without separating the suits. And talk about poker faces. Mac's was carved in stone, while Jack found it impossible to conceal moments of elation or depression.

I was fairly confident I was the reason Mac kept coming back. And I didn't want to shut the door on the one possibility I had of moving up in the business. Although it would be almost worth chucking it to have Jack in an optimistic frame of mind again.

This night I noticed the two of them were huddled longer than usual at the bar. Between sets I joined them to find out what was going on.

I figured Jack would be down to his last cent. Instead, he flashed a wad and grinned. He was rolling.

I glanced at Mac. His usually taciturn expression came close to approximating a smile.

What could have pleased them both?

The explanation, which they were equally eager to give, stunned me. Mac had just bought my contract for seven hundred dollars—most of it, probably *all* of it, our own money.

Fury mounted, blotting out everything, including good sense. Jack got it first. "You did this without consulting me? Without asking how I felt about it? You did this behind my back?" Mac was next. "You think you've made yourself a deal? Well, you're mistaken. I'll never sing a note until you tear that thing up. So now you know what you bought—a big fat nothing!"

"Kathy . . ." Jack tried to take my arm, but I shook him off.

"Selling me like meat, like something you buy at the market. You're nothing but a pimp, and I will never let you in my life again."

"For God's sake, Kathy, I thought you'd be pleased."

"Pleased? I *am* pleased. I'm pleased to find out how low you can sink. You gambled me away, and I'm gone."

I slammed doors in their faces and took a cab. I wound up in another motel; they're all alike, aren't they?

It was time for one of my talks with Abram. "I walked out on them, Abram, and it feels good. Jack Sullivan is scum. I don't need him in my life. But I need someone. A singer can't just waltz into a club and say, 'I sing. I'm good. Hire me.'

She needs someone to say that for her. It could be that's Mac. I don't really know him. He owns my contract. Maybe if we kept it strictly business. What do you think, Abram?"

Of course Abram wouldn't know anything about situations like this, but then neither did I. Still, it was good to talk it out, and I stopped being angry and stopped fretting about things, and had a good sleep.

In the morning I went back for my things. I saw right away by the cars parked out front that both men were there. I took a deep breath and sailed in like a prima donna.

Mac had sacked out here and they occupied the twin beds. They were still in them. When they saw me they drew the covers up to their necks. They were probably stark naked, and trapped where they were.

I remembered when the situation had been reversed, and took my time getting my stuff together.

"What are you doing?" Jack was the first to recover himself.

I didn't see the need to reply.

Then Mac tried. "I told Jack after you left that you were right to be ticked off. You certainly should have had a say in the matter."

Again there was no need to reply.

"So." Jack forced an upbeat note. "I thought we'd go out for breakfast and discuss our future."

"I'll be happy to go out for coffee with Mac and discuss my future, but only if you stay strictly away."

"But—"

"You heard her," Mac said.

"Now hold on a minute . . ."

I threw the last of my clothes into the suitcase. "I'll meet you in the car, Mac."

"Wait a minute," Jack yelled. "That's my suitcase!"

Five minutes later Mac came out. Jack was right behind him, tucking the tail of his shirt into his jeans, talking fast. And that's the way we left him, doing what he did best, talking.

▼ ▲ ▼

I HAD a few things I wanted to say up front.

"I want you to know this is business between us, Mac. I don't want any personal junk to get in the way. Because if it does, contract or no contract, I'm gone."

"Well, if those are your terms, that's the way it will be."

"You'll hold the money. But it's only fair to warn you, I know your history. So I'm going to keep a close watch, what we take in, what goes out. And I'll go over it with you the end of each week."

"That's fine with me."

"And when we travel, separate rooms."

"Okay, if that's how you want it."

"That's how I want it," I said firmly.

Then it was his turn. He laid out his plans. And beautiful plans they were. We put them into effect that afternoon. Going to a music store, Mac rented their equipment and in a little side room, accompanying myself picking guitar, I recorded my three best numbers. Mac, who had a good, well-placed speaking voice, announced them and presented me.

"This is what I was born to do," I told him. Because it

was a take the first time. "God, I'm good," I said, listening to it objectively.

Mac laughed and agreed.

He pointed out a couple of things, though. A note he felt I could give more emphasis and a spot where my diction was muddy. We did a second demo, and I had to admit it was improved. So at the outset I leaned on Mac as I never had on Jack, and trusted his opinion. His general plan was to work our way south, head for Chicago, stop at radio stations and pitch my tapes. Our distant goal was to wind up with a recording contract.

Mac was a pro. He knew how to go about things and how to name-drop. Jack only knew about ponies and how to lose at cards. One of the first things Mac did was to sit me down and list all the places I'd sung. There were a lot of them, mostly holes in the wall. But a reader of the prospectus wouldn't know that. They were credits, and added up to an impressive total.

Next came photographs. Mac had an expensive 35-mm camera. He said you could scrimp on lodgings and transportation, but never cut corners on professional equipment. He bought rolls of high-quality film and we shot poses in every conceivable light. My lips ached from the different smiles I tried. When we finally got a good negative, we had it enlarged and fifty copies made. I wanted copies of the three or four best, but Mac educated me. "Just one. You keep pushing that one, and eventually people will recognize it."

I scrutinized the photo. It was sexy, in a clean-cut, windblown country way. Mac had pulled my blouse down and there was plenty of cleavage. My lips curled provocatively, and my black eyes snapped. But you knew deep down I was a decent, small-town gal.

"Is this me?" I asked.

"It's what we're selling," he said.

After making the demo, listing my credits, and printing the photos, Mac discussed what he called "the bottom line."

"It's the last line on every financial statement, and sums up the whole operation. It's the score, the result, the finish, the ball game. Better known as Profit or Loss. You were getting nowhere with Jack. Why? You never looked at the bottom line. You were making it; as a matter of fact you were doing great. But the faster the money came in, the faster it leaked out. If you got holes in the bottom of your boat, it won't help to rev up the motor. Income is important, but Income *minus* Outgo, that's what sinks you. The Profit factor is what you got to keep your eye on."

I nodded sagely, although I could see that this deep financial wisdom wasn't any different from what Mum dinned into me at age six. Mac took it seriously, though, and purchased a used trailer so we could save on motels. That was okay with me as long as I could lock my door.

The more I got to know Mac, the better I liked him. There weren't the ups and downs there had been with Jack. Mac was on an even keel. He lacked Jack's sense of fun and high good humor, but there weren't the sulks and the despondencies.

We got to be buddies. He was as good as his word. He never came on to me or made a pass, except once when he was drunk. Best of all, he discussed things with me. We talked over strategies. They were mostly his ideas and his knowledge of the business, but it made me feel I had a say in the matter, and he was quick to praise me when I came up with a good suggestion. He was ambitious but realistic in assessing our chances. All in all, I felt I'd made a move for the better. At first Jack dogged our steps, showing up where I was singing, trying to horn in. But I never considered relenting. Anyone who would sneak behind my back, who thought he could buy and sell me! It made my blood boil to think of it, and I'd start getting mad all over again.

"But we're married." It was a refrain he brought up constantly.

Mac made the decision; it was a bottom-line, strictly-business decision. "It will cost something, but you've got to make the separation legal."

When Jack showed up next I told him.

"Divorce?" he said, looking pained.

Giving every word its own emphasis, I said clearly and emphatically, "You and I are history."

He saw it was true and gave in. "All right. But there's something you ought to know."

His air of satisfaction over what he was about to say scared me.

"You're dead, Kathy."

I stared back at him, not knowing why but feeling a death chill around my heart.

"That's right, when I took you from the hospital, that's what I told the Masons. They think you died in childbirth, and that's what they'll tell Kathy. Your daughter will grow up thinking you're dead."

The cold spread through my body. I was dead.

Alarmed, Jack took a step toward me. But something warned him back.

When I spoke it came out a toneless whisper. "The Cree say there's a death spot in each person. Touch it and the person dies. When you lied to the Masons you touched that spot in me. It's not a lie anymore. If I'm dead to my daughter I *am* dead. You did this to me, Jack Sullivan, you murdered me."

"You're mad," he muttered, "stark, raving mad."

He stopped following us after that.

Knowing I was dead to Kathy produced a numbness when I thought of her. I was so upset that I turned to Abram. He would mull it over in typical Abram fashion. He did, and eventually came up with a solution. "You need to talk to someone about it. What about Mac?"

I couldn't do it. I didn't know him well enough. I couldn't take him into my confidence or confess the terrible guilt I felt about my baby. My impulse to go get her was something I fought every day. But there was no way a two-year-old could fit into this rough-and-tumble life. I worked till one, didn't get to bed until two in the morning, slept till noon, and then most likely we'd hit the road.

There was no help for it; Kathy would grow up thinking I was dead. In a way, that whitewashed me, made a good person of me. I was no longer a mother who deserted her child. I was a good mother *because* I was a dead mother.

This seemed a circular bit of reasoning and I wished I

could explain it to Mum. Thinking of Mum brought my thoughts to Erich von Kerll, my father. Mum had thought he should know about me. And I thought he should know that he had a granddaughter.

On impulse I wrote what would be a crazy sort of letter to receive, and I didn't know if he would receive it.

I wrote:

Dear Erich von Kerll,

I know it will come as a shock to learn you have a daughter, and recently, a granddaughter as well. We are both named Kathy, which won't surprise you when you think back to another Kathy—Kathy Forquet, whom you married at the end of the war.

I'm sure you know the same stories I do about Mrs. Mike, and how we are all named for her. Mum told me many things about you too. I know you have gray eyes. I know you had a sailboat you used to take out on the Bodensee, and that you were second officer on U-186. I know you lost a leg, and I could hum you any number of little Austrian folk songs that you taught my Mum. And you know nothing about me.

That's the way it has to be, for now at any rate. You are a very distinguished man, a government official. And I must tell you that right now I am nothing at all, except a mother. I did bring into this world a beautiful little girl. Did I tell you she has red hair? I hope someday to meet you, but that's a long way in the future when I'm standing on my own feet. I won't come to you in the way my husband wanted. I want us to be equals. In that way you'll know I don't want anything from you and we can be friends.

I hope you loved my Mum. I loved her very much. She's dead now.

I hope this finds you well.

Yours sincerely,
Kathy

I was glad I wrote this new letter. I couldn't send it, but I saved it to show him someday. I couldn't send it because he could probably track me down. If you were rich you could do that kind of thing. And right now I didn't want to be found.

▼ ▲ ▼

I WAS sitting in a Denny's with Mac, having a sandwich. He was discussing a makeover for me. "Get rid of the bangs," he was saying. "Makes you look too much a kid."

"I may look like a kid, but I'm not a kid. I *have* a kid." I'd kept it bottled up so long that now it came spilling out. "A daughter. Her name is Kathy, and she lives with the Masons on Oakdale Street in St. Paul, Minnesota. They think I'm dead."

He just looked at me. I hadn't meant to let it out. But it was said, and nothing I could do about it.

"Is that true," he asked, "or are you conning me?"

"It's true. She's two years old."

"I'll be damned." It was meant as consolation.

"She thinks I'm dead," I repeated.

"Hey, she isn't old enough to think."

"That's what they'll tell her when she is old enough. That's what they believe."

"Well now, that's a shame."

"Oh, I don't know. Maybe it's a good thing." Why was I always posturing, posing, making a show of things when inside I felt miserable? Mac wasn't the right person. I couldn't really open my heart to him. I could tell him the bare facts, but nothing of the gnawing emptiness.

▼ ▲ ▼

ONE spring day in 1966 as we drove along I heard my own voice coming to me from the country music station.

I grabbed Mac's arm and he nearly went off the road. "Hey Kathy!" he whooped. "You did it!"

"Shhh," I said, and settled back to listen. "I could have picked up the tempo a shade, but it was good."

"It was damn good." From the minute he bought my contract, Mac concentrated solely on me, putting his other enterprises on hold. He was fond of reminding me of all his expenditures: financing the trailer, food, gas and oil, clothes, photos, demos, fees, the works. So far the club dates brought us even, with a little extra. I had gone a notch higher in the class of clubs we played, although I usually didn't get top billing. Mac didn't agree with the old saying that it's better to be a big frog in a small puddle than a small frog in a big puddle. We both knew I was going to be a big frog in the biggest puddle in the world, and the only way to get there was to dive in and fight it out with the best.

All we had to do was convince a couple hundred million people. Mac intensified his campaign, mailing my demos to deejays and, when possible, stopping to go into a studio and twist arms. He was always plugging me, and it was beginning to pay off.

"Being played on radio is the break we've been waiting for. The next thing on the agenda is to get some songs written for you. Most of your numbers are too old and beaten to death. And what's worse, they're identified with other voices. We need a hit that's yours."

"Oh Mac, there *is* music I want to sing." And it came out that my Mum was Cree, that I used to spend time on the res and learned the songs of the earth. "I can bring a whole world to an audience. That's what I want to do. Only people seem offended, they stiffen up, they're afraid to hear, they don't want to know there's a world out there that they know nothing of."

Right then Mac asked me to sing my Cree repertoire.

I did. I threw myself into it. But stopped short at the reprise. I'd lost him. He too didn't know what to make of it. "Well, it's different. Too different, that's the trouble. Not enough melody. Hard to hum, too much of it off-key, strange." Seeing the effect this was having on me, he stopped and went on in a more conciliatory tone, but it meant the same thing—he hated it.

"Later," he said, "when you're established, that's the time to introduce something new. Who knows, it might be a novelty. Ethnic might be big by then."

I nodded, accepting for now.

The problem of material remained. How were we to come by a good songwriter we couldn't pay?

"We'll be in Chicago in a couple of weeks," Mac said. "Plenty of talent there. I have some friends at WGN. And I'll drop by the Morris office. Of course the real action is New York, but Chicago is a big step. It might be easier to pick up an agent there."

"You're my manager. What do I need an agent for?"

Mac roared with laughter. "Kiddo, when you get there, you're going to have a manager *and* an agent *and* a business manager *and* an investment counselor *and* an advance man *and* a makeup gal *and* a costume designer *and* a voice coach *and* a driver *and* hey, your own private plane plus pilot. You'll be cut up so many ways, you'll be lucky to keep ten percent of you. But I'll tell you something. That ten percent will make you rich. And my twenty percent of your ten percent will put me in offices in Beverly Hills and a condo in Acapulco. Never forget what I'm going to tell you. A hundred percent of nothing is nothing. Ten percent of a fortune is a fortune."

All this maneuvering was new to me. I hoped it wasn't new to Mac. I hoped he knew what he was doing. I hoped he could revive his old contacts. I knew he was counting on me as much as I counted on him. I was his ticket back.

We added my radio exposure to my credits, and I pulled down another twenty dollars a night. The latest club was a lot more elegant than any I'd sung in, and Mac persuaded a couple of people in the business to drive up from Chi to hear me.

Catastrophe.

I never get colds. But I woke up unable to swallow. Total panic. I put on my bathrobe and went into the middle section of the trailer, where the kitchen was. Tea with lemon, that's what Mum had given us kids when we had sore throats. I filled the kettle and sat disconsolately waiting for it to boil.

Maybe it wasn't a cold. More likely I'd strained my voice singing in all these smoke-filled bars. And Mac was always urging me to do more belting, get that earthy tone into it. That was hard on the voice, but the audience loved it and I kept doing it. What if I'd damaged my vocal cords? It happened.

Had it happened to me? The kettle began to whistle. I took it off the coils and poured it over a tea bag. I stirred a while, then sipped the tea from a spoon. At first it hurt awfully, but gradually my throat opened and felt better. What should I do about tonight, and the people coming from Decca?

Mac's advice, when he got over being exasperated, was to give me a Smith Bros. cough drop and tell me to sing through it.

That's what I did. As I heard those muffled, grainy notes fall like wounded soldiers, I wanted to break off—stop, run and hide somewhere. But you don't do that. You finish. You pretend it's all right. The Decca exec who listened with his eyes closed, pretended too. But he left before my next set.

So my big chance came and went.

Mac was worried now. He canceled right and left and, instead of reproaching me, tried to buck me up. But in the depths of me, trussed up in sargasso weed, were my dreams of singing. I wouldn't allow myself to think past it; there was nothing past it.

At the end of the week I was able to coax a few of my sounds back. I did it cautiously, my heart leaping with a tentative joy at each note.

"We lost Decca," Mac said, "but there are other labels out there."

To prepare Chicago for us he ran an ad in the *Tribune* in the form of a songwriting contest, the winning song to be sung by me. With that as payment, we hoped no money would be required.

"We've got to find a name for you," Mac said. "Something out of the ordinary. McCartney, Lennon, Harrison were going nowhere. They name themselves the Beatles, and bang! They own the world."

"I had another name," I said, thinking back. "Little Bird."

"Little Bird . . ." He rolled it around. "Cree?"

"Yes."

"Well, we'll keep that part under our hat. Besides, you don't look Indian . . . So that's what they called you? Kathy Little Bird?"

"My friend on the res did, when I was eight."

"I like it."

So did I.

It brought Elk Woman and Mum and a little girl standing outside the church in the snow singing.

▼ ▲ ▼

CHICAGO!

Mac sold the trailer and purchased a fourth-hand Buick. It looked impressive, but we had all sorts of trouble with it. However, we drove through the Loop, past the zoo, and came out on Michigan Avenue. Broad, beautiful, with trees planted in the cement of the sidewalk. Magnificent, stately hotels with doormen, awnings, and facades of fieldstone, brick, and glass.

Of course we didn't stay in any of them, just looked. We looked at the lake, dancing with yachts and sailboats riding at anchor, bouncing over choppy little waves. Mac, who was embarked on a progam of educating me, recited a poem by Carl Sandburg. "Hog Butcher to the World." It had the smell of stockyards in it, and the sweat of men and animals. It wasn't the Chicago I saw.

We wound up in a shabby apartment in an Italian neighborhood on the city's west side. "You won't be here much," Mac said apologetically, and it was true. We were on the go from the moment we got up in the morning.

Running around Chicago in August isn't the most comfortable thing in the world. Half the population were trying for a little air by getting out of sweltering apartments onto the fire escapes. We saw them as we passed on the El, lounging on mattresses and beach chairs. One enterprising guy had dragged out a sofa. The rest of Chicago was fighting for a spot on the beach. Mac, the optimist, said it was off-season, our best chance to get in to see people.

Much to my surprise, several songwriters entered Mac's contest, and the first thing I knew I had material to look over. With a nip here and a tuck there, they fit my style pretty well.

Meanwhile the Decca scout we thought we'd lost showed up with a Decca producer. Apparently there were some things he'd liked well enough to give it a second try. This time it went smoothly and an audition was arranged.

From that moment my world began spinning.

"From the top!" came the directive from the glass booth. "From the top," because the balance was wrong.

Like the record I cut, it was all part of the Chicago Loop. The Loop spun round and round, Michigan Avenue, the Blackstone. We moved in to have a good address. It was awesome. The lobby was out of an MGM spectacular, enormous sprays of flowers in what Mac told me were Ming dynasty vases, and a fountain to throw pennies in. My room reflected none of this luxury; it was small, ordinary, and the view was the brick wall of the hotel next door. But I was just an elevator ride away from glamour. Studio technicians sat behind glass, twiddling dials, mixing my sound on a Gates board. I was getting close.

I'd never sung with a real band, just pickup musicians or me and my guitar. But, hey, this was big time. There were five instrumentalists backing me. I loved the beat of the drum and the unexpected cry you get out of amplified guitars and a slap bass. I had my mike, they had theirs, and in the booth they mixed and matched.

That first session they didn't get what they wanted in their cans. "Cans" was the name for the earphones we were all plugged into. They sent everybody home with an early-morning call.

I'd sung my heart out and it hadn't been right. They'd drowned me out, the drums that I'd jived to, and the electrified stuff. "What do they expect?" I stormed at Mac. "Five to one, and I'm up against drums. It's impossible. I can't do it. I'm not going back. Tell them that. Tell them no singer on God's earth can compete with drums. Do you want me to tear my throat out again? No good to anyone, washed up, through?"

"It's tough with house musicians," Mac soothed. "You'll get the hang of it. It will go better tomorrow."

"There isn't going to be a tomorrow. Don't you listen when I talk to you? If I belt the way they want, I won't have a voice. Don't you remember what it was like? I couldn't even whisper. I won't wreck my voice—to please you or them or anybody."

We both knew I was letting off steam, that I wasn't about to tell off a booth full of Decca executives. No way was I going to spoil my big chance. Still, I was frightened. Most other musicians wrapped their instruments in silk scarves and warm flannels, kept them safe in cases, while a singer exposes her voice to all manner of hazards. No matter how vulnerable and fragile, it goes where she goes and is not shielded from weather, illness, pollution, or accident.

In the morning when I walked onto the soundstage, not only was the band there, but they were affable and friendly, as though they had not drowned me out. The guy on steel who had dragged the tempo and thrown me off offered me a Styrofoam cup of coffee. But I was still leery. I had my eye on half a dozen female singers. Were they here to replace me?

"Your backup," Mac whispered.

I was utterly panicked; probably most of them were better than I was. One of the Decca officials confirmed this by telling me they were from the Chicago Lyric Opera chorus.

That was it, that was the last straw. They were out to show me up, to make me look ridiculous, to scuttle me before I started.

I took an unobtrusive breath from the waist, from the diaphragm, a singer's breath. I took another. And another. It was the best way to fight nerves. I knew I had to psych myself up.

Don't let them get to you, I told myself. They may be from the Lyric Opera, but they're here to *back you up*. They are just backup sound—to *you*.

Having talked myself into the Kathy Little Bird persona, I went over to my mike and tapped it with my finger to see if it was live. I'd been waiting for a chance to do that.

The QUIET sign flashed. The bandleader, who looked like an animated blowup of a fly—small, hairy, and ugly—lifted his stick, and we started to make music. The backup singers produced an echo effect. It sounded good.

In fact it was great, really compelling. Once again I sang my heart out. Let them sit behind glass, let them twiddle the dials. I didn't care what they did. I was doing what I did, and I was doing it well.

Decca records signed me, and Mac said we could stay on at the Blackstone. I still hadn't time to explore the lobby, stand before Ming vases, sink into plush divans, gawk in front of shops and elegant boutiques, toss pennies in the fountain. "Loop the loop," I murmured, singing it all under my breath. I was evolving a plan. A great and wonderful plan.

Now that money was coming in I wanted to set aside enough for Kathy to go to college. I wanted her to have things, advantages like piano lessons, whatever she wanted. After all, she was almost three years old. She'd need nice things, clothes, a good warm coat. Stuff like insurance to cover medical and dental bills.

That was the plan. I was dead, and it was best that way. I didn't want to upset anything, but how precisely did one give money anonymously?

Mac had just brought an entertainment lawyer aboard, someone called Harriman, whose main job was to tinker with Mac's income tax return, on which Jack, who was in Vietnam, was listed as a dependent. Several long-distance phone calls and a deal was struck. Jack agreed to keep his mouth shut. It cost us, but the money was well worth the peace of mind.

When it came to Kathy, I was afraid to go through Harriman; I didn't want him or Mac to know my plans for her. So I had recourse to the Yellow Pages. Wanamaker, Adams and Markham, sixteenth floor, sounded impressive. When I got there it appeared much too grand. There was a samovar in the waiting room. I was preparing to back out when a vigilant secretary caught me and brought me to Jonathan Markham's office.

Young, bright, and hawk-faced, he listened intently to my problem and asked a few questions about the Masons. His solution was to take advantage of Mrs. Mason's Swedish ancestry. "An inheritance," he decided, "to be disbursed periodically by a firm in Stockholm or Uppsala. I'll do some research. It should prove out at a casual glance, and that's all one gives, a casual glance at a stroke of luck like this."

"You mean, it supposedly comes from a distant relative?"

"Exactly. Having no immediate family . . . You deposit the requisite amount with us, we forward it to Stockholm, they invest it and send quarterly payments to St. Paul."

And so it was arranged. That part of it anyhow. But how to account for my monthly expenditure in a manner that wouldn't alert Mac? He approved of expensive clothes, of getting my teeth straightened. In fact he insisted on it. But he'd be dead set against sending money to my kid. Mostly because he'd be afraid it would somehow leak out. "Rising young singer abandons child." That kind of publicity would be fatal. I had just completed my first single, and a big promo was scheduled to hype it onto the charts. Simultaneously, Mac was angling for a guest spot on a national radio show. But it was all tentative; it hadn't happened yet.

Mornings I memorized leadsheets and sang them in the bathroom so people in the next room wouldn't bang on the wall. Afternoons I shopped for and bought a watch and a tennis bracelet. Buying top of the line, I had paste copies made, pawning the originals and sending the cash to the Wanamaker, Adams and Markham office. I was reminded of my early days with Jack, all the subterfuges I'd practiced so we could stay afloat. Why was life so complicated? It was my money. Anyone would think I was stealing it.

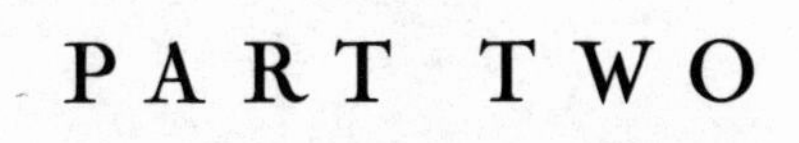

PART TWO

Chapter Ten

I WAS Cree dreaming again, a habit that had kept me going these last twelve years.

Having breakfast in Central Park and dreaming . . . Had I been hasty in not accepting Mac's proposal of marriage? He would provide what they call "a stable home." A home I could bring a teenager to. Or perhaps, watching the riders come by on beautifully groomed horses, bobbing up and down in elegant English style, holding the reins with careless wrist . . . perhaps I could do it without Mac, do it on my own.

Mac thought I wanted to live at the Beresford because of its address, because of its three towers, and because it was supersharp and meant I had arrived. No, I wanted it for Kathy because it looked out over the park and I could picture her riding on this bridle path, or sitting with me in this little outdoor cafe I'd found. I'd be studying my music, and she'd be doing homework—she was in high school now—studying algebra? Or maybe poetry? We were comfortable together, we could talk or not talk, the way it is with a friend.

This was the day of the evening of the Carson show. Johnny Carson was in New York to oblige a big star who was promoting the opening of his current blockbuster. That was the chance Mac had been waiting for. He shoehorned me in.

Rehearsal was called for two o'clock. I thought it would relax me to sit here, have a latte and bagel, and enjoy the sun.

A nearby clock struck two. But that was wrong; it was only one. I looked at my watch to verify this, then shook it. The watch had stopped.

Already on my feet, I threw money on the table as I ran. Rehearsal for the biggest step in my career and I was sitting in Central Park munching a bagel.

Mac was gearing up for success. Autographed glossies were piled on his desk, and he'd hired someone to answer the anticipated ton of fan mail. He'd worked out a standard reply, customizing it to fit the age and sex of the writer. In it I thanked all those who had helped me—especially Johnny Carson, who had plucked me out of nowhere. We didn't mention the arm twisting of the show's producers, the lunches with agents hinting at a double commission, and a promised kickback to one of the expediters. Probably more went into it that I didn't know about. And here I was about to blow it.

I ran till my side hurt and hailed a cab. It didn't stop. I practically stepped in front of another. "It's an emergency," I shouted, "Can you take me to Fifty-sixth and Avenue of the Americas?"

I climbed in beside the driver, a very surprised young man. I sized him up as being impoverished. The hack was on its last legs, but I didn't care as long as it got us there. He told me his name was Freddy, and that he was only driving a cab until he could find something better.

"It's your lucky day," I said. "You can work for me, if you get me there before my number. But you've got to hurry. "

He'd never heard of me, but was galvanized by the name Johnny Carson.

"I'm just starting out, when it comes to a national show like this, so I can't pay much."

That was all right with him. His career behind the wheel had so far netted him two deadbeat fares and one mugging. He was delighted at the thought of chucking it.

While he'd never heard of me, he remembered my single, "I Thought It Couldn't Happen to Me," and when I told him that was me singing, he didn't believe it. I took Freddy into the studio with me and, in the break, talked to Mac, who took him on as a gofer. His first job was to find the coffee machine.

It turned out I hadn't held anything up. They were fixing some glitch in the lighting equipment.

That night I psyched myself up, saying, "Just do what you've been doing for years—sing!" The difference was, there were forty million people in the audience. And a latte in the park, even hiring my cabdriver, plus a session with makeup fussing over me, didn't fill the chinks completely. It only took an instant for panic to mount, my throat to tighten, and the song to get stuck. I battled this attack of nerves with vocal exercises and deep singer's breaths, walked out on stage, and sang.

I was a hit; the anticipated fan mail arrived, along with dozens of offers. I let Mac sort it out and we settled into the Gotham. The Beresford condo was out of my league; I'd need a long-term contract or my own show to afford that.

All sorts of people entered my life. Al Lennox was hired to arrange and facilitate. Everything mechanical was coordinated by him. He leased a van, which he drove on short hops, and hired a cab to hang around in front of the hotel when we were in town. He booked flights when it was necessary, and battled desk clerks and headwaiters for the sheer joy of it. Wrestling luggage was beneath him; he employed local talent for that.

Anabel Trimble was suggested by MCA and brought on board as my handler, responsible for clothes, shade of hair, color of nails, deodorant, and moisturizer. She had the final say on how I appeared on stage, TV, or album covers.

Mac, of course, ran the whole show. This was what he called "making it." He no longer thought of himself as a manager but as an impresario. His contracts became famous for their escalation clauses.

I almost forgot Freddy. As a mark of special esteem he was assigned my guitar, which he carried in a reinforced case. Mac wanted to get me a decent guitar, as he put it. They didn't know that Mum travelled with me in that old beat-up instrument.

My press agent, Danny, planted a story about how the guitar and I had grown up together. We insured it with Lloyds of London for three million dollars, and got a squib in *Variety*. The guitar got a new bass E string out of it. What do you think of your guitar now, Mum? It was half prayer, half mantra, because I didn't dare ask what she thought of me. There wasn't much left of the Kathy she'd taught me to be.

I'd brought up ethnic several times over the years, but Mac acted as though I hadn't any idea how I sounded or what was best for me to sing.

Last time he didn't reply verbally, but waved a check for a thousand dollars under my nose. In short—you don't meddle with success.

There was no dearth of songwriters now. Lyricists and composers flocked around, pushing songs and special material. The agency people working on my new album wanted me to do a little patter between numbers, "project personality," in the hope Hollywood might beckon. I turned down the idea. They had an all-day conference, sending out for sandwiches and beer, but I wouldn't change my mind. They picked apart every syllable I sang, croaking out melodies in whiskey voices to second-guess possible movie moguls. A dozen Svengalis pulled my strings. I capitulated.

Once in a while their choice of material was good; mostly it was bad. It wasn't that they didn't know their business. It was the committee system. A committee always plays it safe. They opt for the standard stuff. So the new, the daring, the controversial, the interesting, gets passed up.

The audience I wanted to sing to were young people, who

were falling in love or falling out of it, who were alone and lonely, or in a crowd and lonely. They wanted excitement, passion, they wanted to laugh and cry and make things happen. And my singing had to give that to them.

The material I was getting didn't.

▼ ▲ ▼

I BROACHED the problem from a different angle. I suggested that I do some songwriting, thinking maybe I could slip in just a suggestion of Cree music in the tonalities and syncopation. Mac cut me off: "We have a sweet setup." He ended with the admonition about rocking the boat. So I shut up. But that didn't mean I stopped thinking about it. I bought a music notebook, and delved seriously into Cree music from the old days and played what I remembered by ear, concentrating on the Wind Song. Like many Cree themes, it was about being lonely and talking to the trees and hearing them answer, talking to water currents and listening to their murmured reply. The original ended on a low G; I took it up an octave.

I wished I knew how to get it down on paper. I hungered to know not just the melody line but the orchestration.

Words came second. All my life I have been happier without the words. No matter how clever, they didn't seem to add to the music. The emotion was in the notes, the longing. The sorrow, the joy, the bitterness, hold a depth and subtlety words can never express.

Jim Gentle came by and looked over my shoulder. I was

embarrassed and tried to shield my elementary effort with my arm. Of course, the notation gave me away.

"Let's see what you've got there." He lifted the pad from my lap.

"I was just fooling around," I said defensively.

"Come over to the piano, and I'll show you some interesting chord progressions."

I followed Jim across the rehearsal room. He'd only been with us a couple of weeks. He was a special-material writer: lyrics, patter, jokes, intros. He really dug music and could pinch-hit for any instrument in the band. He'd sold stuff to Bob Dylan, but the rumor was they had a fight over politics. Mac thought he was good and was buying from him pretty consistently.

Jim was a big guy, six foot four or five, and Mac called him the Gentle Giant, a switch on the Jolly Green Giant. Although I thought of him more as a fairy-tale giant. Anyway, the name took. Everybody liked him. I did too. I had the feeling he didn't belong in a rehearsal hall. He didn't belong indoors at all. I kept seeing him against the high prairie background I'd grown up in. His gestures were broad and large as he was. He was always running into things, tripping over extension cords, knocking into music stands. "They made the world a size too small for you, Jim," Mac kept telling him.

As I followed him to the piano, I couldn't help turning him into music. He was an easy person to sing; just go up the scale, pause on the leading tone, and hit the tonic with all you had, honest and clear. I thought I was doing this in my mind, but humming must have escaped me, for he turned around and looked down on me with a quirky smile.

He made me sit beside him at the piano and took me through the basics, beginning with the diatonic scale. He showed me the two-three pattern of black keys on the piano that helps locate the octaves. "The whole idea behind harmony is that the harmonics are hidden in the original note, so if I sing an octave above you, my sound sounds inside your sound. The octave is the first overtone. The next is the twelfth, after that the double octave, and then the third above that. All these harmonics are inside the original note, but in different mixes. That's what timbre is. For instance, the way a sax mixes the harmonics is different from how the fiddle does it."

For the first time I had a glimpse of what was happening when music took hold of me. It was like my soul was pouring out through all these notes and their combinations. No wonder I liked it better without words. Pure sound is pure emotion. Octaves, *cool.* Twelfths and fifths, *lonely.* Thirds and sixths, *sexy.* Seconds, *trouble.* Sevenths, *freaked out.* Ninths and elevenths, *fury.* Diminished sevenths, *tears.* The unison, *death.*

Jim played "Three Blind Mice" in octaves, then thirds, then triads, and finally chords with added sixths and chromatic changes. I leaned across him, trying to imitate the pattern of his fingers on the ivories. I definitely liked this big gentle man, and I forgot to be self-conscious about my lack of formal musical training.

"With your sense of musicianship you'll make huge strides," he told me. Fifteen minutes and eight bars later he stood up. "Well, I'm off to jail."

"What?"

"Just visiting."

"Who?"

"Nobody in particular. I pick a little guitar, try some of my vocals out. The guys seem to like it, you know, it's contact with the outside."

I was intrigued. "But why do you do it?"

"I'll tell you about it sometime. Right now I'm late."

During the mixing when I had a breather I asked Freddy about him. "Jim Gentle? Stay away from him. Don't be fooled by his name, he's trouble."

"What do you mean, trouble?"

"He hangs with the wrong crowd." Before he could clarify this, Fitzpatrick was calling, "From the top," and I was up again.

But when I like somebody, my antenna is out, and I knew the minute I came on the soundstage whether or not Jim was sitting in on the rehearsal.

Several days later there he was again. I went up to him at the coffee machine, and without a word he dropped change in for another cup and handed it to me. We gravitated to a quiet corner and picked up where we'd left off. "About prisoners . . . ," he said, "I don't place special emphasis on them. It's wherever there's a need, that's where music should be."

I frowned slightly, trying to understand.

"When the war was being protested back in the sixties, when they raised money for Montgomery, Selma, the civil rights movement. Wherever people struggle," he reiterated, "that's where music should be."

"That isn't music, that's politics. What has music to do with it?"

He looked at me in surprise. "You ask that? You? Music unifies, it gives courage. The Christians sang when they faced the lions. War protesters sang when fire hoses were turned on them. Prisoners sing to forget they're caged."

Now I knew what Freddy meant when he said he was in with the wrong people. "The do-gooders," Mac scoffingly called them. Joan Baez, Pete Seeger, Peter, Paul and Mary, Stevie Wonder, Crosby, Stills and Nash had sung for peace and given voice to civil rights.

"We thought the world would be different." Jim laughed in an unhappy way. "But something *did* come of it: the idea of singing for causes. The benefit as a forum definitely caught on." Jim looked at me speculatively. "Were you ever part of that scene?"

"Me? Good heavens, no. I was just getting started." But—a thought occurred to me. Maybe, just maybe . . . it might be an opportunity to sing the songs I wanted to sing. The well-heeled habitues of clubs in Manhattan were no different than the old-timers and barflies I had sung for in the past. No one knew what to make of them. Perhaps this was my dream audience, young people searching for answers. It could be they were the ones the earth breathed for, the ones who could hear the song the wind carried. I was dizzy at the possibility.

Sensing the confusion he had created in me, Jim apologized. "I get carried away, it's not for everybody."

"No, no," I said, "it's a magnificent idea." Now that I was beginning to know him, I would sing Jim Gentle differently. I'd sing him reaching out in great chords in many directions. Not only was he a big man, his concepts were big. When he suggested dinner, I said yes.

That night, sitting in a basement, candlelit Italian restaurant over scallopini and a bottle of chianti, he continued the conversation. "Pop music has done more for world peace than all the churches, the UN, and political leaders put together."

I sat there trying to figure him out. I thought maybe he was someone who would understand and sympathize with what I wanted to do. But, while open and forthcoming, he was at the same time hard to know. One moment in pursuit of the holy grail, the next he was telling me wild stories. Like Brian Wilson, who once put a sandbox in his living room, got into it when record people came to talk business, and built sand castles as they discussed million-dollar deals.

Or Skip Spence, who was locked up in Bellevue when he wrote *Oar.* "He was stoned out of his gourd on Quaaludes and cut through a hotel door with that fire axe they have behind glass. So they carted him off to the funny farm and there in a padded cell he went crazy all over again, this time because of the music in his head. When they let him out he recorded the album in his garage, laying down the tracks and playing all the instruments himself. As you know, today *Oar* is a collector's item."

Music fascinated Gentle, any music. He knew a group in Harlem, the Furious Five, who were experimenting with two turntables, hopping back and forth.

"And that's it?" I couldn't stop laughing. I thought I'd stump him, so I brought up "scratching." But he knew about that as well. "It was an accident, like penicillin. The turntable was jiggled and you got a needle that's slipping and sliding all over the place. But it kind of added to the mood. The trick is to do it in rhythm. Anyway, there's a real craze for it."

One of Jim's weirder stories was about a guy, very talented, but he had a bad drug habit. "Well, this one night he turns up dead. Overdosed. So they take him to the morgue, go through the whole routine, stick the body in one of those pull-out metal drawers. They're just putting the tag on his big toe when he lets out a hoot and sits up. That experience straightened him out for good. Today he writes for some of the biggest cats in the business."

Jim wanted me to laugh at this, but I didn't. I shivered. I was afraid of drugs. They were endemic in the music world, I knew that. But I stayed clear. I tried to explain this to him. "It's like a horror film where they transplant another person's eyes into your eye sockets. You see—but not through your eyes. Then they give you his brain. You think—but not with your mind."

He fell in with this. "Yeah, like the zombies in the Caribbean, who have no soul."

I decided Jim Gentle was one of the most interesting men I'd met in years.

After that first dinner there were more, and I found myself telling him about me, as far back as Skayo Little Bird sitting on the porch of Elk Woman's government-built house and smoking. "She sang me the cries and chants of the Cree. She said they nourished the soul." I broke off because he was staring at me.

"I understand now! You have Indian blood somewhere in your background."

"My mother was three-quarters Cree."

"The eyes, of course, deep-rimmed, black on black. Why didn't I see it before?"

"I don't know anything about First Nation people except for Elk Woman and my grandfather when I was little."

"I was never little," the gentle giant said, "but I was young. I wasn't Indian, but I was part of the Indian movement. I was a kid just out of college when seventy-eight Indians from a dozen tribes claimed a disused crumbling prison and the rock it stood on as Indian territory. They backed this up by an ancient treaty—just one in the long trail of broken treaties. This one, signed at Fort Laramie in 1868 between the Sioux Nation and the United States government, ceded all surplus and abandoned federal property to the tribe."

"Alcatraz?" I breathed, vaguely recalling newspaper accounts.

"Alcatraz . . . sitting on seven acres in the middle of San Francisco Bay. Alcatraz . . . flashing by, segmented by the frame of a car window, an Indian car in need of body work and a paint job, plastered with decals from a dozen nearby states featuring national parks and monuments. . . . This glimpse from the Golden Gate Bridge of the lowering penal institution, brooding choppy waters, ignited a dream. Like a lit match to gunpowder—a flame exploded in hearts and minds. It was discussed in psychedelic cafes along the Haight. Wine and drugs and idealism united students from Berkeley and Santa Cruz. Crow and Sioux formed a crazy sort of alliance that included Osage, Creek, Ponca, Mohawk, Comanche, Rincon, Chippewa, Lakota, Paiute, and Navajo."

"And you," I supplied as he drew breath.

"Me. For sure. That's where the action was. I bummed a ride to the West Coast, and when I hit San Francisco, made for Pier 39. It was Thanksgiving and the Indians on the Rock were hosting a big party. The press was there; so were the celebs. Hollywood turned out big-time. Jane Fonda. Dick Gregory came later and Marlon Brando. The cast of *Hair* passed the hat at intermission to raise money for the action.

"The climax, though, was the Proclamation they posted:

> "'We, the Native Americans, reclaim the land known as Alcatraz Island in the name of all American Indians by right of discovery.
>
> We wish to be fair and honorable in our dealings with the Caucasian inhabitants of this land, and hereby offer the following treaty:
>
> We will purchase said Alcatraz Island for twenty-four dollars in glass beads and red cloth . . .'"

"Why twenty-four dollars?"

"That's three dollars and thirty cents an acre more than we paid for Louisiana." And he went on reading.

> "'We will give to the white inhabitants a portion of the land for their own to be held in trust by the American Indian Government in perpetuity—for as long as the sun shall rise and the rivers go down to the sea. We will further guide the inhabitants in the proper way of living. We will offer them our religion, our education, our life-ways, in order to help them achieve our level of civilization and thus raise them and all their white brothers up from their savage and unhappy state.'"

I was laughing too hard to comment.

"That's more or less the gist of it," he said. "No one knew whether it was guerrilla theater or history. But it made a hell of an impression on me, reoriented my life, started me off. I muscled in on a Buffy Sainte-Marie fundraiser, and I've been doing pretty much the same sort of thing ever since." He grinned broadly. "It made me what I am today."

I couldn't get the occupation of Alcatraz out of my mind. "How long did they stay?"

"Nineteen months."

"Almost two years. I don't suppose they left of their own accord?"

"Most did. The new term started and the college kids left. It was no picnic, you know. There was no electricity, no telephone, no heat, no running water, the kitchen was locked away behind iron bars and they had to cook over an open fire. The toilets were flushed with seawater. It was cold and it was grim. And once the spotlight was off them, they went hungry a good part of the time.

"Still they held on. The government at first attempted to ameliorate the situation by suggesting the area be turned into a park. The occupiers were incensed. Were they to be zoo-like creatures for tourists to stare at and feed peanuts? It was the government's turn to be incensed. Their best offer, which they were ready to fund and maintain as a cultural center, had been dismissed out of hand. Their reply was thirty agents who descended on the island, backed by a Coast Guard cutter and a helicopter. The Indians had dwindled to a mere fifteen. They were arrested on charges of trespass, interfering with navigation, and destruction of federal property."

I considered this. "It was so quixotic. Did they really think they could move in, establish squatter's rights, and be allowed to keep the island?"

"Alcatraz was a statement. Symbolism. The world was reminded that by treaty it was Indian. The first land sighted by ships entering San Francisco Bay was Indian land. The sit-in was a defiant shout to the white man that they were a nation that had never surrendered."

"Indians can be rather wonderful. They admit they're people of dreams. They're proud of it. Like my friend Elk Woman. She was my Mum's friend really, but I considered her mine. She kept me centered."

"Centered?"

"She didn't let me go off the deep end. She was there when Mum died. She was the one who taught me to sing people."

We went to his apartment. I didn't know whether it was to sing or make love. I wanted to do both.

It had been a long time since I'd loved or been loved in a meaningful way. I wanted it to happen, and I wanted it to be with this gentle giant who felt a brotherhood with the entire universe, and who lived and breathed music.

His apartment was in the Village, ground floor. It had a green door. He took my coat and I looked around. Neat, spare, definitely a male bastion. Nothing had been tacked to the walls, no pictures, nothing. It was as impersonal as the day he moved in.

I sat on the futon and he dropped down beside me. "I'm going to tell you about Duke Ellington and Billy Strayhorn."

"Why?"

"It may be important. It may be very important. His name was Edward Kennedy 'Duke' Ellington, and as you will see, a good deal of his music, and his life, were tied into Billy Strayhorn. Billy was just a kid when the Duke found him performing in some West Side dive. The Duke heard the exceptional quality of the music he made and knew that he wanted this talent near him.

"So then and there he offers Billy a job with him, and he writes out the directions to his apartment on one of those little drink napkins—take the commuter train to Grand Central Station, shuttle over to Times Square, then the A train to the Bronx, get off in Harlem at the second stop. Billy Strayhorn takes down these directions. Next thing you know he turns them into what becomes a hit single."

"Of course . . ." I joined in, excited, " 'Take the 'A' Train.' "

Gentle nodded approvingly. "Billy was a hell of a lyricist, and tops as a composer. He and the Duke collaborated on everything. When Ellington was asked who wrote what, he'd reply, 'One of us must have.' They were inseparable in their musical life and their personal life. No one knew for sure whether they were lovers. They were in the truest sense one person." He paused, then started talking about Mac.

He didn't think Mac was right for me. "He's too limiting. For instance, the country you're into so heavily. Haven't you noticed that sooner or later everything ends up being about death? Dead mothers, dead fathers, dead babies, dead dogs. And what you want to sing about is life."

I couldn't help smiling at his characterization, and admitted I would like to edge a bit more into pop. "But we're doing so great, and Mac tells me not to rock the boat."

"That's what he would say. I'd like to see you experiment. Keep the country sound as a base, but venture into other modalities."

"You mean right now—make a move into pop? Are you saying that?"

He shrugged. "Not to wind up there; pop is essentially a three-chord affair. I could hear your sound in R&B. The way you move suggests that to me. So what do you think?"

"What do I think about what?"

"Me being Strayhorn. Writing for you. Writing with you."

"Are you serious?"

"I'd move you in the right direction. Think about it."

"I couldn't do it, Jim. Mac's been with me from the beginning. It's been his game plan that's got us this far."

"Right," Jim said. "I wasn't trying to muscle in on Mac. I don't want to be your manager. Just help you grow as an artist. Make it possible for you to sing the music you should be singing. It's kind of too bad that you're not just any girl singer starting out. Then when I say something like that it wouldn't sound as though I was trying to ingratiate myself."

"I never thought that for a minute."

"But let's examine the situation. If you were just any girl, we'd have kissed and hugged and gone to bed before this."

"You think so?"

"I know so." He was a funny guy, one of the few men who could talk sex in the abstract, without acting on it. Instead of moving on me, he poured us each a glass of wine.

"So you sing people?"

"Well, I sing the way they look and I sing the way they are."

"Show me how you would sing me."

I stood up, threw my head back, pretended I was six-four, and began a column of notes, going up in good order, then a riff, because something had happened to him somewhere along the way to make him feel so strongly, to make him reach out. For my ending I simulated pulling the world in on top of me.

He finished his wine in silence. It seemed to me he was struggling with himself. Then he broke out, "Kathy, how does it happen in such a short time you know all of me, theme and variations?" He wanted to leave it at that. He didn't want to say more, but suddenly he was talking about himself, no longer hiding behind his stories. "'Nam changed me." His voice was hoarse, rasping, I'd never heard it like that. "Yeah, I was there, stoned most of the time so I wouldn't have to ask myself questions. But eventually you've got to ask, and answer them too." He spoke close to my ear, but far away. "I try to make up for what I did over there. I can't. It's never enough." He was shaking as though with fever.

I held him, and stroked and kissed him. That seemed the best answer. He'd been badly hurt, they'd damaged his soul. I let my kisses do what they could, say the things one doesn't know how to say.

The next moment I was gathered into him. I lay back, accepting his broken words, accepting his touch. He brought out the longing that had lain in me so long. Sweetest chords and wild discordant ones played over me, creating a pitch of frenzy that catapulted us beyond ourselves.

Sharing a ground-zero experience can do that for you.

Chapter Eleven

WEEKS followed during which we were scarcely out of one another's sight. Gentle attended my rehearsals, recording sessions, club and show appearances. This, over Mac's protests, as I turned more and more to Jim. His opinion was important to me. If Mac knew the workings of show biz, Jim Gentle understood its soul. For it does have one. Vulnerable and in constant flight, it comes up now and again with brave ideas.

Was my idea for Cree songs one? I broached it once more in a tentative way to Mac, and got another put-down. So far I hadn't brought it up with Jim in any serious way. I'd held back because if he rejected my music, he rejected me. But I didn't think he'd do that. Jim would understand where no one else seemed to, that this music was part of me and lay behind everything I did.

I found it impossible to avoid comparisons. Mac hadn't an artistic bone in his body and was known as a "no-talent guy." Still, he had an uncanny knack for touching the pulse of the public, a sixth sense of what it wanted, what it would go for and what it wouldn't.

Jim, on the other hand, was open to new ideas, took them seriously, explored them. That, and the special relationship that had developed between us, gave me courage. I decided to put my career in his hands. Without preparation or explanation I plunged in. "Jim," I said, uncurling on the futon and unwinding my legs from his long ones, "I want you to imagine an old Indian woman muttering between her teeth, not bothering to remove her pipe, but lifting her voice to the Creator as she plants a patch of garden behind her house. Or a shaman, tall, lean, even older, white hair straggling to his shoulders, eyes burning fierce as embers, who breathes with the breath of the universe."

"Can these things be sung?" Jim asked.

"Jonathan Forquet was old then; he must be dead many years. But he is a shaman, a Grandfather who touches both sides. Listen . . ." It was time to let loose. I sang my grandfather, introducing Gentle to him through the Wind Song with its stirring of trees and lifting of boughs. I closed my eyes and sang the Shadow Song, and the girl who hung around and took it all in.

I didn't stop. I sang my grandfather's invisible gift. I revealed it with all its tender unseeable glory to Gentle.

I finished and he sat shaking his head. When at last he

spoke, it was to respond as he always did when something touched him deeply, "Yeah."

▼ ▲ ▼

FROM then on we were one person, like the Duke and Strayhorn, in love with music and each other. He understood my struggle with musical notation and showed me how to get on with it. He was a master teacher. He made a drawing of the circle of fifths depicting the relationship between keys. With this to navigate by I was able to transpose. He kept me at it, and soon, in spite of my hectic schedule, I had a full notebook.

He was in no hurry for me to sever my ties with Mac. On the contrary, he didn't even want it. Instead of losing Mac, he thought of ways to add himself to the team. One idea we developed jointly—when he felt I was ready he would arrange a benefit concert where I could perform—yes—Cree songs.

I heard him say the very things I'd thought. "It's a different audience, youthful, daring. They want the new, the innovative. I have a gut feeling that the stuff you want to do would go over big-time."

Teacher, mentor, lover—Gentle laid traps for me to see how much I studied, to see how much I loved, to see how much I lived. Loving though they were, they were nonetheless traps. He would confront me suddenly and ask, "Why do you love me?" And I would have to come up with a reasoned answer that he found acceptable. One day I stopped at a little Jewish deli and brought him strudel. I heated coffee and we munched. It was a great way to kill an hour before rehearsal. He leaned over to wipe a crumb from my chin and asked another of those Delphic questions.

"Tell me," he demanded, "why do you want to sing First Nation music? What does it mean to you? Can you tell me? Do you even know?"

"Of course I know. I already told you. Can I help it if you aren't satisfied with the answer? I picked it up when I was a kid and it's always stayed with me."

"Go on," he urged. "You're on the right track."

I hunted in my mind. "I guess I want everyone to know it and feel about it the way I do, that it's mystic and holy. First music, sung by first people."

"Ahhh," he said, "that's what I thought. But look how I had to drag it out of you."

"That's because everyone is so unreceptive, even hostile. Yes, actively hostile about my singing it, or even writing it."

"By everyone you mean Mac?"

"I guess so—and audiences."

He didn't pursue this but said, "You'll need program notes. You can't just spring this kind of stuff on people. It can't be out of the blue. They have to be prepared, told about it, its antecedents, what it means, that it's sacred. And at the same time wild and not to be tamed. Keep working, you're closing in on it."

"And then? Eventually? It will be part of my repertoire?"

Jim backed off a bit. "Go slow, it's a successful career we'd be tampering with. All I'm suggesting is that you try them out in a benefit situation, see how they're received."

"When do you think, Jim?"

"You've more work to do. The songs need polish and arrangement. I can handle the rest. It will mean raising funds. Mac has to let you do one outside show a year, that's guild rules. So if we don't ask him or any of the agency people for anything, they've got no beef. I think your songs could start a trend, whip up interest among other artists. And we'd put it on for First Nation people. I know a cat in P.R. who will act as front man. You, my girl, would have to be your own dresser and makeup expert."

"Just like the old days," I said, rather liking the idea. "Actually I'm fairly good at it. Watching Trimble, I've learned to paint and highlight my exterior self. And the other I've given up on."

I saw our love in a new way, a giving way . . . like any lovers that have so much there is bounty to share.

If you want to make the devil laugh, they say, make plans. Or was it Loki the Trickster, in hiding all this time, who saw to it that I forgot my purse? I knew where I'd left it, on the futon in Gentle's living room. I went back and rang the bell. He didn't answer.

He had to be there; I'd just left him. I rang again. This time I heard footsteps.

"Hey," he said, "it's my love."

It wasn't what he said, but the way he said it, in a thick, mumbled tone that didn't sound like him.

From a sunny day I stepped into a darkened room. I squinted to see his face. It was twisted into a foolish grin. He was totally spaced out.

I stiffened.

I knew of course about the smack he'd taken in Vietnam, but I thought that was then . . . I should have realized. The psychedelic counterculture was cool, part of the music world, Timothy Leary, the whole bit. But I kept clear of druggies. Mac reinforced this. He was like a maiden aunt on the subject, pointing out the careers it trashed and reading obits with relish, especially those resulting from overdoses and suicides. But it wasn't Mac; everything about the drug scene scared me. I didn't want to attain greater awareness. I dreaded greater awareness. I wanted it to be *me* who thought my thoughts, felt my music. And the dreams I had I wanted to be my own.

"I left my purse," I said, and, walking past him, retrieved it from the floor. I saw the cocaine on the side table, looking like spilled sugar.

"Little Bird, Little Bird." He bent over me. "How'd you like to be a snowbird and fly with me?" There was a foolish laugh that went with the foolish grin.

Was this the man who had become part of my life?

▼ ▲ ▼

I WAS angry with myself and remained angry for days.

At least I told myself it was anger. Anger was what I hid in. When it subsided I was left empty and arid. The snow came down black with dirt. I was glad; it matched my mood. New Yorkers hardly noticed. Pollution up, pollution down, what was the difference? I took aspirin and food supplements in an effort to feel better. When they didn't work I stormed, "When will you stop fighting with yourself, Little Bird?"

The reply was easy . . . when I stop being an idiot. Because I should have known; anyone with half a brain would have known.

Gentle didn't come around for a week. When he did, he came straight up to me. "Did it mean anything," he asked, "that you didn't bother to sit down? That you left immediately?"

"I would say so. It meant that I don't want to see you again."

"You don't mean that."

I stared at him stonily.

"But why? At least tell me that. Was it the sex?"

I shook my head.

"The music?"

The same nonverbal response.

"The drugs, then?"

"Bull's-eye."

"I knew it was the drugs. But everyone drops a little acid or sniffs a little coke. Why, right here in your own group . . ."

"I don't want to hear. As far as I'm concerned, anyone who messes with junk is on another planet."

Now that he was here, looking like Jim, sounding like Jim, it was hard to force myself to remember him as I had seen him. It was hard to walk away from Gentle.

I had built too fast and too much with this man. His love of music and my love of music. His willingness to share his talent . . . Then the other Jim intruded, vacant eyes, slobbering, "Little Bird, Snow Bird. Fly with me."

It was a wracking experience. I didn't know how to stop

loving. I tore him out of my life while I still loved him. It was like burying someone who is alive and won't stay dead. At too many unexpected moments he would force himself into my mind. Too many things and places reminded me of Jim. I mean, when even the coffee machine brings a pang of heartache, what can you do?

Mac must have gotten wind of something. He knew I'd broken up with Gentle. Rumors circulate about everyone, but in this case, with Gentle staying away, it wasn't difficult to figure. Mac chose this time for what he called a heart-to-heart.

There is a point in every conversation of this sort where you know what's coming, and try to stave it off. Mac was working himself up to another proposal. I preferred him censorious and nagging to romantic. But I couldn't stop him.

He segued into, "What you want, honey, is the right sort of guy. Not necessarily another musician, or even some good-looking stud, but a mogul, a CEO, someone who's made it in the industry." He meant himself, of course. "What do you say, Kathy? You need someone, otherwise there's bound to be . . . episodes. Hell, you're lonely. I'm lonely. What do you say?"

I took one of his hands and squeezed it. I wished I could say yes.

I did need someone, he was right about that. I looked around. Freddy came to mind. He was a sweet guy. He had stopped his hack for me with a row of cars, horns blaring, behind him. He had taken good care of my guitar. I was not going to live my life in New York, unhappy and wiped out.

There were clubs to take in, shows to see, music to hear. I ended by asking Freddy for a date, knowing he'd never get up nerve to ask me.

I was surprised when he called for me with a friend in tow, a nice chap who had a puppet theater in the Village. His puppets had the distinction of having been arrested. The charge, indecent exposure. We dropped in at several places, heard Deborah Benedict give a smash rendition of Piaf songs, listened to an exciting Tex-Mex bunch who also did Cajun, and wound up in a little dive that served up Basin Street blues.

There were moments when I sank into music. Even with other people making it, my feet tapped along. I pretended there was no such person as Jim Gentle. I pretended I was happy.

When at the end of the evening I was escorted through the lobby and up to my door, I turned to say I'd had a lovely evening, the two of them were kissing each other good night.

Again I was alone.

▼ ▲ ▼

THE initial impetus the Johnny Carson show gave my career had run its brief course. Nashville was beckoning, and since things looked more promising there, we packed up. Much of my time during the next year was spent there, with stretches in both Chicago and New York. But wherever I was physically, things settled down to their usual norm—a crisis every other day, forgotten by the end of the week. Better described as maniacal. Maniacal in Chicago. Maniacal in New York. Maniacal in Nashville.

Time seemed to compress. I worked in tandem with myself, carrying on with all routines, keeping appointments, cutting tapes and demos. I thought of getting a benefit together on my own. It seemed the only way I could sing my ethnic songs. But Jim Gentle was too closely associated with that particular project. I hadn't gotten over him. He wasn't an easy guy to get over.

So I didn't object to the killing schedule Trimble laid out for me. Mornings she brought out her ledger book, embossed with my name in gold leaf, and read off my obligations for the day.

It did seem there wasn't enough of me to go around. But at first I was pleased that I never had an afternoon to myself. And as long as there were people surrounding me, I was "on." Being "on" meant looking good, standing tall, and smiling cheerily no matter what. I couldn't slouch about in sweats. If something itched, I couldn't scratch. Above all, I had to be unfailingly pleasant, always hard for me. There were moments when I needed to glower and gloom and carry on, but my schedule didn't allow for letting off steam.

I was listening to Trimble inform me the pedicurist had arrived, and remind me that at four o'clock a writer from *Cosmo* was dropping by . . . after that, a rehearsal with my backup . . . then dinner with some visiting big shots from Las Vegas, and I was to be at the studio nine A.M. sharp. The room began to swim. It was time to yell—Enough yet! I had to be by myself. To think.

No, to *not* think. Just to lie down and not think. Not plan, not arrange, not commit, not promise, not impress, not argue, not convince, not agree, not fight, not make up, not laugh, not cry—simply lie down and look at the ceiling and blank out.

I put the pedicurist off to another day, sent everyone away, and told a probing Trimble to cancel all appointments.

I went to my room and lay down on the bed. There. I'd done it. It was easy. I was alone. Finally.

Instead of feeling peaceful, I was distressed. I had made too good a job of it, cut myself off from everyone, from Abram, from my daughter, from Jack, from Gentle, even from my brothers. I often wondered about them. At one point I'd written Jason, but the letter came back. He no longer lived there. There was no human being I had any connection with, no one I cared for or who gave a damn about me.

I recalled the various cats and dogs I'd gone to sleep with when I was little: Nicky, an enormous, docile Newfoundland who resembled the nurse in Peter Pan; Beau, a white Sami who kept my feet warm; my kitten Pitty Sing from the *Mikado*. Abram ended up with her because Jellet claimed he was allergic. I wished I had one of them now.

A few days later I was in my dressing room, taking a break. I picked up a *Reader's Digest*. The jokes didn't seem funny and the true stories didn't seem true. I tossed it back on the table, trading it for a slightly rumpled newspaper. Yesterday's. Oh well, I suppose the world was pretty much the same today as yesterday. The same problems unresolved, Israel and the Palestinians, the troubles in Ireland. I thumbed through the pages methodically.

My eye was caught by a handsome, distinguished-looking

man about to board a plane. I read the caption and snapped to attention. It was my father. Erich von Kerll, trade commissioner. Yes, that was right. I tried to read it all at once, to absorb what they said about him. "... divides his time between Austria and the United States ... expedited export of American engineering technology. Responsible for ... his daughter ..."

His daughter? Me?

"... his daughter, Elizabeth Brillianna Kerll ... killed in a blinding blizzard when the car in which she was a passenger ..."

My God, a sister! I'd had a sister. Her name was Elizabeth, and she was dead. My poor father. Poor Erich. How awful it was to lose someone out of your life, especially a daughter.

I recalled the Austrian folk melodies Mum used to put me to bed with, the ones von Kerll taught her. Folding the picture all around and creasing it with my nails, I very carefully tore it out.

The man who was my father looked back at me, very handsome, a touch of gray at his temples. And his eyes, gray like Mum said.

Would he come back to America? I wanted to help him through this terrible time. I wanted him to know, in spite of what had happened, that he still had a daughter.

On the instant I hunted up pen and paper and wrote to Erich von Kerll at the Austrian consulate. PLEASE FORWARD, I printed in block capitals. I started my letter.

I wrote you twice before. Once in 1963 and later. The 1963 letter came back, and the other I didn't send. So you never knew you have another daughter.

Oh Be Joyful's Daughter didn't tell you because she didn't want anything from you. But she did want me to be in contact at some period of my life. This seems to be the right time. I don't mean that I can in any way replace the daughter you lost. We lost, for I lost a sister I didn't know I had. Mother died some years back, so I am able to understand your grief and that of your wife. Have you perhaps other children as well?

If you return to this country and want to be in touch, I enclose my address and phone number. I hope it isn't too late. I hope we can still meet, and you can learn more of my Mum—and I, of you. I want very much to know you. I hope this attempt to write will reach you, although I am not too confident about it. I send a Cree prayer for the soul of Elizabeth.

Your daughter, Kathy (as if it could be anything else)

I stuffed my letter into an envelope and took it to the post office myself. I watched it being weighed, watched the postage go on.

Why hadn't I done this before?

What was wrong with me? Why had I allowed those dissonant chords Elk Woman sang to describe me, prevail, when what I wanted was a yodel, mountain peaks, snow valleys, and my father, Erich von Kerll?

Mac had been after me to let him arrange a European tour. Why not? Why not meet my father, second-in-command of a U-boat in Hitler's navy?

I tempered my enthusiasm with a dose of reality. Simply because I liked his pretty Tyrolean folk songs did not negate the fact that he had left Mum.

Mum had not been lucky in her choice of men. The one she really loved died on her, von Kerll went back to Austria, and the third, Jellet, the less said of him . . . I reflected that so far I had not done better.

Why had I ever left home? Why had I wanted to sing, to make love to audiences? Why had I wanted to bring Cree songs to the world? I should have stayed in St. Alban's with the only person who ever loved me.

I could do it now. I could go back, take my share of the bankroll and go home. I could settle down and send for my daughter. I brought myself up sharply. I knew where that ended.

I felt a strong need to fight with somebody, but there was no one I liked well enough.

Chapter Twelve

MAC was insistent that we attend the ACM awards. I wouldn't have thought much about it, except for Trimble. She dressed me with exceptional care and fussed over makeup until I looked like Barbie.

"Anabel," I said exasperated, "what's all this about?"

"I'm not supposed to say anything. But rumor has it . . . you're in line for an award."

My heart did a kind of flutter. "I don't have any platinums. I don't have a chance."

In the taxi I challenged Mac. "Do you know something about the ACM awards that I don't?"

He chortled. "Let's say you're an odds-on favorite."

"Really? Me?"

"How would Best Female Vocalist strike you?"

I hugged him. "Oh Mac. If it's true, it's wonderful." And a second later I burst out with, "I can't believe it."

And I couldn't. This happened to top people. Had I climbed into that league? Was I there? My spirits shot into the stratosphere. Years of fleabag motels, smoky clubs, running up and down the country in that old jalopy pitching my vocals. The work, the turndowns, it all paid off tonight. If only Mum were here. I needed someone to share it with. I was teaching myself not to think *Gentle,* not to think *Abram.* Gentle was lost. And Abram was married by now—some Mennonite girl with thick ankles and a dozen kids.

Shared or not, the award was the best thing that could ever happen to me. It meant I'd made it. I'd really made it.

We pulled up in front of the theater. The presentation first and dinner afterward. Mac squired me past screaming fans to where police guarded the door. It was unreal.

Inside Mac led me to the third row. "Not too far to walk," he grinned. My group and backup singers were there, some big names, the media, agency people, staff people, and studio heads. Mac kept whispering names as he pointed them out.

The program began; a stand-up comic warmed up the audience and the speeches got underway. I sat in a daze.

"Best Female Vocalist!" Mac squeezed my arm.

The spot swung around. I sat forward in my seat, ready to rise. But something was wrong. They didn't call my name.

Dear God, it was a mistake. It wasn't me at all. The spot picked up a blonde, beautifully coiffured. But—but—it was one of the girls who sang backup for me.

Flashlights went off in my face as a dozen cameras caught my expression of dismay, chagrin, and bewilderment.

Everyone laughed except the comic, who mimicked my expression of dismay.

"It's a roast!" Mac shouted, laughing with the rest.

I stared at him, still not comprehending.

"A joke! A gag!"

Dozens of people surrounded me. "You should have seen your face!" "Priceless!"

Laughter.

All eyes on me . . . how was I taking it? The laughter mounted, shafting me.

I tried for brittle, I tried for sophistication, the bright amused smile. "So clever. Hilarious."

They congratulated themselves. They couldn't talk of anything else.

The doors were opened to let in the audience, and the actual ceremony got underway. When I won Best Female Vocalist I stood woodenly, and woodenly accepted my plaque.

On the way home I remembered Mum telling me of something that happened to her. "My mum had a roast once," I told Mac. "She was in nursing school, and when grades were posted, she had the highest score. So her classmates honored her with a practical joke."

"Oh? What was it?"

"She left her patient to see about his medication and when she came back they had planted a corpse in the bed. You know, the screen around it, the sheet drawn over the face."

I regarded Mac carefully, from the wen on his forehead to his nose hairs. "Which gag do you think was funnier?"

▾ ▴ ▾

HOLLYWOOD.

There it was, spelled out on the sign in the hills, just as you see it in movies. And there was Mann's Chinese, gilt and plush, mirrors and deep carpets, and the twisted colonnades which, Mac instructed me, were Romanesque. Outside, handprints and footprints of the old movie stars forever encased in cement. I wondered if the women brought extra-small shoes for the occasion and crammed their feet into them, because they were sizes smaller than mine. If I became famous enough to do my feet, even Anabel wouldn't be able to help.

Since I'd given up on benefits, perhaps Hollywood was the answer, churning up innumerable possibilities. The first appointment was a continuation of our sightseeing: offices on the MGM lot. What a thrill when the great gate clanged behind us.

The meeting was upbeat, gracious, with coffee served. I was just what they were looking for, a new talent, box-office gold, and on and on. We left, glowing.

The fabulous deal that simply required a signature fell through. The producer we were negotiating with was fired. Mac, never at a loss, had another hot contact, and we did lunch, this time with both producer and director. Everything was go. Then we got word that the male star they were angling for got a better offer and the picture was shelved. A third possibility demanded a piece of my contract. We went back to middle America and club work. My permanent home was Nashville, if you can call an apartment hotel permanent or homey.

Then RCA bought my contract and I began rehearsals for a two-album release, and signed for a slot on a weekly variety hour, with my own TV show in the offing.

I insisted on continuing to sing to live audiences. I liked singing to people, and I pulled them in. Saturday night after my club date I was amazed to find a large crowd assembled outside. These were people who hadn't the price to get in. An indelible memory was revived—a little girl standing outside singing, a little girl who never went inside or sang with the choir as a regular member—but stood outside.

I stopped where I was on the stairs. I told Freddy to hook up a mike and speakers. Then and there, practically on the street, I gave a concert. My voice rang out, it floated, it sobbed, it exulted. For an hour I gave them everything, ballads from the forties to my latest album, song after song. They cheered, clapped, and stamped their feet in the slush. It was exhilarating. Finally Mac plucked my arm. Only when I quit did I realize how exhausted I was.

Mac passed me on to Trimble, who got me into bed, telling me I would ruin my voice, citing examples of singers who abused their instrument. She enumerated the various ways it could happen: the smoke in bars, or forcing your voice through a cold. Plain greed ended many a career, and she'd seen it: over-booking, too many commitments, grabbing for the brass ring one time too often.

She was still talking when I dozed off. And when I woke

up, it was morning. Trimble tumbled half a dozen papers into my lap. "The free concert you gave the other evening was terrific P.R., but standing out in the chilly night is not something to repeat; it could lead to pneumonia."

My glamor pictures looked up at me as I read of my generous response to ordinary people.

"You're very clever," Trimble said. "You can't buy that kind of publicity—providing you don't kill yourself, of course."

I didn't bother to explain that I hadn't planned it, that it just happened. What was the use? Everything was scripted.

The syndicated variety show I was guesting on these days and the new sponsors insisted on a delivery that was belted out, stylized, not me, not me at all. The one thing that had been mine, the singing itself, the magic, they took. That wonderful time that had been mine from the moment I first stood outside the Mennonite church, they took away. They wanted a new tone.

I no longer sang to please myself.

I was making fabulous money, racking up a fortune, and the bank in Uppsala increased the flow to the bank in St. Paul.

▼ ▲ ▼

It was Mac who told me. "Gentle's here in Nashville. Been here a couple of weeks, I understand. He hasn't tried getting in touch, has he?"

"No. Of course not. Why should he?" I listened to my own words, cool, controlled, giving no indication of the schismatic quake below the surface. Fracturing, rupturing, but invisible.

His being here could have nothing to do with me. It had

been a full year; we weren't the same people. So why the inner turmoil? He'd been in town several weeks and hadn't called. On the off chance that he might, I'd tell Trimble to add him to the list of people I didn't take calls from.

That feeble resolution came to nothing, because when I got home there was a note from him. I recognized the writing. He held the pen hard and pressed hard. The strokes were thick, black, and decisive.

Kathy,
What you did by breaking things off, that was right. It was a tonic chord. But a new theme has entered. We should allow it to play. What was right then, may not be right now. You took something very important away from me—you.

I want to call and tell you I've been off the stuff all this time, but I'm afraid of Trimble, your phone answerer, whose job it is to tell people—especially me—to get lost.

When I read that I laughed out loud. How close he had things figured. He ended asking me to phone him.

Not on your life, Gentle. I refuse to get on that merry-go-round again.

A phone call the very next afternoon changed my life.

Not Gentle.

My father.

I knew it was him, even before he told me. It wasn't an accent exactly, but the English was too perfect.

He'd received the letter, was now back in New York, and

wanted to see me. He proposed flying to Nashville next Friday and spending the weekend.

I made reservations at the hotel I stayed at, and upset Trimble by cancelling appointments right and left. I insisted on uninterrupted time with my father. There were two lifetimes to catch up on, his and mine.

When the time came to meet his plane, I had as bad a case of stage fright as I've ever experienced. I stood with a little crowd of expectant greeters and watched passengers deplane.

They straggled out, and then came in bunches. The knot of greeters was quickly diminishing, as friends, family, and lovers met, embraced, and left. Finally the gentleman with a cane I had been waiting for all my life. The different ways in which I had imagined this meeting coalesced. The reality was, I walked up to him, we looked at each other and knew each other.

I started to shake his hand, but he pulled me to him in a warm hug and kissed my cheek. "Kathy."

I started to cry. It was the last thing I wanted to do.

"Let's stop at one of these little places for coffee," he suggested.

I blew my nose and nodded.

We ducked into a garish little cafe, one of many that line the aisles of an airport terminal. This was nicer than some; it had booths. I slid across the plastic seat. He did the same, but from the other side, so we faced each other.

"I knew you by your eyes," he said. "You have your mother's eyes."

The waitress came to take our order. "Coffee, and some kind of sweet roll." He looked across at me, "Or would you prefer a sandwich?"

"No, coffee and a roll will be fine."

There was a slight pause. Where to begin? "Mum described you to me, many times."

"You wrote she is dead." He brought the fingers of his hands together, each touching the opposing one. "She was a unique person. Quite wonderful. She deserved a good life. Did she have one?"

"She made it good," I said evasively.

"Did she marry again?"

"Yes," I told him, and saw that he didn't like this answer. For Mum's sake I took pleasure in it. Then I remembered his loss and became gentler.

"Now can we hear about you?" he was saying. How nice he was. How glad I was he was my father. It was so easy to talk to him that I found myself telling him all sorts of things I hadn't intended.

About Kathy. I didn't want him to form a bad impression of me, but I had to tell him.

He listened, took my hand in his. "I see how it was."

That simple sentence went a long way toward absolving me.

We had supper that evening in my suite and he ordered a bottle of merlot. I poured coffee, which we took to the couch. There was so much to say, so much to tell. We wanted to know each other and perhaps ourselves. "Elizabeth," he said, drawing out the name as though behind it pictures formed.

"Her mother chose her schools, checked her friends, later her boyfriends." He laughed. "She always lost boyfriends because she constantly beat them at tennis. She was a lefty, you see."

"She too? I used to be left-handed."

I could tell this simple, crazy happenstance endeared me to him. "Really? Now we know which side of the family it comes from."

Elizabeth was a subject he kept returning to. He needed to talk about her, and until now I don't think he had. ". . . Something of a tomboy growing up. Then when she shed her braces, suddenly she was this lovely, attractive young lady. I remember, on one of my trips back from New York, hardly recognizing her. Her mother took over at that point. But Liz and I got in some great times. A camping trip. We climbed Pizza Leone, went looking for fragoli, rode, pitched our tent under a waterfall. Then to give ourselves a rest, put up at The Elephant. Rupert Hapsburg's one-time hunting lodge. Wonderful old place, I'll take you there sometime. . . ."

I leaned back and closed my eyes, wrapped in the old dream, my father supplying the details that had been missing all these years.

"A fireplace that extended over an entire wall. At one end it had built-in shelves that were used as beds. The actual opening where a fire would blaze was at your feet."

Yes, yes. How many times I had been there. Slept in that wonderful chamber.

The last night of his stay, he told me about her death. He

brought out a picture from his wallet and I gazed into the eyes of my sister. She was lovely. Clear gray eyes like his, and a forehead like his, broad and high. A patrician face, with a touch of hauteur about the lips. What would she have thought of me, a part-Cree sister? Could we have been friends? The candid gray eyes claimed me, but I wondered.

"She came home from boarding school. And as a reward I wanted to take her with me the last trip to New York. But it was inconvenient. Her mother had planned a coming-out party, and all manner of things." He paused, as though determining just how to proceed.

"I feel at this point I should explain Natalie, and perhaps myself a bit. I came back to Austria from a sense of duty. It's not good to be on the losing side of a war. There was a great deal that needed doing, and my family had always served the government in one capacity or another. That was the rift between your mother and me. She understood, or said she did. But she felt strongly that she could have no part in such a life, such an endeavor. And she felt a Cree wife would be an insurmountable handicap for me. I did not agree with any of this, but at the same time I couldn't escape what I conceived as my duty to return. Another factor was my mother, too old and frail to run the estate, or even track down its assets, which had been hidden during the war. It was quite a job, as you can well imagine."

What I wanted to know was whether he had loved Mum. "It must have been hard, your decision to leave Canada, I mean."

"I don't know if I can explain it, but your mother and this great new continent were fused, one with the other. I was ready to start a new life. I won't deny it was hard after the war—being an Austrian. I'd been trained as a naval engineer and an expert stress analyst and draftsman, but there weren't many openings for a man with a German name, lacking one leg, and who might have torpedoed someone you knew. I don't blame them. I was prepared to stick it out and prove myself. I was already starting to break through, and given time I would have, of that I'm quite sure. But my mother came, a perilous trip then when commercial air routes were in their infancy. But come she did. And made me see that my help was crucial if the family was to survive. I have no brothers, and my father was a casualty of the war, mentally that is."

I nodded. His version pretty much tallied with Mum's.

"As for the annulment, it was the only sensible step to take. We were separated by a continent and an ocean, and by our separate worlds. But one can't annul feelings; those remained. Remain to this day.

"Eventually I married. Natalie was from an old family. In Europe that still means something. I am proud of the home she keeps. She has a place in Austria's politics; no function is complete without her. She is, if anything, busier than I am."

He was circling his intent, but he needed to tell me.

"Elizabeth was on vacation in the Italian Alps. She'd gotten engaged, you know. Her fiancé was driving, and there was another couple with them. I remember when she was old enough I taught her to drive. She was an excellent driver, cautious without being overly so, and with splendid reflexes. The trouble is, the man generally does the driving. I remember at first, when some young wet-behind-the-ears chap would come calling, I'd make him take me for a test spin. Natalie laughed at me. 'Do you suppose the way he drives with her father is the way he drives with her?' But what can one do?

"It was on the road to Cortina. It's spectacular driving, exhilarating, with sheer drops at every turn. I've driven it many times, you feel the sun on your face, the wind in your hair. Of course it's not banked as an American road would be. It's built by Italians with a small stone guardrail that comes maybe as high as your knee . . . a warning perhaps, but no protection if your car goes out of control. They never found her body. The wreckage was totally unrecoverable."

After this there was nothing we could not say to each other. I told him the story of how I came to be dead to my daughter, about life on the road, about Jim Gentle.

He took my hand and began to stroke it. "You're well out of that relationship, Kathy. A drug addict is almost always hooked for life. They are unreliable, desperate people."

"I know, I know. And he had such dreams . . ." I went back further in my life—I was leaning out the window waving good-bye to Abram. But he wouldn't wave back.

"I left the only person that ever loved me," I told my father. "I married someone who took me out of St. Alban's. My mother was dead, and I didn't get on with my stepfather. So I left Abram to get away.

"You don't want to know about the ups and downs, the

crazy life I led—still lead—like a gypsy, hardly ever laying my head down in the same place twice. My husband and I divorced . . ."

"And you still think of your first love, what was his name, Abram?"

"And he still thinks of me, even though he's probably married to a nice Mennonite girl and has half a dozen kids. You see, we traded shadows."

The evening couldn't break up until we sang some of the Austrian folk songs he had taught my mother:

Wenn i komm, wenn i komm,
Wenn i wiedrum komm
Kehr i ein, mein Schatz,
Bei dir.

"Here's one you don't know." And I launched into a Cree song. I sang it to the end with its strange dissonant wailings and its patter sections, its listening and its telling, its questions and its answers.

My father sat in amazement. He'd never heard anything like it. "It washes over you like wind, like rain," he blurted out.

I hugged him. "Yes, that's it. Oh Be Joyful's father, my grandfather, would have said you have the soul of a Cree."

When the weekend was ended we were a father and daughter who had found each other. We parted with promises to get together. I would work on Mac to get a gig in New York. "Don't worry about it," my father said, "I'll be back in the new year. In the meantime I'm going to give myself the pleasure of buying up all your albums, and any singles I can find."

He phoned me later in the week to say he had become a fan. "I love your voice, Kathy. It's filled with warmth and longing. It made me realize I don't know you yet." We settled on two weeks from now for his next visit.

That night I dreamed of my sister. Her life was so formal: boarding school, the right clothes, the proper friends. She was so protected. Yet I, who grew up hit or miss, was the one who lived, and Elizabeth the one to die. How odd the world was, and no one, not Catholic priest or Indian shaman, could tell the why of things.

Chapter Thirteen

A PHONE call from Jim Gentle. I knew his voice instantly. And how well he knew me; he knew his name would be on the list of calls I didn't receive. And it would have been, except through some Freudian oversight I never did tell Trimble, and she patched him through.

The moment I heard him, time telescoped. It wasn't a year ago we'd made love on his half-collapsed futon, it was yesterday.

"Before you hang up," he said, "this is a 911 call."

"Oh?"

"Ever hear of Wounded Knee?"

"What?"

"That's what I thought. Ever hear of the Trail of Broken Treaties?"

"I think I'll hang up now."

"No, please. This is serious. In 1890 Red Cloud affixed his thumbprint to the Fort Laramie Treaty. Except, except this call isn't about him."

"Gentle, you're not making sense."

"I told you it's a 911 call."

"I'm listening."

"I'm in trouble. I got into a brawl with the police. Nothing serious, just my motorcycle against theirs. They threw me in the slammer, where I spent New Year's making good resolutions. That's why I'm calling, actually. When I got out, a friend gave me some high-grade stuff. I'm sitting here looking at it. Looking at it and not taking it. I've been clean ever since we broke up, I swear it. But now I'm going to need a little help. Will you come over, Kathy?"

"No."

"I thought maybe you would."

"No."

There was a long pause. Had he hung up?

Then, "Billy Strayhorn would have come."

"I thought *you* were Billy Strayhorn."

"They were like one person. Kathy, I don't know how much longer I can hold out."

"Flush it down the toilet. What's the address?"

I banged the phone down. Calling myself an idiot I threw on a coat, jammed my feet into galoshes, and grabbed an umbrella. The wind turned it inside out.

What was I doing? Over is over. But when he met me at the door and pulled me to him, heart to heart, I felt I belonged there.

I drew back. I was here in response to a 911 call. "Well, let's see what needs to be done." I sat down with him and got him through the night.

The next night we had sex and the next. It was warm and wonderful and I allowed myself to hope. So did Gentle.

"What was that business about Wounded Knee? Is that for real?"

As Gentle told it, there were two Wounded Knees. In 1890 it was the site at which a Pauite prophet, Wovoda, proclaimed that white men would disappear and the buffalo return, if the rites and rituals of the Ghost Dance were faithfully performed. At this messianic promise, the Indians fell into a self-induced hypnotic state. They danced without food or drink. They danced until their feet bled. They danced until they fell. The government, fearing the ecstatic cult and the fanaticism it bred, sent in the Seventh Cavalry.

The Indians were greatly outnumbered and surrendered. But there was a skirmish and Sitting Bull was killed while being arrested. This led to several hundred Sioux fleeing the reservation and hiding in the Badlands. They were pursued and surrounded as they camped at Wounded Knee.

The Indians again surrendered. But as they were being disarmed, a young brave refused to give over his new rifle. The trooper tried to take it from him, it discharged, and the trooper fell dead. That did it.

Machine guns fired into the disarmed Indians. A hundred and fifty-four died there, including forty-four women and sixteen children. They weren't buried until the following spring, when weather permitted and the army returned to clean up the mess.

"Well, that was the Wounded Knee massacre that took place in December of 1890. The second Wounded Knee occured six years ago—February 27, 1973—when two hundred members of AIM, the American Indian Movement, took the present hamlet of Wounded Knee by force and occupied it. Their leaders, Russell Means and Dennis Banks, vowed to stay until the United States threw out the government-appointed tribal leaders, who ran the res like a penal colony. They further demanded a judicial review of all Indian treaties and an impartial commission to investigate government treatment of Indians."

"Where did all this happen? Where is Wounded Knee?"

"South Dakota. It's a tiny place on the edge of the Pine Wood Indian Reservation."

"So how did it end up?"

"With a reign of terror. A seventy-one-day siege by federal marshals, who surrounded them and let no food in. It was pathetic. Hunger versus resolution . . . with hunger winning."

"It's all so sad. I suppose the land was worthless anyway?"

Gentle laughed. "That's what the U.S. government thought initially when they ceded it to the Indians. It was for sure no good for farming. But here's the catch. As it turned out, the Good Lord deposited something far more valuable than gold—uranium—in the Black Hills.

"Naturally, the government wanted to remove the Indians and start mining. Congress, falling into step, passed legislation aimed at getting the Indians off welfare and integrating them into urban life. To most people, this seemed a laudable goal, and the ancient treaty was abrogated. To nudge the Indians to leave, their welfare checks were cut. When they began to starve, the Indians themselves brought the matter before a federal judge, who ruled in their favor, saying, 'The waters of justice have been polluted.'"

"That's good. The ruling was in their favor."

"The *ruling* was, but nothing happened. The mining goes on. That's what we're giving this concert for—to reinstate the Fort Laramie Treaty. I thought of you immediately. Would you," Gentle finished up, "donate your time, be one of the headline singers?"

"Could I sing my Cree songs?"

In answer Gentle swung me off my feet and polkaed around the room to the triumphant strains of Beethoven's Ninth. "I do believe you are waking to this great world around you. Yes, I do believe it."

On top of everything I was doing, Gentle and I took our plans out of cold storage. I was to write and sing my indigenous material. An Indian repertoire was certainly appropriate for a benefit seeking the restoration of Indian land. Jim would get it together. As for me, the sheer thrill of working on the pieces I had dreamed of doing for so long kept me going, allowed me to do without sleep, kept me on my feet.

I had to call my father and postpone our get-together by a week.

"I'm heading a delegation to Mexico City and I'm leaving

that Sunday. But if I can make decent connections from Nashville, I'll leave from there."

"Would you! It's just that I have an opportunity to sing my Cree songs. You know what that means to me."

"Don't worry. I'll work it out."

Half-truths must be what the road to purgatory is lined with. Or was it Loki, once again, who lured me into it?

Because when we got together, I had to tell my father that the Cree songs were for a benefit.

And when he asked more specifically about the benefit, it came out that Jim was organizing it.

"Jim Gentle? The one on drugs? You're back with him?"

"He's been clean for a year. And when he was tempted to go back on them he called me, and I was able to help him. He fought it off. He'll be okay now."

"I wish you could hear yourself, Kathy. For God's sake, don't get in too deep with this person."

"I don't know what you mean, too deep. But I'll tell you this about me, I don't do things by halves. It's all the way with me. I'm back with him, and we're going to bring this concert off together. I know everyone at the Ole Opry, and I'll help him recruit other headliners."

"Kathy, can't you see he is using you? You want to sing your Cree songs . . . but he has his own agenda. He's a dangerous man."

"How can you make such a judgment? You don't even know him."

"I'm looking out for your welfare, Kathy."

"Are you? Don't you think the father bit is somewhat overdone? Like maybe thirty years too late?"

"You're quite right, I haven't earned the right to criticize." He stood up. "Well, I've an early flight in the morning."

A few awkward words on both sides, and he was gone. I knew I'd fought not only with my father, but with myself. He was probably right and I was probably wrong. I didn't care. I was betting on Gentle.

▼ ▲ ▼

To get a feel for the background, Jim sat me down and had me tell him every scrap of conversation I'd ever had with Elk Woman about music. He took copious notes and drew black boxes around sections he thought particularly valuable, such as when Elk Woman compared Cree singing with pop and rock. "White people listen with half an ear to music, while doing something else. With us, when the spirits give you a song, you pay attention."

Gentle ploughed into research, taking the phone off the hook to study. When I saw him next he was primed with prairie and Northwest Indian cultures. "Instead of being crafted note by note and bar by bar, their songs come in a vision, all at once."

"Yes, yes. That's how it is with me too."

"Their word for 'singing' means musical sounds. Even drumming is a kind of singing. In American and European music, the drums beat out the rhythm, which the voices follow. Not in Indian music; there drum and voice can beat to totally different pulses."

"Yes, that's true of words, too. Indian music goes for ideas that can't be put into words. Like what you feel when you're desperately lonely, or someone dies that shouldn't—like my sister Elizabeth."

"Do you know how to put a scream into words?" he asked. "Because that's what you'll have to do, Little Bird. Turn this whole rotten life into music, the way First Nation people do."

"I can do it. I know I can. Still, for an American audience, I'll have to throw in a few words—or they'll walk. Another thing I remember about Indian music, the silences. Toward the end of the wildest celebration or the sweetest love song—sudden silence! Then crescendo to the climax." I leaped up and dragged him into a howling and a growling Indian-style dance.

There was special joy in working so closely with another human being. I realized I had come to look on this benefit Jim was organizing as a contribution, a public service, which no one else was doing: not the politicians, not the newspapers or TV, only a few churches and us, the music community. We were a voice for the underdog, for the victims, for those who got caught in the machinery and ground up.

An unexpected plus was the many fine musicians Gentle assembled. Their willingness to give of their time and their talent to help regain treaty land was very touching to me. Not an Indian among them, but they felt injustice. And they wanted to stand up for what was right. They were willing to sing and play for people who had no way of speaking out for themselves.

And who were these performers? Professionals. Many of

them big names. We got together, never all at once, but as we could, and everyone ran through their numbers, which Gentle tried to put into some sort of framework and make into a show. His first thought was to hold it outdoors at Wounded Knee itself. But there was no way the Bureau of Indian Affairs would let us into a reservation. The state of South Dakota was a different matter, however. There were several little towns in the vicinity, under the same northern sky and awe-inspiring Black Hills. Jim found a natural amphitheater belonging to a defunct gold-mining operation, whose absentee owner was happy to rent it for a day and get his name in the papers.

Jim's other thought was to make the date May Day. South Dakota weather scotched that. We settled for June. From the various points of the globe performers would assemble, along with Indians, journalists, and we hoped a large audience.

▼ ▲ ▼

"WHEN you make plans, the devil laughs," is the way whites phrase it. But for the Indian, Loki the Trickster hides in the shadows.

Trimble picked up the phone and handed it to me. "One of the band."

I took it carelessly. Rono Hart said in a voice without tone or inflection, "It's Gentle. I'm calling from the hospital . . ."

I remember a sort of gasping sound. I didn't know it came from me. The next thing I remember was asking for his room. He didn't have a room. He hadn't been admitted. They told me they were working on him in emergency—an overdose.

A nurse with a stripe on her cap showed me to the waiting room. "We'll call you," she said.

"He's going to make it," I replied. If this was a question, no one answered. If aphorism, it was ignored.

I sat down. There was a goldfish swimming aimlessly in an aerated tank with dyed shells and colored seaweed. It came to the surface and gulped air. I picked up a magazine, well worn. Somebody had torn something out. What could it have been? Something that in some way applied to their life? Or was it simply a recipe? But a recipe might not be simple. It might be profound, a recipe for life.

You don't get off drugs, that's what my father said. It was what I'd always been told. It's stronger than willpower, stronger than the person. Vietnam had done this to him. He'd seen inhuman things, taken part in them. No amount of expiation eradicated them. Only drugs could drive the scene back into hidden recesses of his brain.

I'd known this a year ago. I knew it when I started up with him again. I hadn't known he might end up dead.

If Gentle died I couldn't bring myself to face the waste. A guy so loving, so full of ideas for helping, improving, making better. I couldn't think of him except as reaching out . . . teaching through music, me for instance.

I thought of the 911 call, and further back to the foolish grin. "Snowbird, come fly with me." I had the feeling then, and I had it now, that he was rushing to meet death, anxious to shake hands with it.

. . . And here was I, sitting on a vinyl couch in a sterile waiting room with a small, trapped fish and a pile of magazines whose pages were sized with the imprint of dread and fear. The nurse with the stripe on her cap was coming back. Had he been brought in too late? Had they given up?

I got to my feet. I wanted to be on my feet when she told me. I tried to ask, but no sound came.

The nurse smiled. "He's going to be okay. You can go in now, but only for a minute."

I turned away from her, away from the ER, away from Gentle. Outside I took a deep breath of rain. How odd it felt to be crying from outside myself.

▼ ▲ ▼

I WOULDN'T see Jim, or take his calls. This time I made it clear to Trimble he was at the top of the "No" list.

But I did work like a dog to save his reputation. If the benefit was allowed to collapse, that would be the end of him in the business. I spent hours on the phone soothing everyone down. I saw to it that no hint of drugs ever came up. Gentle's hospitalization was attributed to a flare-up of last winter's bronchitis, coupled with the pressure and the threats he had been receiving. This was the first I heard of threats. Apparently, Rono Hart told me, he was a target for every skinhead in Tennessee. Which made me all the more determined that the benefit take place.

It was less than a week to countdown. The work was essentially done, the P.R. released, the fees paid, reservations made. So I worked the phones, reassuring everyone that the concert was on track. Rono Hart, whom I had hardly spoken to, turned out to be a pillar of strength.

Gentle's sense of drama in choosing the large, flat valley floor, was unerring. It was, he had told me, the ancestral home of the Lakota.

My part in all this was to sing, to release the ethnic songs that had been bottled up in me so long. My mum's people would hear them. Indians know no border; they slip back and forth between Canada and the States, and many would be in attendance at the concert. As for the rest, it was the kind of audience I had always imagined. "Young," Gentle had said, "idealistic. They live in alternative worlds. They stopped the killing in Vietnam with flowers—make love not war."

Mac was horrified by the whole affair. He was horrified that I had taken up with Jim Gentle again, and doubly horrified to see me swept up in something as stupid as Indian causes. He skulked about and would barely speak to me. I don't know how he found out about the drugs. Maybe it was a guess, but he exploded in a series of grunts and stomped out. Was I a crazy woman, as he maintained? I didn't have time to think about it.

The moment I met up with the little group of musicians at the airport, I felt I had done the right thing and that we would make it through. I asked Rono to phone the hospital and tell Gentle we were on our way to Wounded Knee. That, I knew, would help him in his fight back. "And oh, Rono, tell him this time it's final. He'll understand."

I'd booked a commercial flight with an extra seat for the bass fiddle. Those of us coming from Nashville all sat together and went over entrance cues and tempo. Mostly we joked around, Willie did card tricks, and we got into Chicago, which was the hub, and out again without any mishaps.

The last leg of the flight I slept. It was a little one-horse town with a single motel, whose sign had a letter missing. All evening they kept pouring in, arriving by taxi, by motorcycle, by limo, by bus. There were hugs and kissses and people who had only heard about each other, meeting, and going off to pick a little guitar.

I was up early to look the place over. I rented a truck and drove to the location, passing a used auto lot filled with rusting skeletons.

What man had made was rather depressing, but what God had made was magnificent. I saw immediately how wise Gentle had been to turn down theaters and hold out for this spot. An oval meadow against a backdrop of hills cutting patterns in the sky made an acoustically favorable setting. Intuitively Gentle knew an open-air spot was right for open-air music. There'd be light breezes, and puffs of clouds . . . nature speaking. And my songs answering back in a kind of dialogue. Tomorrow there would be blankets and beach chairs and cushions strewn colorfully and haphazardly, as people listened to a sound they had never heard before. Of course there were a plethora of other groups and individual performers to balance what I did, but I concentrated on me.

A stage had been erected, and a truck stood by with our electrical grid. I tested the mikes, and the curve of the hillsides reverberated. It couldn't be better; the place was alive to sound. Any worries I had about an al fresco performance being risky were put to rest.

I'd been too busy to notice the old car that rattled up, but when I turned around—there was Gentle.

I was shocked. Shocked that he was here, but shocked equally at his appearance. He looked as though he'd been buried, left in the ground for a week, and dug up. His long frame was skeletal, his eyes recessed, hooded over by a drooping lid.

"Hi, Little Bird," he said, letting me know by his avoidance of "Kathy" that he abided by my rules. "Now," turning to the others, "let's get the show on the road."

We had a good rehearsal without too many glitches. This did not reassure me, for stage lore has it that a good rehearsal means trouble during the show.

During the run-through Gentle had not uttered a private word to me. For my part, I was relieved. I didn't want to fight with him. He looked as though he could barely stand on his feet as it was. But now he came up to me. I shaded my eyes and looked up, way up, as you have to with Gentle.

"I wanted to say thanks for seeing the concert through, for not letting it fold. It means a lot to me, as you know. And I believe it will mean a great deal to you too. I think it will bring you the audience you've been looking for. I think tomorrow your Cree songs will have found a home."

I held out my hand. "We almost made it, Jim. We almost did."

"About tomorrow, there may be trouble. That's why I'm here. A bunch of Lakota are acting as lookouts. They should be able to spot any local gangs and keep them at a distance. Should a few rednecks slip in, they'll be handled. So don't worry about it. If there is a disturbance, it will be throwing some guy out on his ear. Keep right on singing. Leave the rest to me."

I looked into the eyes that I had so often kissed, and the thick hair I had so often caressed, and the two sides of my nature sparred, the left-handed and the right-handed. It was an intense battle, but short. "Have you notified the police? Maybe they should be on hand."

"Oh Little Bird, Little Bird." He smiled and crossed himself. "The police are the last people we want here tomorrow."

"I understand you had that kind of trouble back in Nashville."

"You never leave it behind. It's a war, and it's on-going."

We all went back to town and Gentle bought ice cream cones, which he handed around, for a job well done.

I went to the motel to rest. Having my lover of only a few days before turn up as an impersonal director was unsettling. The two Gentles kept overlapping. I kept seeing the sweetness and the laughter, while keeping my mind stony against him.

And what was all this about trouble, security, lookouts? Had he thrown me to the wolves? Growing up in Alberta, I knew about wolves. You hear them howl in the night; in the day you see their tracks and their scat. Sometimes you come across a carcass they've left. Wolves aren't kind. They rip their prey apart. Would the audience do that to me? To my songs? To the message we sent?

I tried to analyze the various possibilities separately. The message of the benefit quite simply asked that a wrong be righted, that what had been taken be given back. I couldn't see the harm in that. Yet this was the source of the threats against Jim, the potential violence.

The rest of what I felt was pure nerves. But putting a name to it didn't seem to help. It didn't change the fact that I'd be experimenting before thousands of people with a strange, atavistic kind of music. I remembered how it had struck the band when they first heard it. It was a rocky start. The intonation, the beat of the Cree threw them. Timing was off, entrances missed . . . a debacle. I remember Gentle holding up his hand, calling for quiet. Then he asked if I would start the Wind Song a capella.

Somehow I got it together—a few bars and the drum fell into sync, the slap bass followed, the guitar was with me. We were making music. The question was, would this audience here in South Dakota, lying, sitting, sprawled on blankets in a high valley, surrounded by the Black Hills, which at the noon concert would be starkly white . . . would they get it?

I laughed ruefully; in the old days I would have gone on stage withut turning a hair and sung my songs. Now I worry about everything. I think it's finally being grown up.

Gentle joined us for dinner at a sort of refrito-tortilla cafe, where there was plenty of beer and red wine. The performers crowded in with the electrical crew and some of our local sponsors. The upcoming performance was heady for everyone, but it meant different things to each of us.

The day was perfect, not a cloud in the sky. The word was, a large audience was assembling.

I did a couple of runs and then a trill in the bathroom to limber my instrument and psych myself up. I looked in the mirror and tied a wind-band across my forehead. Remembering Mac's mantra, I repeated, "Start high and go higher."

Kissing my reflection, I told myself, "You're great, Kathy Little Bird, and you're going to wow them." I went out determined to give the performance of my life. After all, I was singing for Mum and her people . . . my people.

The crew, working since before dawn, had rigged a backstage area that was very nicely curtained off. The first set was up. I stood listening to the spirit of the music that would enfold me when the moment came and lead me onstage. Just before this happened, Gentle caught me in his arms. His kiss seared my mouth, fierce and loving at the same time. It brought back the turmoil, the love, the passion that had been between us.

But something besides music reached me, raised voices where the prop men and the electricians stood. Something was going on. Was it the trouble Jim had alerted me to? He went over to quell the disturbance.

Three police and a marshal were huddled with the stage manager. When Gentle approached, the marshal took out a sheaf of papers and waved them angrily under his nose.

Someone said they were going to stop the show. Was that how bully boys operated? I could see Jim was furious. He had spent one entire day at the town hall getting proper authorization, putting up bond money, and having the correct people sign off on it.

"Count the house," Jim was saying in a harsh undertone. "Can't you see the crowd we've got out there? There'll be money—money to pay everyone . . ."

The marshal was unmoved. "I have a court order here. It has the force of an injunction."

Apparently someone had gotten to the owner of the property and convinced him he was consorting with radicals. He was now claiming he'd been promised payment in advance.

Desperately, Jim agreed to this and started to take up a collection from the cast while our business manager began counting the receipts in front of witnesses so as to turn them over.

As the argument escalated, several worlds burst into each other's orbit. I heard my cue and walked out on stage, letting that inner force that I could always call on sweep over me. I had to make my audience see Elk Woman smoking her pipe. My sound would ascend with the smoke and I would sing creation stark, after the bombardment and fireworks of the Big Bang.

I let out the first tentative note into a world still barren, waiting for the Creator to bring life. I sang first seeds and first flowering. I sang the animals in nests and burrows.

People came next, the notes rich and resonant but verging on discord. At the lightning-struck climax the audience reacted with a roar . . . pierced instantly by a response that was mechanical, abrupt, harsh. Repetitive, nonhuman.

Gunfire.

Someone was firing into the air.

Gentle had said, "Continue singing." That's what I tried to do.

Pandemonium.

People flung themselves toward the stage, tripped over wires. My mike was disconnected.

They were climbing over each other, screaming, clawing through the press and bulk of bodies. I stood trapped in chaos and horror.

You don't think at such moments. One brutal scene after another is highlighted and brought before your retinas. Someone grabbed me. Thank God, Gentle. But a club of some kind, I think it was a rifle butt, smashed his face. He went down and they were all over him.

Who? Who was? Who were they?

A wave hit me, a living wave, jammed together, surging, screaming, cursing, yelling, striking out with heads, arms, shoulders, beach chairs that had been ripped apart for battering rams.

I fell over something, no—someone.

Looking up I saw boots, and clogs, and patent-leather dress shoes coming down on me. I turned my face to the floor and raised my hands to shield my head.

A blow. A jar through my whole body. Streaks of pain that ran the length of my nerves like the flick of a lash.

The vortex of cries and pain receded and became distant.

A final realization. I'm dying.

Chapter Fourteen

I WOKE up not dead at all, but feeling sick to my stomach and with a miserable headache. I refused to rest there in the hospital as the doctor suggested. I was badly shaken up but had apparently escaped serious injury. I was lucky; half a dozen people had been trampled and there were two fatalities. I inquired after Gentle, only to be told he'd been taken into custody. No one I spoke with knew on what charge.

I couldn't wait to get out of there. I didn't feel too bad; a bit light-headed, as though I walked a foot or so above my body. At the airport I picked up a paper. They came down hard on Gentle, who was described as a well-known radical and troublemaker. Some enterprising reporter found out that he had been hospitalized for "a drug habit."

I didn't fare much better. "Little Bird was the lead singer for this sorry event, which was to be held for the purpose of raising money to overturn recent BIA policies intended to integrate reservation Indians into the general population. Someone should tell Little Bird we don't appreciate Canadians coming here, making a mint, and telling us how to run the U.S. of A. Where oh where is the sweet country girl we know from her many recordings?"

I crumpled the page. But it was only the beginning.

I was met by both Mac and Trimble. Anabel got me to bed, and I slept the clock around. I was just out of the shower and had slipped into a bathrobe when I heard an altercation at the front door. I went in to see Trimble arguing with a young man. "What's going on?"

The young man turned wet, doggie eyes on me. "Kathy Little Bird?"

No sooner had I said yes than a summons was thrust into my hands. I was to appear at an INS deportation hearing on Wednesday, June 13, 1979, at 2:00 P.M., Room 19 Federal Building, Judge Eleanor Cooke.

I sat down slowly.

Trimble looked back at me with a blank expression.

Not Mac, he had plenty to say. He was livid and I-told-you-sos poured out of his mouth. The wen at his temple turned purple. "How could you get hooked up a second time with that druggie? Well, they got the goods on him this time, found a cache of stuff in his apartment. They'll throw the book at him for probation violation."

"He was on parole?" I was aghast.

"He forgot to mention it?" Mac asked sarcastically. "I suppose it slipped his mind. According to the latest edition, he did time for inciting a riot back in the early seventies."

"Oh my God." Nightmare was sucking me under. "But how do I figure in this? I didn't do anything illegal. I just wanted to sing my songs."

"Remember all the phone calls? You held it together while Gentle was ODing—and you're down on the program as organizer."

"But that's ridiculous. Jim did all the work. I only stepped in at the last moment when it looked as though the whole thing would collapse. I couldn't let that happen—we'd put in so much work."

Mac cut through all that, his practical mind in gear and working. "Now you're not to talk to anyone until your lawyer gets here."

"Mr. Harriman?"

"Not him, he's an entertainment lawyer, only good at interpreting commas and semicolons in contracts. He wouldn't be of help here. No, I've hired Wendel Morris. He's the best in the business. Oh, I'll need a five-thousand-dollar retainer for him. And while I was at it, I've rearranged your assets slightly. We may need a large sum of cash. In cases like this, it helps. But not to worry, you've a good hunk that only you can get at—just in case the market falls, or someone drops an H-bomb, or I take off with what I can lay my hands on."

He laughed and I laughed with him. "You're such an idiot, Mac." But I felt better; I felt he would handle everything.

He assured me of this himself. "Leave it all to me, the newspapers, lawyers, your fans."

"My fans? They will make an auto-da-fé of my albums, and toss my singles on for a better blaze."

We waited for Wendel Morris most of the afternoon. He arrived suave and unapologetic, saying to Mac, "I'll need a brief conference with my client."

Mac grudgingly moved to the far side of the living room and poured himself a whiskey.

Wendel took my hand and patted it. "Now then, Kathy." He sounded like a kindly uncle. I'd never set eyes on him before, but if he wanted to be my uncle, that was okay with me. He made a very good uncle. "Now then, my dear, they'll put some questions to you. But it will be in my presence. If there's something improper, something that I feel they've no right to ask, I'll say so. As for the rest, answer straightforwardly and to the best of your ability. Keep your answers short, and do not, I repeat, do *not* volunteer anything."

I went back to bed feeling I was on trial for murder.

It was a full week to the hearing. Everyone pretended it would be fine. They tried to keep the newspapers from me, but I slipped the desk man fifty bucks.

I was unprepared for the deluge of hate-filled articles. Pictures I had posed for and those I hadn't, photos shot from car windows and from behind fences, all appeared in the tabloids. Not only the supermarket scandal sheets but mainstream magazines carried the story.

An ugly story about a Canadian singer who had clawed her

way to the top in this country, became wealthy in this country, and then turned on it. Espousing far-out Indian causes, such as Red Power, she had attempted through an ill-fated concert to raise money to fight the United States government. The article ended with the same refrain: Does Little Bird think she knows better than homegrown U.S. citizens how this country should be run?

The newspapers fell through my fingers. My life had been turned into pulp fiction. And the efforts made to protect me were washed away in the tsunami that engulfed me.

Optimism and good spirits continued to surround me, but I could imagine the gloomy confabs behind my back. Were they looking for new jobs yet?

Because the worst was just beginning to trickle in . . . my fan mail. I had joked that they would turn on me, but I hadn't really believed it. The pleasure they took from my fall from grace was unbelievable. They were howling for my blood.

Mac refused to acknowledge this. "Your fans are out there," he comforted. "They're different now, that's all, a different bunch. They'll be curious to see you now that you're controversial." He went on to propose the old idea of a European tour while this blew over.

"They don't have newspapers in Europe?" I snapped.

"In Europe they're sophisticated. They don't give a damn about stuff like this."

My head was aching. "All right. Maybe," I said to get him off my back.

The thirteenth came, and I fortified myself with Valium. It

was an ordeal, although not what I expected. The press was there en masse, along with a crowd waving signs. My troops, consisting of Mac, Morris, Trimble, and Freddy, closed around me and attempted to spearhead our way through.

They led me with what decorum they could muster to Room 19. It wasn't grand enough to be a courtroom, just a plain room with chairs and a table, like a teacher's at the head of the class. The judge, a woman of about sixty, conducted the proceedings under an American flag.

People were called up before her. A federal marshal came in and stood beside them and a court reporter took everything down, but they spoke too low for me to hear what was happening. As far as I could tell—nothing.

We waited around until lunchtime. Everyone ate in the cafeteria. A sort of cease-fire was in evidence; lawyers from opposing sides shared a table.

Back in Room 19, Wendel Morris smiled soothingly and murmured the mantra of the day: "Don't worry, Kathy, everything will be all right." He made a very good uncle.

More people came in and took seats. Everyone spoke in whispers. The judge entered and the clerk rapped for order. I decided Eleanor Cooke looked like a judge. She had youthful brown hair framing an old, lined face. She looked intelligent, but on the grim side.

We were sitting closer now and I could hear better. I intended to pay strict attention. But they spoke in paragraphs, long, dry, and boring. This, from what I could gather, concerned people who were convicted felons, people who had overstayed their green cards, and people here in the country illegally.

That was the extent of it. Hour after hour wore away. Finally, at about four o'clock, Wendel Morris was allowed to approach the judge. They talked at length. Afterward I was told they wouldn't get to my case today, that the hearing was postponed to the twentieth.

Mac was pleased. He told Morris things had gone well, and explained to me, "We've got a continuance. Time to prepare our case and for things to die down."

I got up, stretched, got into my coat, and turned to see the deputy at the rear of the room attempting to evict someone. That someone was . . . Abram.

"Abram!" I shrieked.

He tried to wave, but the bailiff caught his arm.

"Abram!" I ran up the aisle and flung myself at him and the bailiff and hugged them both. Part of this configuration squirmed loose, but Abram hugged back.

Abram stood there looking big and blond and solid and—and Mennonite. He had a beard. Sure enough, "Praise the Lord!" were the first words from his lips.

I patted his arm and kept patting it, to make sure this was my Abram who had come to get me out of this mess. For the first time I had a flash of hope that I might weather the storm and not flounder and go under.

Mac and Morris, Freddy and Anabel all came up.

"This is my friend Abram Willems," I said, and didn't let go of his arm and didn't stop patting it.

My coterie of semi-friends-semi-employees didn't like someone from my past showing up. They were cool and unhelpful. This was wasted on Abram. He didn't notice.

Between us time stood still. I was seventeen again and he was Abram as he had always been.

I didn't want to talk about what the papers had done to me. I didn't want to think about it.

I took Abram back with me to the hotel. Mac was being purposely difficult. He refused to be shucked off and stuck like glue, not leaving us alone for a second. I could see he was trying to figure Abram's angle. For Mac everyone had an angle. I was impatient with that and said pointedly that Abram and I had a lot to catch up on.

When we were alone I couldn't stop talking. I talked so I wouldn't have to say anything.

"So what are you doing these days, Abram?"

"I work in a bookstore."

"A bookstore. I like that. You and books always went together. Does it make money?"

"Well, we've added a line of stationery and greeting cards, and it's doing better."

"I bet you've read every book in the place."

He grinned a shy acknowledgment.

"I knew it!"

I couldn't keep it up. I suddenly felt the most vicious contempt for myself. "You think I'm the old Kathy, don't you? Well, I'm not. I'm nothing like her. If you met me now for the first time you'd see that. You wouldn't even want to know me. I don't sing now when I'm happy or when I'm sad. I sing for money, lots of it. And the songs I sing are their songs, not mine. You wouldn't like me at all, Abram, you wouldn't."

In reply he opened his arms wide and set me in them. I turned my face against him, and they closed around me.

"Oh, Abram."

"Shhh," he said, "shhh." He held and rocked me. "Little Bird." His words were murmured into my hair. "You should never have flown away." After a moment he took me by the shoulders and set me at arm's length, looking long and carefully into my face. "Don't tell me that you're not Kathy. You *are* Kathy. I see the old fire, and the soft lights in your eyes. They tell me more than you do who you are."

"And you think I'm that Kathy? You really do?"

"Praise the Lord," he answered me.

▼ ▲ ▼

I PERSUADED Abram to stay with me in the suite. I did this by holding on to him and not letting him go.

"I know what you're afraid of, Abram," I whispered fiercely. "You're afraid of me. You're afraid you'll be tempted to 'know' me in the biblical sense. That should have happened a long time ago between us, and you know it. But I agree to your sleeping here on the couch. Is that okay with you?"

"I came to be with you," he pointed out. "We're going to see this through together."

"I'm washed up, Abram. The whole world hates me. It's unbelievable the letters I get, the vituperous, raging hate that spills out. Yesterday they loved me. It doesn't make sense—there's no more bookings, Abram. I never thought there'd be a time in my life when I couldn't sing."

"They can't stop you singing. All they can do is stop your bookings."

"See what I mean, Abram? You think you're talking to the old Kathy. This is the Kathy I am now. Prettier, because they straightened my teeth, taught me makeovers and clothes coordination. Wealthier, because I made money and Mac invested it. Wiser, because I came up the hard way. I'm a professional—just like a prostitute. I never give it away free."

Abram winced. He didn't like it when I talked like this. And I couldn't help but bait him. He was incontestably Abram, thinking it all through, making up his mind. And by the time he did I had danced a mile ahead of him.

"Do you ever wonder what it would have been like if I'd stayed and never run off with Jack?"

I couldn't get him to speculate. I think maybe he had, many times, to himself. He wasn't eager, either, to talk about the present situation: where I stood legally and what was apt to happen. It was best, in his opinion, to let things unfold.

"When they do," he said, "that is the time to deal with them."

We sent out for Chinese, and ate at the kitchen table. He made an actual fire in the fireplace; no one had ever done that. And we stretched out in front of it on the floor, my head on his knees. We didn't talk much; mostly we watched the flames.

"That blue at the bottom, that's caused by an excess of carbon monoxide."

"Hmm."

A log burned through and tumbled to a new position.

"You're not married, are you, Abram? You don't have a dozen kids and lilacs twined above the kitchen door?"

"No kids. No lilacs. I was married. She died."

"I'm sorry, Abram. It's hard to lose people."

"Ummm—" he said.

We watched embers flake off the log and settle in its heart. "How come it's so comfortable with you? I mean, we can talk or not talk."

"When it's right for two people to be together, they don't have to do much about it, just let it alone, let it be."

"And you think that's us?"

He didn't answer but his hand stroked my hair. As the fire died into ashes I began to realize that one of the things I had run from was my feeling for Abram.

He was like a mountain, solid, intractable, and I loved him for it. But that was nothing new; I'd always known it.

I wasn't the only one with Abram on their mind. Mac chafed at his presence. At our usual Thursday planning session, he confined his animosity to a few unpleasant remarks, such as "that Willems guy seems to have taken over," or how he wished "that Willems character" wouldn't keep shoving his nose in where it didn't belong. All this because Abram had joined us for lunch.

Then he came out with it. "Kathy, I don't like to intrude on anything personal, anything that isn't my business, but this Willems seems to have a lot of influence with you. You say he's an old friend, you grew up together. Is that the extent of it? I mean, he's staying in the suite. I feel I have a right to know. Are you serious about the guy? There's no danger you'll up and marry him, is there?"

"Marry Abram? What an idea! I like him too much for that. Besides, he hasn't asked me."

"Then I'm right. You have given it some thought?"

"Of course I have. Since I was eight years old."

"It would be the worst move you could possibly make. It never works out, marrying outside the business. The hours, the pressure . . ."

"I don't think we have to worry about that."

"Of course we do. This is a temporary slump. All the adverse publicity will die away and you'll be back on top, bigger than ever. We can't have some corn-fed hayseed muscling in."

I laughed. "Is that a description of Abram? My wonderful Abram?" Then in an effort to propitiate Mac and get him off my back, I said, "Abram should be the least of your worries. He doesn't want anything. He's just here to help me through a bad time."

A sarcastic expression crept into his face, and I realized to him that sounded like a con. He would, I believe, actually have been relieved if he could figure out what piece of the pie Abram was after.

I walked to the window and stood looking out. I wanted him to understand. "Do you know what the Mennonites are?"

"Aren't they sort of like the Amish?"

"They're quiet, calm, thoughtful people. Abram, whom I've loved since I was eight years old, is a refuge for me."

"He's a dream. You've climbed into a dream and pulled the covers over your head."

"You may be right. But he means more to me than fans, or career, or music, or anything. I'll let everything else go, but I won't let go of him."

I expected a big blowup. It didn't happen. He took it rather well. He shook my hand and said, "I hope you can forgive me. I really do wish you well, and I'm sorry about Anabel."

Anabel? She was the first defection. I hadn't seen her all day, but I hadn't realized she was gone for good. She was.

▼ ▲ ▼

JACK used to say when your luck turns, everything goes against you. In the midst of this debacle, Mac, Mac the dependable, the steadfast, the guy I counted on, was the next to leave the sinking ship. He absconded, left with all the securities and cash he could lay his hands on.

The way I found out—a heliotrope and platinum card came in the mail inviting me to our usual New Year's Eve party. When I phoned to talk it over, there was no answer. Not even the answering machine.

Half an hour later my lawyer, the one he had gotten for me, Wendel Morris, telephoned the news. I was stunned. The theft amounted to hundreds of thousands of dollars. Maybe more. He was gone and it was gone. Morris ended the conversation by informing me that he was submitting his bill.

I hung up, dazed.

Abram was at my elbow.

"No one came this morning, did they?" First Trimble, then Mac. Freddy too, hadn't shown up. I clutched Abram's jacket. "They won't come, Abram. They won't come anymore."

I told him what had happened. I realized it was a lot to throw at him.

He sat rather heavily. Reaching for my hand he drew me down beside him. "You know, Kathy, you never saw that money. The only thing it did was to bring you all those people, the ones who aren't here this morning. I think you can do without them, don't you?"

"But . . ." I stumbled over the words. "I don't know what's left. Maybe nothing. I worked damn hard for that money, getting up at all hours, rehearsals, run-throughs, I sang my heart out. It isn't fair."

Abram smiled. "That's why it's a crime," he said.

"Don't make jokes. I don't know if there's enough to pay the rent . . . Mac, of all people. But you know, he gave me fair warning. In a way, he told me what he was going to do and asked my pardon in advance. Mac wasn't your ordinary bargain-basement embezzler. He had his code of ethics and lived up to it. From his point of view he was justified. He built Kathy Little Bird step by step, recording by recording, album by album, concert by concert, adding that long string of guest spots, finagling the TV show. He had a big piece of me, which he was entitled to. Why did he want the whole enchilada? Why didn't he talk to me? I didn't know he felt like that. I hadn't a clue. We could have reached some agreement."

"I don't think so, Kathy. I think you hit the nail on the

head when you said he wanted the whole thing. You can't negotiate that."

"He was worried about you, Abram. That precipitated it."

"Maybe so."

"Oh Abram, all those years bumming around, scrounging. Mac, my old buddy, the guy who taught me the fine points of the business, the one I've been through so much with. I feel sick to my stomach."

Abram called downstairs and told them to run across the street and bring me a bottle of Tums. I grabbed the phone. "Not Tums. Make it a bottle of Mumm's."

I explained to Abram the theory I operated under, which had originally been Jack's. "Always celebrate bad luck."

He considered this carefully, as Abram did anything that was new to him. "I like it," was his verdict.

I knew he didn't drink, but when the champagne came he had a glass with me. It reminded me of the old days when we broke into the storeroom of the Eight Bells and swilled beer.

That evening there I was, this time on television. All major stations picked up on Mac. There were shots of us, at functions, at the Grammy awards, and another huddled together outside the courthouse, trying to make our way through the press. I turned it off.

"I hope they don't find him," I said.

"You don't want him caught?"

"No. He'd do much better sunbathing in Cancun or Moorea."

Abram kissed me. He hadn't done that in sixteen years.

That kiss made me understand why he kept himself so

strictly to the straight and narrow—when he left it, the world stood still, the sun too as it did for Joshua. We were hungry for each other. I bit his lip and slipped my hands inside his shirt.

He lifted me off my feet. I wound my legs around him. His need was my own. I wanted him now, this minute.

But he wrenched away, setting me firmly and deliberately on the floor.

"Forgive me," he said. "I don't know what came over me."

"You're a man, Abram, under all that psalm singing." I tried to approach, but with one stiff arm he held me from him. I had to laugh. It was as though I were a tiger and with a chair he kept me at bay. I laughed until tears came to my eyes. "Oh, Abram, you are so funny."

"I must move immediately from this apartment, Kathy. It is impossible for me to even be in the same room with you without . . ."

"Yes, yes, I know what you mean."

"I'll let you know where I'm staying."

"Damn you, Abram. You haven't improved since you were ten years old. You suspect I'm upset, but you have the wrong reason. You think it's because you went too far. You idiot, it's because you didn't go all the way."

"Oh."

"*Oh?* Just *oh?* Is that what you have to say? Such scintillating dialogue sweeps me off my feet. But you're right, you'd better go. Thanks for coming, and standing by me. I do thank you for that. I can face whatever they throw at me. I'm strong now, I really am."

By way of stopping me, because words were gushing out and I couldn't stop them, he took both my hands and held them.

"Marry me, Kathy."

"Oh no, I'm not strong enough for that."

"Marry me."

"Why?"

"Because it says in the Bible, 'created He them.' We were created to be together. Adam was lonely and alone. And I am his true son. Have pity on me, Kathy. I'm distracted and out of control."

"What if they deport me as an undesirable alien, or an enemy alien, or whatever it is they think I am?"

"Why think of it like that? Marry me and come home to Montreal. Would that be so terrible?"

I found it hard to focus on anything but now—right now. "Give it to me straight, Abram—you can't, you absolutely can't sleep with me? This minute, for instance?"

"Without marriage it's fornication. Have patience, Little Bird—your perch is with me."

"Is it?" I wanted him to convince me. But when they changed me from left-handedness I don't think they changed me all the way. "Do you really think you could put up with me, Abram? I mean, have you thought about it?"

"I've prayed about it."

"What if I told you I was still married to Jack?"

"I know you're not. That's the first thing I asked Mac. He told me the divorce was uncontested."

"So you made sure of that, first thing?"

"I did."

I looked around the room with its copy of a T'ang horse on a small pedestal and the Flemish tapestry and a Picasso lithograph—a hodgepodge, like my life.

"Is there anyone here," I called into this doleful effort at an artistic setting, "that knows why this man and this woman may not be joined in holy matrimony?"

I raised my hand. I stood up. "I have a daughter," I said to the T'ang horse. "She's being brought up by Mr. and Mrs. Mason." This I directed to the Flemish tapestry. "They live on Oakdale Street in St. Paul, Minnesota," I informed a modern print.

Silence reverberated against the walls, shrieked in the fireplace.

"You have a daughter?" Abram repeated slowly.

"You hate me, I knew you would. Despise, that's closer to what you feel. And that's what I feel for myself. She's a teenager now, and she's grown up thinking I'm dead. I've never done anything about it. The time was never right, and then it was too late."

"Hold on, Kathy, hold on. Let's get a handle on this. You have a daughter? The Lord has blessed you with a daughter?"

I was totally impaled by this statement. "You think so?" I asked uncertainly.

"When is a child not a blessing?"

"When you can't raise it. When you have to give it away. When she thinks you're dead. When it's been an agony in your heart for fifteen years."

"I'm not speaking of what happened afterward. But the child itself is a miracle."

I jumped to Mac's bottom line. "Then you think it would be the right thing to do, to go get her? When this trial blows over, if it ever does?"

"No. No, not necessarily. No, I don't. She's grown up with these people, they're her family. You shouldn't disturb that relationship out of your need to feel better about her, but out of *her* need."

"Her need? How could I possibly know if she needs me?"

"Have faith that the Lord will tell you."

Abram seemed so calm and sure that looking at the love in his honest face, I did have faith. Only it was in him. "I'm sorry I interrupted you," I said in an effort to bring him back to the proposal.

I could see the twinkling look in his eyes when he asked, "What were we talking about?"

"You had just asked me to marry you."

"And what was your answer going to be?"

"My answer was going to be yes. Yes, yes, yes!"

I knew what he was going to say, and hollered out along with him, "Praise the Lord!"

▼ ▲ ▼

It was Tuesday evening and the Wednesday of the deportation hearing only hours away. In an effort to nudge a little luck my way, I made a resolution to be less self-absorbed. We were sitting on the couch, my head on Abram's shoulder, when I deliberately put aside *my* and *me* and *Kathy*, and prepared to listen to him and learn more of his inner life as well as fill in the gaps in the external one.

Abram wasn't used to talking about himself, and he did it awkwardly. I persisted and bit by bit drew him out. I began by asking about his wife, wondering if he had been very much in love—after all, not all Mennonite girls were dumpy with thick ankles.

He began his account of Laura with a shy recounting of her father, his good friend, John Wertheimer. "He is a brother in Christ, a wonderful man, Kathy. You'll love him as I do. He has acted as guide and mentor to me. It's his bookshop, and through his kindness he has made me a junior partner. Upon his retirement he has undertaken to leave the bookstore to me. It's a rare opportunity, Kathy."

I smiled into his face. I knew he undoubtedly did all the work and at something like janitorial wages, but he was happy. And on the instant I made another resolution . . . to defend Abram, in case they laughed at his outmoded clothes, or made fun of his considered, methodical speech, or despised him for being poor.

Who "they" were, who would do these things, I had no idea. But it might happen, and if it did, they'd have to walk over my dead body first.

I prompted Abram here and there with questions, while he filled in the missing years. He gave a candid, complete account. It took exactly three minutes. In all these years absolutely nothing had happened in his life.

I thought of my life, how crowded and crazy, going from

one extreme to the other. All this time Abram had not gone to college, not gone to war, or pursued a career or made money or dropped out, or anything.

He'd left home, it's true, but without quarreling with his parents or defying the church. In fact, he'd sought out another Mennonite congregation in Montreal and was a member in good standing. He quietly got a quiet job in a quiet little bookstore on a quiet out-of-the-way street.

In telling me about this, his voice became soft and mellow, and I realized this was where his life was centered. I probed a bit more and discovered that the bookshop didn't do much business. A beneficent look crossed his face as he confided that most of the time he sat on a stool reading out-of-print volumes before they were remaindered.

And that was it. Oatmeal with raisins for breakfast, peanut butter and jelly sandwich for lunch, stew for dinner, and a store full of books nobody wanted.

Abram tightened his arms around me and smiled into my face. "You can see what an exciting life it's been, filled with discovery and once in a while true revelation."

I gulped and nodded. His books. That was the world he lived in. And not only what they contained, but the books themselves were important. Old ragged cloth or worn leather binding didn't matter to him. The whisper of pages turning was for him what music was for me. On rainy or icy days—and a Montreal winter has plenty of those—the steep street banked with slush deterred customers, and Abram would lose himself in whatever world the print dictated.

Bit by bit, as I listened, I shed the skin I'd wrapped myself in all these years. I hoped the new one would prove to be a better fit. I wanted the little musty bookshop, where I could close the door on a hurtful world and be alone with Abram. And this is what I told him.

"If you're sure," Abram said, "then you won't be upset tomorrow if things go wrong."

"I'm very positive about this. What I want more than anything on earth is that musty old bookshop and you."

Abram told me about Montreal ". . . intellectual and creative capital of Canada. Artists flock to it. There's a keen interest in music, and . . ."

"And books," I finished for him.

He nodded with utmost seriousness. "Everything in the shop has its proper place and designation. It's all been codified: History, Biography, Reference, Fiction, and in the northeast corner, Classics, arranged by subject and under that by author."

"I wouldn't dare touch one."

"Of course you'll touch them and read them. If you get stuck, I can lay my hand on anything from the World Atlas to Macaulay's *Quotations*. And our flat is directly behind the shop."

"So I can be with you all day in the bookstore?"

"There's a stepstool that slides along the entire back wall. That's where you'll sit."

"While you explain this obsession you have for reading."

"That's easy. I'll explain now. It's a way of finding out what people make of themselves and to what extent they've figured out the world."

"Have you figured it out, Abram?"

"Not yet."

"By the end of your life?"

"Maybe."

"When you find out, tell me."

"I will," he promised.

I was teasing; he was serious.

▾ ▴ ▾

WEDNESDAY morning. That's when I discovered that absconding was not the worst thing Mac had done. It seems he had neglected to renew my green card, or so Wendel Morris's assistant told me—the great man himself was conveniently sick with the flu.

I knew Mac didn't do it on purpose. He was never petty—he had his eye on the big things, the important things—and he just forgot.

Eleanor Cooke did not like me. I was young. She was old and dried up. Even worse, I was part of that suspect world of music and entertainment.

I was classified as an undesirable alien, and ordered deported to my country of origin. I don't really think she, or anyone, believed for a moment I was a threat to the United States government, but they'd found the ammunition they needed.

I held my head high, looked her in the eye, and made the peace sign.

It was over. Over, over, over.

Abram was right, it was no punishment to go home to

Canada. It was to be our honeymoon. So what if my career was in shambles, my fans hated me, and I'd lost my money? I had a new role to play in life as Mrs. Abram Willems.

I took Abram's arm. He wouldn't look for a back way. Together we strode out the double glass doors and faced the press. I blew kisses and called out that I was getting married.

Chapter Fifteen

We went straight home and made wedding plans. That is, Abram made them and I said yes to everything. None of it sounded real. But I knew it was everything else that wasn't real, and that this was. This was the life I should have lived, could have lived, long ago.

"We will fly to Montreal. You will stay with my friends the Wertheimers until we can fix the wedding day. They will stand up for us. We will be married in my church. And I think it would be nice if your father gave you away. Why don't you write and ask him?"

"You think he might? That would make it perfect." After a moment I plucked his sleeve. "Abram," I said, "I want a honeymoon."

"A honeymoon?" he repeated, as though this word were

not in his vocabulary. Probably it wasn't. Abram never had even a vacation in his entire life.

"I want to run away with you, just like we always said. I want it to be the way we planned when we were kids."

I could see he was catching fire slowly, as Abram did. "I'd have to refigure things, calculate more carefully . . ."

"If it's money, Abram, I . . ."

I saw his jaw jut out. "No, that's out of the question."

"Do you know what I was thinking of doing with the pittance Mac left me? I was thinking of starting a big bonfire and tossing it on." I could see the thought of this was painful to Abram. "So instead, why don't we pool it with whatever you've got for a real honeymoon, a honeymoon to remember! Please, Abram."

"It would mean starting out without a dime," he said considering it.

"Absolutely." I was overjoyed. I'd dreamed of running off with Abram since I was eight. "That's the best way to start out. Then we make everything we have together."

"It means being poor. It's been a long time since you were poor."

"Was I poor?" I asked, laughing up at him. "I don't remember that."

A long kiss sealed the discussion.

Coming back to terra firma, I asked, "Where will we go?"

"What would you think of B.C.—Vancouver Island? It's wonderfully beautiful from all I've heard. Then . . ." He stretched out the word and grinned.

"Then?" I said impatiently.

"Then on to Alberta to a little place known by you and me, and scarcely anyone one else, where you will visit your brothers, Jas and Morrie. And if you'd like, your friend Elk Woman. I will say hello to my parents and introduce you to them. And then . . ."

He didn't finish; I'd thrown my arms around him and smothered him in kisses. "Oh Abram, will we really? Will we do that?"

"You think that's a good addition to the plan, do you?"

I nodded. I couldn't talk.

That evening I wrote my father.

Dear Father,

I hope by now you have forgiven me. I haven't had much practice in being a daughter. I'm sure in time I'll get better at it. You'll be pleased to know I didn't marry Jim. I'm going to marry Abram. I told you about him. Remember? Yes, he is the one I traded shadows with. The ceremony will be in Montreal where he lives.

If you've read an American paper recently, you know about the fracas here. I got deported, and I'm not guilty of anything except wanting to sing my kind of music. The press treated me very badly and my fans deserted me. Mac ran out on me. Can you believe that? He took a huge amount of money with him.

But I am as happy as any bride ever was. Isn't that strange, considering. But I am. If you can possibly share my wedding day with me, and give me away, I will feel that we have truly found each other and will be father and daughter for the rest of our lives.

I love you very much.
Kathy

I dreamed our wedding plans over and over to myself. I wanted to devote myself entirely to Abram, to wonderful Abram, who had come to my rescue from Mennonite Canada to save my life and my sanity.

I thought it touching that his heart was now set on a honeymoon as much as mine, although I think he considered it in the category of minor miracles. "A honeymoon," he'd told me, "when I married Laura, was out of the question. At that time I had nothing saved. And even now," he said, by way of apologizing for his not very substantial contribution. "Still, a honeymoon is a fine old tradition; it's served a lot of folks well for a very long time."

"I suppose it gives people a chance to know each other," I chimed in. "After all, most of them haven't been in love since they were eight."

"Do you think you loved me then?" He was deliciously serious.

This time I was too. "I know I did."

▼ ▲ ▼

THINGS I had paid no attention to, or shrugged off as not important, now loomed large. For instance, what about the

Mennonite church? Would I be able to take my place on the women's side of the aisle?

What if Abram's brethren in Christ didn't approve of his choice? What if John Wertheimer and sister Lucinda didn't? What if they expected another Laura? I remembered how eager I had been to defend Abram against insults and disparagements. What if the only person I had to defend him against was myself?

That night I had a nightmare.

I saw myself in a wedding gown, marching along a street that I knew was in Montreal. Church bells were ringing, and to either side parishioners made way for the bride and groom. But I kept my eyes averted. I couldn't meet their glances. I tried to loosen the grip Abram had on my arm and run. He held me tight, and together we came to the white wooden church of my childhood. I had never entered it, and I knew I would not enter it now. I made an effort to communicate this to Abram. He didn't hear me. He mounted the stairs, pulling me with him.

A group of elders stood before the doors, blocking the entrance. Abram confronted them. "Good day, brothers," he said. "Will you stand aside? We are the bridal couple, here to be married before God and this assemblage, and we wish to enter."

The answer pelted me like stones, knocking me to my knees. "There is no place for that woman in God's tabernacle. We deny her entry."

Abram stood his ground. "This church is not your house. It is God's house."

Oracular mouths opened to denounce me. I woke myself up to escape the nightmare. I was afraid to sleep the rest of the night, but kept my eyes open and fixed on the ceiling.

To erase the dream, tear it out of my mind, I brought the subject up with Abram as we breakfasted in the hotel dining room. I made it casual, as though it had just occurred to me. "Are you sure the Mennonite church will recognize a marriage with a divorced woman?"

"I checked that out before I came."

"You mean you came with the idea of marrying me?"

"If you'd have me—yes. But to answer your question—until quite recently the church was intractable on the subject. But even the Mennonites have to give a little."

I knew why I had dreamed that ghastly dream. There were things I needed to tell him that I still hadn't. If I hoped to start my life in that murky little bookshop I had to make a clean breast of everything.

As he reached for a piece of toast, just for a second I saw him on the steps of the Mennonite church facing the elders.

"Abram, I was wondering. What do you think they'll make of me at church?"

"They'll love you, of course."

"What if they don't?" I leaned toward him across the table. "Oh Abram, I don't think I'll fit in."

"You'll fit in. Don't worry about it."

"But shouldn't we have talked things out? I don't think we talked things out enough, Abram."

"What things?"

"How many children should we have?" I said desperately. "Two, three, four?"

"Kathy, do we have to settle that right now? Can't we finish breakfast? By the way," he added, "I want to phone John Wertheimer at three. Will you remind me?"

"Three. That's prophetic. You said three, that's a good number. We'll have three."

"Fine." And by his expression I was quite sure he hadn't any idea what he had agreed to.

I watched him butter his toast and add jam. I started to tell him—and couldn't.

"You were going to say something?"

"I was wondering what it would be like to have a home. Home is just a word to me."

"Home," Abram said, "is something you make. We'll make ours together."

"I want so much to start my life in Montreal. I want to take long walks with you, go down to the docks, watch the fishermen unload the day's catch. I want to skate in the winter on the little pond near the bookstore. I want you to teach me chess and read to me while I drowse into different times and different places. I want to do all the things you've been telling me of."

He smiled, and I plunged on. "I want to sit on that stepstool that runs along one entire side, and slide back and forth looking at the volumes that make up your life. I want to start being Mrs. Willems."

I received a kiss on each of my fingers for these sentiments.

I had come up to it again, and this time got it out. "I've something to tell you, Abram. I didn't tell you before because, well, it's difficult."

"Spinoza said, 'All things excellent are difficult as they are rare.' "

I knew that was right. Because what I had to tell him now was in the difficult category.

I moved my chair back so I could look into his face. "In the beginning I didn't tell you because there were so many things coming at you right and left. Jim Gentle was my lover."

Abram continued to look at me, and his expression did not alter. "I rather thought that was the case," he said. "I'm glad you told me. But that's in the past, before you agreed to become my wife."

I marveled at this remarkable, brilliant, knowledgeable man, who was as trusting as a child. My hand found his across the table. "Did you miss me all these long years?" I asked.

"No," was the surprising answer.

"No?"

"The reason," Abram soothed, "has to do with photons."

"What are they?"

He pushed back his chair. "Let's take a walk and I'll tell you. They're the fundamental particles of light. Physicists have discovered a fascinating phenomenon: nonlocality. Which, in the case of photons, means if they've ever been together, even though they are separated by millions of light years, they communicate. Stimulate one and the other will react."

"Really? Is that true?"

"It's true."

"And it doesn't matter how far apart they are?" I thought that over and began pummeling his chest, right there for the passing world to see. It was a titmouse attacking an oak. "You've been holding out on me, hugging the greatest scientific breakthrough of the century to yourself all this time."

He caught my fists, straightened and kissed them. Abram didn't care either about the cars and trucks and traffic going by.

This made me unaccountably happy.

▼ ▲ ▼

ABRAM looked up from a tourist brochure. He had decided on Tomahawk, a resort on Vancouver Island, with the Strait of Georgia lapping at its shore. I leaned over him studying the picture showing cabins at the edge of a wood, hiking trails and moonlight horseback rides. It resembled dozens of other colorful pamphlets promoting summer hideaways, but Abram saw something special in this one, and I left it to him.

The INS agent who escorted us to Immigration at the airport shook hands, wished us well, and before turning us over to his Canadian counterpart, asked for my autograph.

▼ ▲ ▼

I STRAINED for a look at my new home—Montreal.

"A city of dichotomies," Abram said, as the cab took us through it. "French and English, saintly and crime ridden."

"Why crime ridden?"

"Its location. Europe has always been hungry for anything

American: jeans, tape cassettes, cars, you name it. The St. Lawrence river flows west to east out of the Great Lakes connecting Chicago, Detroit, Cleveland, and Buffalo with Montreal, Quebec, and Toronto, which invites smuggling. And there's always been a brisk traffic."

"Okay." That question was settled. Now I wanted to know about the French influence.

"You mean the English influence. The French were here first. There was a French trading post in Montreal before the *Mayflower* landed."

It was an island city of bridges and waterways dominated by a cresting hill, graduated and terraced. As I craned from the window of the cab to keep it in view, Abram explained to the driver and me how it came about. "Montreal sits on a glacial moraine blanketed over by a volcanic flow. The lava hardened and trapped the debris in sheets of ice."

Like me, the city was ice and fire.

"The main feature you see in front of you, Mont Royal, was named by Jacques Cartier, the French explorer. I'll take you there for a picnic. From a number of vantage points you can look down on skyscrapers."

But I was more interested in a great cross that seemed to bless the city. It was planted partway to the summit, as though, like Jesus, someone got tired of carrying it.

Our decrepit taxi struggled a bit on a hill. "We're in what's known as Old Montreal." Abram felt for my hand as we turned into a cobbled street. "Rue St. Paul. We're almost home."

Once again I hung out of the window, straining for a look at my new home.

"There. There!" Abram pointed to a narrow building with larger ones leaning on it from either side. It had a curved window that faced the street, filled with books. I tried to take it in all at once, from its fieldstone facade to its dormer window. How familiar it was bound to become.

Abram bent his head and whispered, "I'm going to carry you over the threshold." It did seem appropriate, as this was the first time I would enter the home Abram had brought me to.

There was a bell on top of the door that tinkled as he unlocked and opened it. The door itself had a large oval glass panel at its center, with a frosted design of leaf sprays. Abram flicked the sign from CLOSED and we were open for business. The main business being to scoop me up and set me down inside the shop. "Here it is." He gestured broadly. "This is it. Pretty much as I told you, isn't it?"

A pleasant little shop with rows of books, and tables with special books on display. He tugged at my hand; I'd only time to observe that past the books, by the cash register, there was a small display of stationery and a rack of postcards with scenes of the city and its bridges.

Abram didn't pause, but took me through the rear door into the parlor of the living quarters. A warm, friendly room, with a fire crackling in the fireplace. The furnishings gave it an old-fashioned appearance. The pieces were mahogany, dark and heavy. A few bright pillows would do wonders. The floor was covered by a somewhat threadbare carpet, but chances were underneath they were hardwood.

"What do you think, Kathy?" Abram asked anxiously. "It's nothing fancy, but . . ."

I cut him short. "I love my home. I love it, Abram."

"I very much suspect John and Lucinda have been here. I'm not exactly Sherlock Holmes, but look, a fire blazing away, the house is warm and cozy. And do you smell something?"

I sniffed. "Smells good."

"Let's investigate, shall we?"

We went into the kitchen, a marvelous kitchen, with a breakfast nook. It was painted a cheery yellow-and-white, so even on the gloomiest days it would give the effect of sunlight.

Then I spotted tea things laid out on a little rolling tray. Everything was prepared, there were dainty slices of cake, and the kettle was still warm. "It will be ready in a jiffy," I said. "Talk about a welcome!" I reached my arms out to him. "We're going to be happy here."

We had our tea and cake by the fireplace and watched the logs crumble and embers nestle in its heart. Afterward we washed up in the yellow-and-white kitchen with its trim of oak. I washed and Abram dried. It was like playing house.

I didn't want to leave—ever. But Abram said it was closing time and the Wertheimers would be waiting for us. "They're up the street a few blocks."

Their house was of the same fieldstone. Most of the buildings around here were. The feature that distinguished it was a roof so steep that it reached almost to the ground.

We were met at the door. I found it hard to believe I was seeing them for the first time, they were so like Abram's description. John had a rufous cowlick that wouldn't be plastered down, and his bright eyes took in every detail. Lucinda was the tall, gaunt keeper of the flame. She spoke with asperity, but everything she said and did was kind.

I realized that it might be hard for them to welcome me. After all, his daughter Laura had been Abram's wife. Their kindness to me was proof of their devotion to him.

I was given a small room under the eaves, and cautioned not to bump my head on the sloping ceiling. That night I drew a homemade quilt over me. The stitches were large, like a child's. I wondered if it was Laura who had selected and worked at all the crazy pieces that went together so well.

In the morning I stared into a window pane of small cut diamonds; a multitude of Kathys looked back at me, iridescent, quivering with rainbow.

In the three days I stayed with the Wertheimers, they were unfailingly thoughtful and loving toward me. And that could be said of the friends that dropped in. I was welcomed by everyone. I felt ashamed remembering the nightmare.

The following day Abram brought a letter from my father. He was flying in this evening. He wrote that nothing could make him miss my wedding. I kissed Abram and kissed the letter. I couldn't believe this was me, Kathy, who was the center of so much love. Here they were, Abram, my father, friends. And not a single one employed by me.

Abram and I went to the airport and I was proud to introduce the two men in my life. With the first handclasp they took each other's measure, and I could see they would be friends.

We brought Erich back to the little flat behind the bookstore. The three of us spent the evening talking, getting to know each other. My father wanted to know what had happened at the benefit concert. I began by explaining the Fort Laramie treaty. "So, you see, it was to right the wrongs done the Indian . . ."

My father smiled. "And a wonderful opportunity to sing your Cree songs. How amazed your mother would have been, and how proud."

"Really? You think that?"

"That's what I think," Erich said.

The next morning my father walked me down the aisle to the strains of the organ. Abram waited beside the minister. My father put my hand in his.

▼ ▲ ▼

THANK God for a Mennonite marriage. It was solemn, heartfelt, and over by eleven. There was plenty of time to catch the plane to Vancouver, then ferry to Victoria. I love boats; I loved standing beside Abram, my face to the wind, my hair blown back. Victoria was a quaint little city with flower boxes at every window. We had dinner at the Hotel Victoria and rented a car for the drive to Tomahawk, which signaled to us the honeymoon had begun.

We were shown to a little cabin, but it was too late and too dark to glimpse the water or the scalloped curve of the cove. That would wait until tomorrow. Abram being Abram, one of our two grips was packed with books. He rummaged in this, found the volume he was looking for, and read to me for over an hour until, conscious of his body warmth, I was the one to press against him.

There is something about body warmth, and something about Abram. He let me make the advances, allowed me to stroke him, to rouse him from dreamy somnolescence. He showed me another dimension of love, touching me with wonder as though he were the first man and I the first woman, and this had never been before.

It hadn't. Not like this.

My boy scout husband was wild as Mum's Mohawk ever was. We fit ourselves into each other in every way we could think of. Rapture followed each experiment. Tides, waves, and swells caught us up. Such moments are like birth, like death, like heaven.

Mrs. Willems, Abram's wife, loved being married to Abram. It extended to everything. I loved the beautiful little bay we were on. I loved the fact that the bottom steps of our cabin were covered when the tide was in. The magic of that first night continued to wrap our days.

Lazy days. The main event was to take a boat out, Abram at the oars. I navigated across a drowned forest, past stumps, blackened stags, and moss-entangled branches through which small fish swam. The challenge was not to rip open the bottom of the boat. I leaned far over the side, trailing a hand in the water. Schools of minnows passed beneath, wheeling for no apparent reason, darting in the opposite direction. Like me. I had been as fast-moving, phoning my agent before breakfast, doing photo shoots, attending galas, preparing concerts, singing club dates, lending my name to foundations—and all the time this calm little cove reflected its pines with only an occasional flash of silver as a fish broke the surface. Whoa! We almost got snagged. "Hard right!" I called, and Abram swerved.

"Time out of mind, Shakespeare calls it."

My bookish husband had the history of the planet and the development of stars at his fingertips. He didn't give a rap for the world I came from. He couldn't understand why anyone would want to amass money.

"Think of all the books you could buy, Abram."

"I don't need first editions. The content is all that's important, and I can get that, no matter how ragged the cover."

I had been the one to dream of presenting him volumes with gilt edges and silk-watermarked endpapers. He didn't want that at all. He told me more about the Wertheimers. "John has a decidedly philosophical turn of mind. So while he interprets scripture, you probably noticed it is Lucinda who runs the house, pays the bills, and makes sure he doesn't confuse Sunday with Monday."

"In other words, she is the practical one. They're like bookends out of a Dickens novel and I adore them."

We pulled our boat up on shore for a picnic. "Now tell me about his daughter, your wife."

Abram thought about this for a while. "Laura was a really good person. Her mother died when she was quite small, and John and Lucinda raised the girl. Laura made little routines for our lives. Hot cereal in winter. Pancakes Sunday morning, and a walk after services. She did a lot of church work, helped organize socials, visited members who were ill, or who for some reason couldn't attend services. She brought them books, did marketing, things like that. Her favorite occupation was at the daycare center, reading to the children. She was distressed that we had none, and never gave up hoping."

"Do you think we'll have children?" I asked.

"I'm sure we will."

I peered into the picnic hamper—It would seem strange to have other children; I wondered if I could be a good Mum—cold chicken with mayo and relish, the whole picnic put together by the woman who ran the resort.

"We don't do anything for ourselves," I observed. "How does a honeymoon prepare us to be married?"

"Do you always complain when things are perfect?" Abram teased.

"Always. Inevitably and indubitably."

"Indubitably? Where did that come from?"

"You shouldn't leave books lying around. I'll get to be as smart as you."

We made love on sun-warmed sand and sifted it onto each other in cascades and showers. On the way back we made love in the rowboat and almost tipped over.

Another afternoon I was laid low by another of those headaches I thought I was through with. But we made up for the lost day. The next morning we went into the little town, which consisted of a gas station and a small cafe, with three or four houses scattered about. I'd noticed some lovely quilts hanging over a porch railing and went to see if they were for sale. While I spoke with the woman, Abram had a discussion with her husband, the filling station attendant. It turned out they were Mennonites, that there was a congregation here. I'd been talking to their little boy, four or five, with overalls hitched over one shoulder, bare feet, and a straw hat, too large for him.

I bought a quilt, and Abram arranged to rent a sailboat for the following day. When it was sailed around to our cove, the little boy, Jekuthiel, was the crew. So we invited him to come along on our outing. His father agreed, tipped his hat, and left. I took the child into our cabin with me while I picked up a sweater. He was fascinated by the TV, and jumped when I turned it on and it blasted into color and sound, but settled down when I convinced him they weren't real people, that he could turn them off any time he wanted. Then I switched on our battery-operated radio, and again he was amazed. It was strange to find a pocket of the Middle Ages in the twentieth century.

Abram, Jekuthiel, and I got in the little boat, a trim fourteen-foot Sabot. Abram set her nose to the wind and we seemed to fly. I hadn't realized he was a good sailor. There were many things about my husband I didn't know.

The water danced in diamond patterns and I trailed my hand. I must have dozed, for suddenly Jekuthiel was shouting, dancing up and down and pointing.

I stared in disbelief at a sea monster cleaving the water, making straight for us. Shiny and black, it was a whale, spouting from a blowhole. But this creature must be two blocks long. It was near enough for me to see oblong patches of white on its head. There was its head, fifty feet from us, little eyes peering . . . and further down the strait, its tail lifted from the water.

I didn't know a boat could change tacks as fast as this one did. I grabbed Jekuthiel to keep him from flying over the side, and ducked to escape the boom. Were we modern Jonahs to be swallowed by a whale in Georgia Strait on our honeymoon?

Then I saw other heads rearing in what I had taken to be the monster's underbelly. It was a school of killer whales. Abram and Jekuthiel were ecstatic. Jekuthiel wanted to pet them, Abram simply to look. I wanted to get to shore.

We let our passenger off at his home dock, saw his father in charge of him, and sailed back. That was all the adventure I wanted for that day, but there was more in store.

The last thing on our minds was the weather, but we should have been paying attention. A summer squall caught us; choppy whitecaps fought Abram as he headed back. Lightning streaks scissored the sky, thunder so close it reverberated through me. However, I knew it was the lightning I should be afraid of out on the water. "Tell me about lightning, Abram."

"I did."

"I know, but I was eight and I didn't understand it too well."

"It's like this, the clouds rubbing against each other generate static electricity."

"Something like us?"

He grinned. "The lightning and the thunder start at the same moment, but since thunder lumbers along at the speed of sound, the lightning gets here first, almost instantaneously. Then you count, and wait for the thunder."

Another light streak. He counted deliberately, "One, two, three, four, five."

Bang. Almost on cue—thunder. "That puts the lightning flash at five seconds, about a mile away, a little more."

"That's good to know. Thanks, Abram." I watched the rain bead and glisten on his arms. Abram has powerful arms for a bookseller. We landed, secured the boat, and ran for the cabin.

Once inside we stripped off our wet clothes and with a single impulse climbed into bed. Abram read aloud to me. Since our first night this had become our custom. We elaborated it into a game. Neither of us had played much as children; now we reverted to those kids we should have been. I was eight and he ten. Now we played. There was no schedule, no alarm clocks, no appointments, no courtroom, no accusations. Abram had banished them. It was amazing the baggage I got rid of, like friends who disappear and take your money with them. That so-called real world was barred from intruding here.

Everything in the room outside the bed was designated "water." You couldn't get out of bed or you drowned. You had to have everything you might need: cookies, books, cokes, a bottle opener, and condoms.

I learned a lot about Abram during that rainstorm. He

had in many ways moved past the beliefs of the Mennonite Church. His life was a search, an exploration. He took in and made part of himself the spiritual peace he found in identifying with nature.

And he pursued the philosophers: Aquinas, Frankl, Nietzsche, Sartre. The teachings of the Buddha were a way station. I pictured Abram assaulting unclimbed peaks, grasping ideas as handholds. I discovered he didn't exactly read a book as much as argue with it. His questions and refutations filled the margins. It was the most active kind of reading imaginable.

For all its intensity, it was a summer storm, and next day the skies had forgotten the ferocious black banks of clouds. Once again everything was serene.

Time out of mind.

We took a long hike. After a while the trail was overgrown and wild, because not many people went this far. We looked out over the water at a cruise ship headed for Alaska. "We'll make that trip when we're old. It will be fun, we'll lie out on deck with steamer rugs over us."

I had no sooner said this than I tripped and fell. That is, I didn't trip, but I fell.

"Kathy," Abram exclaimed, helping me up. "What happened? Did you stub your toe? There are all these creepers and . . ."

I kept assuring him I was all right. "I don't think I tripped."

He looked worried at that. "If you didn't trip, then . . . Kathy, these headaches you've been having—I think you should see a doctor."

"I'll race you to the point," I said. "If I win, I don't go to the doctor." With that I pushed him hard so he lost his balance. I raced ahead and got to the point first.

Time flew by, we took snapshots of each other, against the bay, under a tree, in the boat, out of the boat. Abram rigged a device whereby, with a string attached to the shutter, he could get in the picture with me and then pull the string. It worked half the time; the other half it pulled the camera over.

Only a few honeymoon days left. I began to wonder—how many times left to take the boat out? The balky outboard motor never took hold until Abram uttered the one oath he allowed himself: "Judas Priest!"—I'd tell myself to remember . . . remember. The sun flowed over your body massaging every part of you. It was in this drowsy relaxed state that I started thinking about what I had put out of my mind the day of the picnic. At the periphery of thought was a question.

What if this unrealistic person who was me, who could so easily become lost in music, made as bad a wife as she had a mother? Had Abram thought of that when I told him about my daughter?

Well, he should have.

I should have.

Abram deserved the best, and what if that wasn't me? I was entering into a new existence with absolutely no preparation. I would never show up for a rehearsal like that. The thought brought on another of my headaches.

Chapter Sixteen

WE took the mail plane to Vancouver, and from there to Edmonton, where we hired a car for the drive to St. Alban's. As the countryside grew familiar, Abram squeezed my hand. We recognized the flowers that came up to the road on both sides, crocus and larkspur. The forest too had its own remembered character. It was not a dark wood but light, with silver aspen fluttering heart-shaped leaves. There was something magical about a pastel forest.

An excitement rose in me as we left the town, the same small town I remembered. Would the Eight Bells be standing? Would my stepfather still be proprietor, or in sixteen years had he perhaps died and passed it on to Jas? Or would it long ago have been sold?

Abram spotted it first.

I wondered if the pub would be open midafternoons. It looked closed. Abram tried the door and it was unlocked.

We peered into the darkness and stepped hesitantly inside. Abram called into the room, which appeared empty.

As my eyes adjusted to the dim light, I discerned a figure slouched on one chair, his feet on another, sound asleep.

"Hello," Abram called again.

The figure roused, stretched, kicked away the second chair and got to its feet, "What the devil . . ."

I went toward him. "Is it Jas? Are you Jas?" This was a big man, six two and hefty. I went up to him and looked into his face. "It is! You are! Oh Jas, I'm so happy to see you! It's Kathy."

"Kathy?"

Yes, it was Jason. It always took him a while to catch on. "You grew, Jas." And I put my arms about him and hugged and kissed him. "I didn't know you'd be so big. Look, I brought Abram. We just got married."

"Wait! Hold on! You're Kathy? . . . My sister Kathy?"

"Don't I look like her?"

"Never! You're this gorgeous lady out of a fashion magazine. Kathy was just a kid in jeans. Here, let me put on the light." He stepped behind the counter and switched it on. "Gee horse-a-feathers, Kathy!" He caught me up in a great bear hug, then extended a hand to Abram. "And Abram. It's great to see you."

"You too," Abram said, as the two shook hands and drew each other into a back-slapping embrace.

"So how the hell are you, Kathy?"

"Jellet's dead, then, if you're running the place?"

"That's right. Four years ago. Morrie's been dead eight years last January."

"Morrie's dead?" The wind was knocked out of me. I felt as though I'd taken a body blow. Mum was at my shoulder. I'd let her down. I should have been here—maybe then . . . but I'd been too ashamed. Too ashamed to contact either of my brothers. I had, to tell them they were uncles—but that was in a dream. When I actually sent Jas a letter, it came back. That must have been before he returned to run the Eight Bells.

Jas was officiating, playing the host. "Sit down, both of you, I'll get you a beer. Here you go. Must have been a thirsty drive."

"Thanks." But I couldn't shake death out of my head. "What happened?"

"He was discouraged. No job, no prospects. He drank more than was good for him. Me? I wouldn't sell him drinks. But others did. He walked into the big light." He broke off to exclaim, "I can't believe I'm talking to you."

"And you, Jas—a big kid trying to hide your sweetness. And now, a big guy—also not letting anyone know you. Are you married?"

"Well, not what you could call married. Polly and I were together six or seven years—it felt like a marriage. Then one day out of the blue, she ups and elopes with a customer."

"What a shame."

"I don't know, I miss the customer more than her."

"Oh Jas, it's terrible about Morrie. I ran off and left you both. I was such an unthinking girl, and I doubt I'm much better now."

"Your being here wouldn't have made a difference. Morrie was always brooding, shut up in himself."

"At least you're here, Jas."

"We're all that's left."

He sounded so downhearted that before I knew it I was telling him—really telling him this time, about Kathy.

"You have a daughter?"

"Yes. You're an uncle."

"Well, what do you know?"

He became silent when I told him I hadn't raised her. He was my brother; I had to tell him the truth.

"So she thinks you're dead?"

"And she has to go on thinking that. Because when she thinks of me, at least she won't hate me."

All this time he hadn't known I was the Little Bird on his jukebox. I went over to the machine, punched up one of my songs, and sang along with it.

Jas was dumbfounded. I think he'd read about the scandal the papers made of the hearing and deportation, because he hadn't much to say on the subject.

As we were leaving he gave me another hug. "I'm mighty glad you finally came to your senses, Kathy, and hooked up with Abram. He'll look after you good and proper, although I don't see you making a Mennonite out of her," he added over my shoulder. Abram wrote out our Montreal address, and they exchanged phone numbers. Abram invited him to visit us over Thanksgiving or Christmas.

It was hard to let go of my big-little brother now that I'd found him. I gave him a last kiss. "And don't wipe that one off."

He grinned as we remembered.

We went back to the motel and were up early and on the pitted old road to the res. It was, like most Indian reservations, a place that time forgot.

I drove because I knew just where her house was, a bit past the others and . . . sure enough with its door open.

Abram stayed with the car; I jumped out, went up the porch steps, and looked in. Elk Woman had a bowl in her lap and was spooning a batter. I threw back my head and began to sing.

I am washed, washed, washed,
In the blood, blood blood . . .

The motion of her hands slowed and she cocked her head. After while she said, "That you, Skayo, Little Bird?"

I flew in and threw my arms around her. It was almost as though I were hugging Mum. I was hugging those times and those days.

"Come out on the back steps and have a smoke," she suggested.

I followed her out and watched as she produced the old pipe and paper matches from her pocket. She lit up, drew in a long aromatic puff, and handed the pipe to me. "There aren't many days left we can sit outside like this. Autumn will be here in colored feathers."

I nodded, handing the pipe back to her.

She inhaled another deep, slow breath. "You been gone a damn long time. Where you been?"

"In big cities."

Elk Woman gathered her saliva into a neat little ball and spat expertly beside her foot.

"They don't want me in the U.S. anymore; they threw me out for trying to raise money to get Indian land back."

Elk Woman looked skeptical. "How'd you propose to do that?"

"Legally, in a court of law."

Elk Woman shook her head. "They're white men's courts, Little Bird."

"But they ceded the land to us in the Fort Laramie Treaty."

Surprisingly Elk Woman knew all about that treaty. "Sarah, who was a friend of Mrs. Mike, who taught me medicine and herbs, she talked of Red Cloud. He was the chief who put his print to that treaty. His grandson, named Red Cloud, is alive today. Ninety-three years old, with five children, eighteen grandchildren, and thirty-two great-grandchildren. It would be good if his old eyes could see this thing."

"It won't happen, Elk Woman. They wouldn't let us raise the money."

"It would take a great deal of money. How did you expect to come by it?"

"I was going to sing."

She nodded approval. "Singing hasn't been tried. War has been tried and it failed. Perhaps singing will succeed. There are some among the elders who say the world came into existence through singing."

"But like I said, it didn't come off. They stopped us."

Elk Woman hugged herself and rocked back and forth. "Yes. It's an old story. Again and again they stop us. But we are still here and the land is still here . . ."

We smoked a while holding this thought.

"I see a wedding band on your finger."

"I have a new husband. Abram Willems, the boy I traded shadows with."

"Then you have stopped fighting yourself?"

"I hope so. Elk Woman, I told my brother, and now I want to tell you that I have a daughter."

She absorbed this along with a draught of smoke. "But not with this man?"

"No, with my first husband. She is fifteen years old."

"Is she with you? Bring her to me and I will ask the blessing of the Grandmothers on her life."

"She doesn't live with me, Elk Woman; I didn't bring her up."

She digested this, and finally said. "But you named her?"

"I named her."

"She is Kathy, like your mother, like Mrs. Mike, like you?"

"She is Kathy Mason."

"Naming is everything." She put her hands over her eyes

and muttered something, then cocked her head as though listening to a reply. When she turned to me again it was to say simply, "The Grandmothers will know her."

"Thank you, Elk Woman." After a few moments I made ready to leave. "I must go, I want to visit Mum's grave."

"Why? She is not there. Better to bring in your second husband; I want to know this Abram."

Abram came in and we were served tea and bannock.

Elk Woman explained to us that when she was eleven she had given my mum a wolf tail. Apparently this gave her proprietary rights in her life and that of her children and even in my redheaded Kathy.

I was amused to see that the unlikely pair, Mennonite husband and old Cree friend, took an instant liking to each other. We stayed late propounding philosophies and putting forth world views. We solved current crises: North Ireland, India and Pakistan, the conflict in the Holy Land. Abram insisted Elk Woman visit us.

"At Thanksgiving or Christmas," I said mischievously.

Before leaving Alberta we called on Abram's parents. I recognized them both. I had seen them many times as a child, but we had never spoken. I don't imagine they read the newspapers, or knew anything about me. I was glad of that; it must have been hard enough to take in a modern young woman wearing heels and lipstick and a stylishly short skirt.

They made a sincere effort, I thought, to be cordial, and I came away with a good opinion of the people Abram came from: decent, God-fearing, hardworking folk. What wild seed sprouted in Abram's makeup, pricked at him and caused him to question and to search, to be, in fact, Abram?

▾ ▴ ▾

ON the flight back to Montreal I developed a headache, far worse than those I'd been having. The ache was so intense it seemed to balloon around me until I was just a head with pain. I attributed it to all the excitement. I dug in my purse, found some Tylenol, and the attendant brought me a glass of water. I leaned against Abram, and by the time we landed felt better.

Deplaning, I staggered and almost fell. Abram steadied me, and I made it into the reception area and into a seat, where I promptly passed out. "As soon as I get you home, you're seeing a doctor."

I knew he was right. Probably it was a migraine.

John and Lucinda found us.

Abram quickly explained the situation and John went to find a wheelchair.

I protested only feebly. I was wheeled to a parking lot and gotten into their car. It was not easy to miss. Polished and buffed, it was the most ancient vehicle in evidence, and John Wertheimer's pride and joy.

Lucinda insisted on sitting beside me in the backseat. She loosened my belt, chafed my hands, and repeatedly told me that I was going to be fine, which made think I was probably quite ill. A strange sensation came over me. Suddenly Lucinda seemed far away, as though I were looking at her through the wrong end of a telescope. Everything seemed to be receding, until it wasn't there at all.

▼ ▲ ▼

A LONG time.

I don't know how I knew it was a long time, but I did.

A long time.

Out of total blackness, streaks of gray differentiated into gradated shades. Sounds came back. They conveyed no meaning, but were made by a human voice.

Time. Empty, passing, slow, painful. No thoughts, but feeling, an elongated, formless feeling . . .

Shapes.

What were they? I almost knew . . . Almost. Not quite. Drifting. Time passing. Time passing. Was I here before? Then I realized, I'm lost. Lost inside my head.

There were partial thoughts, fissures in the blankness, lesions through which time passed. Time passed. I could not find even the illusion of self. I was lost.

Who was this *I* that was used as a reference point? I didn't know. I couldn't remember my name and yet I couldn't force my mind away from the problem of who I was. The effort made me tremble.

Shooting pains in my head. Agony, agony in the back of my neck.

A shape beside my bed.

Shapes shifting, moving . . .

People! Oh my God, shapes and people were the same

thing. That is, the moving shapes were. The rest was furniture. But not always.

To keep from slipping into the void, I let sound into my mind, listening to connected phrases. Over and over, a womb song, soft, protective.

I had no speech and no language and could barely comprehend my own thinking, yet strangely my capacity for feeling was unimpaired, even heightened. Strongest of all was the yearning that overcame me associated with a word. *Abram.* I didn't know what that word meant. I didn't know it *was* a word. I didn't know what words were. But the sound "Abram" brought peace.

▼ ▲ ▼

TALKING was far beyond my powers. I was better at shapes. Some time later I was moved. I didn't move, I was moved. I grew conscious of myself as inhabiting a large, inert mass. People came and went about it.

Certain things became familiar. What had been rasping, unmusical noises became words. They began to convey meaning, and from that moment I made an effort to extract their sense.

With terrible swiftness the bit of world I occupied was sucked into a black hole, the earth standing on end, like a sinking ship being pulled under.

I started to shriek.

"It's all right, Kathy. It's all right."

The shriek was smashing my eardrums, streaking vapor trails across my brain. I was pushed, shoved, crushed against the floor, stepped on, bones and sinews torn out of place, organs struggling for air that wasn't there, breaking apart, dying.

Abram, where are you? Abram!

I'm here, Kathy, I'm here.

Abram came back to me. First as a feeling, a good, warm feeling, a feeling that made me feel safe. The rest began filtering in as I tried to get in touch with myself.

I made an effort and moved my right hand. I couldn't work the fingers. I was better with my left hand; I always had been. I crawled it over to touch my right. When it made contact, I could move that one too.

From then on I concentrated my energy on becoming reacquainted with my body. I blinked my eyes to shut out and readmit light. I gulped air, exhaled it. With tremendous effort I raised my elbows, then let them drop, up, down, up, down, up, down—flapping like a bird.

I was a bird! I was Kathy Little Bird.

My face was wet, I felt tears on my face. That was odd; I was trying to laugh.

Daily I added to the list of those parts of me I recognized. I turned my head, opened and closed my eyes. I coughed.

I learned to swallow and they took the suction tube out of my mouth. I grew dextrous with my fingers, thumb to thumb, index finger to index finger, middle finger to middle finger, fourth and pinky joined in to the tune of "Frere Jacques." With no past and no future, I was fighting for the present. *Frere Jacques, Frere Jacques. Dormez vous? Dormez vous?* The song helped me hold to a sense of myself.

Words were still beyond me. People said them over and over, repeating certain ones. I couldn't hook them up to the pictures of what they were, but I knew I was supposed to make the connection. I knew I had to. I knew the way to survival was remaking connections.

"Kathy" was me. "Abram" was Abram. "Frere Jacques" was song. I started with that. Slowly the things around me found their place in the scheme of things. The chair in the corner had its own name, the bed did, the covers, the window.

I wasn't prepared for someone kneeling on the floor beside my bed. I wasn't prepared for a head on the covers near my arm. I wasn't prepared for sobbing that wasn't my own.

I listened to strangled sounds. There were words in them. My name—"Kathy, Kathy." More words . . . "Love." That was a word I'd known at one time. Now, it floated away.

More words spilled against the covers.

More tears. This time they were mine.

▾ ▴ ▾

It must be another day. Abram was with me. He had shaved off his beard. I knew this was significant, but when I tried to think why he had done it my head began to hurt. He was talking to me. He was talking as though I could understand what he was saying.

It was about the bookstore where we lived. "It has an old-fashioned English look to it. Substantial, built of Queenston and Montreal limestone," he told me. "The roof slopes at a forty-five-degree angle," he told me. "The dormer windows fit just under them. That's where we display the books. Do you remember?"

Static danced in my head as I listened. I recognized most of the words, but had trouble hooking them up.

His voice continued. "Montreal itself is founded on the site of an old Huron village, Hochelaga. It's an enormous flat plain from which Mount Royal humps up like a dinosaur caught in volcanic ash. The amazing thing, although it's a thousand miles from the Atlantic Ocean, it is one of the great seaports. During the war German subs came right up the St. Lawrence. Your father could tell you about that."

I was beginning to take it in, some of it at any rate. Then in one of those startling flashes it occurred to me that you take in information with your whole body, eyes, ears, nose, mouth, all the different parts of you. And I knew Abram would keep telling me about myself and about the world, and that one of those times I would understand.

He was talking about me now, telling me what had happened. I understood that much, but couldn't remember how he got from the island of Montreal and the St. Lawrence to me.

The problem was, he wanted me to say something back. He wanted a word to match his words. Abram wouldn't let me alone. He kept pitching words at me, slowly, articulating exaggeratedly. I turned away and closed my eyes. But I knew he wouldn't give me any peace until I imitated him and managed the same sound.

My mouth had no idea how to form words. It was exasperatingly difficult, especially as I now had lots of things to say. I could make sounds, but I couldn't shape them into words.

I knew I should work at it. But how do you start when you don't know how to begin? I was ready to give up. I did give up. I had sunk to the bottom of that dead water, the Sargasso Sea. What a waste, feeding me, changing my bedding, dumping bedpans, and for what? So I could breathe in and out, match my fingers to their opposite.

Sheaves of thought bumped against each other. An implosion. Like the Big Bang, it all came together. I was born. Like any newborn I let out a cry. Not of pain—pure joy! I was finishing breakfast, chewing on some tasteless, gelatinous muck simply to stay alive, when bang, like a whack on a bass drum, or a baby's bottom, it came together. Everything. I could taste the food. It was scrambled eggs with strawberry jam. Someone was feeding me with a spoon.

That someone was the girl. I saw she was a pretty girl of about eighteen. This must be Pam.

Oh yes, I remember now. Abram told me about Pam. She was the Wertheimers' niece, and she was sweet, and helpful, did such a good job cataloguing books, and, I'm sure, was quite marvelous at looking after me.

This caring, proper Pam leaned toward me to wipe my face. I shook my head and removed the spot of egg myself.

I'd done it! Planned it, executed it, by myself.

"Kathy!" Pam exclaimed, and her eyes filled. She ran out and returned with Abram, chattering to him all the while about what I had done.

But my triumph brought things back to me—boots with laces, descending. Sound splitting me into pieces. Hurtling face down, sticky with blood, the floor against my forehead—can't breathe, patent leather shoes . . .

Abram took me in his arms and held me.

I began to remember. I remembered fainting in the airport. And coming here to my home—I remembered that. Then what had happened to me? What had become of me? . . . They called what I had been a vegetative state. What if I didn't improve?

You should have let me die. Why didn't you let me die, Abram? I wanted to say this, but what came out of my mouth was a jumble.

"You're better, Kathy. Much better. From now on you'll make rapid-fire progress. You'll see."

Then I did get a word out. My first real word.

"No," I said.

Abram hugged me. "That's good. That's terrific."

▼ ▲ ▼

SEVERAL enigmas were solved.

The shapes I had been conscious of almost from the beginning were now sorted into people, things and sounds. On my vanity a music box held the little French tune that had played in my head. Another problem solved; I could put a check after "Frere Jacques."

They moved silently, efficiently about me and around the house. It was time to ask myself who they were. I started with Pam. She was part of this group. They did the chores that needed doing. I was kept clean, wiped, washed, dried, and fed. The linen under and over me was constantly changed and spotless. Medication was measured out and given. And they took turns reading scripture to me. Now I placed them: the Mennonite ladies from the church. They were very kind. I was doubly ashamed, ashamed they had ever figured in my nightmare.

During the afternoon Abram carried me to the couch in the living room. I looked forward to different wallpaper and traced its design endlessly, seeing how far I could get before it repeated. There was a window through which I could see the lower branches of a tree. One day there was a small speck of white on the railing below the tree. I speculated as to what this could be. Then suddenly I knew; there must be a nest in the part of the tree I couldn't see. One of the eggs had been pushed out, and the little white spot was a broken piece of shell. Or maybe a button off one of Abram's shirts.

Abram kept talking to me. Sometimes I would understand better than others.

Every day I tried to ask what had happened, what was wrong with me. I knew my words were jumbled and not words at all. But he replied. Every day he told me again, at length and in great detail. Little by little it sifted through to me.

The initial injury had been when I was knocked down at the concert. At the time it seemed I had recovered completely. Apparently this was not the case.

"Remember your headaches? That was the clue. There

was a lesion from the original concussion, an aneurysm, and leakage into the brain. The doctors are hopeful that given rest and care, it will heal."

The next day I asked him to repeat what he had told me. Even though I didn't like bringing back the breakup of the concert, I thought I should get it all straight . . . the shot into the air. The panic. The surge toward the stage. More shots. No one knew for sure if it was the rioters or the police.

The crowd pushed and shoved to get away.

People went down. People were trampled. The frenzy of the stampede increased; they kept coming on top of the bodies of those who had fallen.

The tide broke over me, smashed me . . . trampled me.

I tried to articulate some of this. Abram guessed. "Is it the other musicians you are worried about? I've told you, but in case you don't remember . . . They escaped, pretty much without a scratch."

The other concern that Abram satisfied was of course, Gentle. "Poor guy, he was in the prison hospital for a week before anyone recognized him as the impresario. He's okay now, more than okay. The concert that almost killed you made him famous. He is in great demand, I understand, back in New York. And yes, he's called several times.

"And what you may not know is that your father has telephoned every week. He keeps close tabs on you, Kathy."

Jim had survived, and I—barely. And Erich had called me. I was his daughter.

What was wrong with me? I tried to ask, will I get better?

How much better? This question was behind the sounds I made and the anguish got through to Abram.

He stroked me and kissed me. "Recover? Is that what you want to know? Of course you will recover."

Another sign that I was coming back was that I was able at times to forget myself and covertly watch Abram. He seemed very troubled. Partly it was over me, but I think there was something else troubling him. I think I remembered, but I wasn't sure, that he had laid his head on the bed beside me and cried.

When he knew I was looking at him, he kept up a cheerful, reassuring front. And with our visitors and helpers he was the same calm, capable, courteous Abram.

There were times, though, when he thought himself hidden behind a book or some routine task, that his expression would darken, his shoulders hunch, and he would seem to shrink. I couldn't bear this, Abram shrinking. A look of utter hopelessness twisted his lips and shrouded his eyes. At the last minute, when the book was about to slip through his hands, he'd rouse himself, straighten his shoulders, and put on the public Abram face.

Something was destroying Abram.

I wished I could help. But I was the cause. If he was grieving over me, so was I.

▼ ▲ ▼

LUCINDA and John Wertheimer were among the good souls who cared daily for me and the house. I remembered they had come to my bed early on and kissed me. They prayed over me too, with a laying on of hands. It must have been hard to see me in Laura's place. But they never let on, neither of them. How did you get to be good and loving like that, I wondered. They were at our door now as part of a delegation of elders.

Abram invited everyone in. They wiped their boots, took off their wide-brimmed hats, and stood awkwardly. Abram motioned them to chairs. They sat stiffly, as though they preferred to stand.

The men spoke of the approaching winter, of snowbound highways, iced-in shipping, loss of business, overstocked inventories due to storm damage. Brother Gildercrest, on the other hand, listened in a sort of smug silence. He sold salt to the province to de-ice streets.

Abram listened politely. He knew why the men were here and so did I. He knew that John and Lucinda did not want to be here, that they came from a sense of duty because Abram had stopped going to church. He had not gone last Sunday. I don't think he went the Sunday before, and I wondered how many Sundays he had missed before that.

The women they sent to tend me were on rotation, so that someone was always here. Abram could have gone. They had expected him. They told him this. They said it saddened them that in a time of crisis he did not turn to God.

Abram heard them out courteously. "I thank you for coming, brethren. I thank you for your concern, both for how we get on physically and our spiritual well-being. If it hadn't been for the help, the baking, the cooking, the washing, the chores that were done . . . You looked after Kathy as though she were a sister. It was generous, caring . . ."

". . . it was only Christian." Jakob, the spokesman of the group, completed the sentence.

"Yes," Abram nodded.

Then John, his friend, spoke. "We have missed you at services, Abram."

There was hurt in Abram's face, as though with those mild words his friend drove in nails. He got up from his place and faced them, saying, "I won't be coming again. It would be hypocritical. I don't believe anymore."

The elders looked at each other in consternation. John Wertheimer's arm fell on Abram's shoulder, and his sister repressed a small cry. The entire company slid from the chairs to their knees. They began to pray for Abram.

The women in the bedroom and kitchen knelt where they were and prayed also. They requested Abram to add his voice. He shook his head in stubborn refusal. He would not kneel.

God was called upon to redeem the soul and open the eyes of this lost sheep, who, bowed by grief and anguish, had given way to despair.

Abram, white and strained, waited it out. As long as the prayers continued, he listened. I recognized that he was in the same place I had been, hearing words but unable to relate to them, having no sense of what they meant. The strict Mennonite passages, ingrained in him since childhood, glided over him, so much meaningless cant. He stood before the barrage of counsel, love and fellowship, with clenched hands.

It was an hour before they left. Reluctantly, with protestations of love, they withdrew their support, taking with them the women who had nursed me. Last to leave were John and Lucinda, who took Pam with them. The girl gave an anguished backward look.

Then they were gone. We were alone with no cooks, no housekeepers, no one.

Abram looked at me and gave a hopeless shrug. "I'm sorry, Kathy. I'm sorry. I couldn't go on taking their charity under false pretenses. I had to be honest."

I was glad I had no speech; I wouldn't have known what to say to him. He looked so desperate, so alone. This is what I had done to Abram.

He made an effort to pull himself together, to reassure me. "We'll be fine. We'll manage. They were wonderful, we couldn't have gotten by without them. But," he muttered, "the price was too high."

He said nothing more for a long time, but sat quietly beside me. When he spoke it was to himself. He didn't believe for a second that I comprehended, which permitted him to say what otherwise he wouldn't.

"All my life I've tried to understand God's ways and how we can best live up to them. I came to take you back, but too late. I was afraid of coming between you and music, and I thought you were too successful to need me. I let pride get in my way when I should have been there. I should have looked after you instead of rows of books. *I* was wrong. *You* were punished. Why?"

He raised his head and gave me a tortured look. "I got

that far in my thinking, when I realized it made perfect sense once I removed God from the equation. God must be just or He is not God. That's it, Kathy. No just and loving God could punish you like this. Me, okay. But that's not what happened. It was you. So I reached the only logical conclusion possible. There is no God."

I saw that Abram was as wounded as I. For him, a world without God was a dark and desolate place.

Chapter Seventeen

In the morning Abram carried our tea to the dormer window so I could see the first, dazzling snowfall, and explained what *aphasic* meant. He had gotten breakfast, bacon and eggs, and burned toast, which he scraped diligently. He was doing his best.

"Aristotle," he said, "believed the mind was located in the heart. The brain is only a three-pound organ the consistency of Jell-O, but it has a wonderful ability. It can rewire itself, send its signals along new axons."

As he talked I became aware that Abram was imitating Abram. He didn't want me to know how frightened he was, or how despairing. I was only able to penetrate to the periphery of his shadow, pretending with him as he pretended with me.

"We're going to be able to cope, Kathy, for the time being anyway." And he told me he had a surprise for me. "Last night after I put you to bed, I made some phone calls. You know who I called? Your father, who's back in New York. Then I phoned Jas, and then Elk Woman. The main office on the res has a phone and I routed out someone who went to fetch her. Do you remember—I invited them to come visit for Thanksgiving or Christmas. But they're coming now. All of them, and we'll call it Thanksgiving. Every one of them is coming; they want to pitch in and give us a hand. Get us over this hump. What do you say to that?"

I tried to speak, but ended simply squeezing his hand.

▼ ▲ ▼

THEY arrived.

Elk Woman came first. She blew in the front door like a gust of wind, undoing layers of shawls with red, unbiddable fingers. She looked me over head to toe, hung a little deerskin pouch of herbs around my neck, chased Abram from the kitchen, and began opening packets secreted in her skirt.

By the aroma that floated to me, I detected . . . wild grasses . . . wheat tassels . . . dried berries . . . and something that smelled like mustard. In the old days she had prepared her mixtures by pounding in the fat of bear. I wondered if that was what she was about in my kitchen. I thought it just as well the Mennonite ladies were not here.

She came in with a cloth soaked with her concoction and wrapped it about my head. It felt warm and comforting.

"Skayo Little Bird," she said, using my res name, "they wounded you in the big cities."

She had a gift for Abram. "Bottled last spring, blackberries put up with sugar and fermented." She poured Abram and herself a glass. "A batch I made at the same time went off like Fourth of July rockets. So I know it's ready. Only not for you, Kathy, you have to get much stronger."

Abram, who was not used to any kind of liquor, tried to disguise the fact that he was coughing.

Later, Elk Woman said to me, "Your man does not need drink to make him wise. He prays different prayers, but the Creator pays attention."

Next to arrive was my father, stamping his feet and unwinding a cashmere muffler. I was very glad to see him, although I felt his shock at seeing me. He attempted to hide it, of course. But I knew. The fact that I didn't speak upset him, and at the first opportunity he took Abram aside to question him. I was glad for Abram to have a chance to really know my handsome, aristocratic father. He carried himself, still, like the naval officer he had been.

While my father and Abram talked as old friends, Erich was somewhat less sure of Elk Woman. But she plied him with her blackberry cordial, and he heartily approved, pronouncing it "very like the berry cordials made in the Ticino. I've had many a glass there in some small *ristorante* looking down on Lago Maggiore."

Elk Woman was so pleased that she imparted the recipe to him. "I can tell you that to this time I have told the secret to no living soul."

Erich bowed and declared himself honored. When his glass had been drained, he inquired of Abram exactly what needed doing and how to apportion chores, so that everyone might be about theirs.

Before this could happen, my brother Jason knocked at the door. He was amazed to see our other guests, and upset to see me. I don't think until that moment he had any idea how ill I was. My inability to greet or talk to him hit him hard. To cover this he made a great show of taking off his gloves with his teeth and shaking the beaded ice from them. "When was the last time you shoveled your steps, Abram?" He accepted a glass of cordial from Elk Woman, and tossed it down. "You should see the cars on the street, each one encased in its own igloo." He also looked for a chance to take Abram aside to find out what the prognosis was.

I know Abram invariably replied that it was only a matter of time before the old Kathy was restored to them. Abram believed this.

Did I?

I was beginning to ask myself if it was simple weakness that kept me from walking. Or paralysis? My body, especially my legs, had no feeling in them.

The disposition of roles waited until morning.

Jas announced his by having a breakfast of Canadian bacon and waffles on the table, along with a side dish of scrambled eggs. "I'm the cook of this ménage. And I think it would be a good idea if I took over the wood chopping. With winter storming at us, you'll be needing it."

Elk Woman had brought a supply of roots, which she would make into medicine to see us through the winter.

Abram said he'd continue to nurse me. I was glad. He was the one I wanted with me, because as I became better and could think about things more clearly, new fears entered my mind.

My father was busy with his contribution . . . flash cards, the kind they used in first grade, with *dog, cat, me, you, him, her* printed on them. He turned to Abram. "Mental health goes with physical fitness. We must keep her mind alive. I have brought books of poetry with me. I've also made a list that perhaps you have in your bookshop. If not, you can get them from your local library. Read to her, read to her at every opportunity. I recommend the classics, and the lives of famous muscians. Especially those where the artist or musician had to contend with—deafness, Beethoven; nodules on the vocal cords, Elizabeth Schumann; depression, Tolstoy. In every case they either overcame, or worked through their problems. Bernhardt, for instance, played *The Eaglet* at seventy with a wooden leg. I was particularly interested in that."

I smiled to myself. So they overcame. Well, bully for them.

My problem was slightly different. Mine was that my brain had been stepped on; it didn't function. I couldn't articulate words. A slam-dunk job had been done on me—my voice, and most of the rest of me.

Had I known what lay ahead, I'm not sure I would have had the courage to go on. Not only flash cards, I had a primer too.

Part of the therapy, Erich explained, he would take on himself. "I think she might like hearing stories of her mother, of our time together." Abram eagerly encouraged him in this. "I also intend," Erich continued, "to do whatever shopping is necessary. You will need a well-stocked larder, and I don't imagine it is always possible to navigate these streets."

"We're snowed in much of the time," Abram admitted cheerfully.

"And *I* will give this place a good dusting and set it to rights." No one noticed Lucinda, as she had come in the back way. Her brother was right behind her. "And I will drive anyone any place they wish to go. If I can get the car started."

So it was arranged.

I saw Abram seek out John and shake his hand. I had witnessed the distress in him when these friends left with the others. But they had thought it over, consulted their conscience and no doubt the Good Book . . . and here they were. "Praise the Lord," as Abram says.

Erich took my hand. "Your mother and I met secretly and married secretly," he said, looking off into a time when he and Oh Be Joyful's Daughter were young.

Jas came, sat beside us, and listened too. I could see that he was fascinated by Erich. "How come you married a First Nation girl like Mum?" he wanted to know.

"She was raised, as she often told me, by a woman known as Mrs. Mike. Being raised by whites, she knew very little of her Indian heritage."

"She may have let go of being Cree," Elk Woman put in,

"but we Cree don't let go of our own. We went to the same schoolhouse and I gave her a wolf tail so she'd know who she was. And in the end, it was Jonathan Forquet who called the Grandmothers together to guide her canoe on the long last journey."

"We realized," Erich continued, "both of us, that we came from widely differing backgrounds. Different worlds, you might say. When I lost my leg I didn't want to go home. I was afraid of pity. And it seemed to me I could trade my old, hidebound, traditional world, for a new, free one, green and young. A world that didn't make distinctions based on color or wholeness of limbs, or anything but the individual worth of the person. Kathy agreed with me, or perhaps I persuaded her. I see now that we were young and naive." He broke off abruptly.

Abram changed the subject with his usual kindness. "I know you are with the trade commission. What is it that you do?"

"I sit in on free-trade talks, representing Austria. As a young man I was trained as an engineer. For a long time I was interested in the nuclear submarines they were developing in the States. Recently I've changed my mind. The waste disposal problem is too horrendous."

"Wind is good," Elk Woman spoke up. "Wind's power is endless and forever."

"You are absolutely right. The form of energy employed should be consonant with the environment. In Austria, geothermal. In California, Florida, and the tropics, India perhaps, solar would be appropriate."

"The sun?" Elk Woman nodded her approval. "That great one, that life-giver is only strengthened by his giving."

We sat together in peaceful agreement until I tired. There was a general shuffling as the company broke up and turned in.

▼ ▲ ▼

IT was inevitable, of course, that they return to their lives. The Grandmothers, in a vision, called Elk Woman to officiate at a naming. Before leaving she replenished the herbs in the little pouch I wore around my neck, and left me fifteen bottles carefully labeled, as to content and purpose. Bear grease and the seeds of the acanthus. Rub on chest for cough, repeat twice in the day and twice in the night. Another unguent was the scrapings of the cherry bark compounded with maggot larvae and roots of ground sassafras. For stomach cramps.

I remembered how she had brought her potions to Mum over the course of her long illness, and how graciously my mother had thanked her. At least that's what I thought then. But my mother was Cree, and in spite of being a trained nurse, she may have believed, as I tended to, in these exotic preparations.

Jas was the next defection. He absolutely had to get back to his pub. Abram assured him he had seen us through the worst of our emergency and we would be able to manage, now that we were so amply provided for. Big hugs, loud goodbyes, and protestations, and my big-little brother was gone. I would miss him. How extraordinary that he had come.

My father and the Wertheimers lingered. It was already

November and the weather had turned stormy. Evenings the men placed me in front of the fire and sat around talking. Lucinda bustled in the kitchen and came in to serve hot chocolate and freshly baked nut bread. My father felt so at home that he unscrewed his leg and propped it against the stone hearth. They were friends.

A telephone call from the commission and he too hurried off. On their departure John and Lucinda had a surprise for us.

"You'll need someone to help you, so we've asked our niece to come stay and give you a hand."

I didn't like the idea, mostly because Abram was so enthusiastic about having her. He couldn't praise her enough. "She was here early to help with your care, and again with the other women from the church. You remember her, I'm sure? A quiet, modest girl. Both John and Lucinda are extremely fond of her. She will be pleasant to have in the house—besides which she helped catalogue my books one summer and did a splendid job."

That finished her in my eyes.

The news that we were to inherit Pam put him in a good mood. He went on and on about it. "With Pam's help, we'll have no problem. She dropped everything to come. You must be very pleased."

Again I employed my new word emphatically. "No."

"If you're worried about her being ostracized at church for helping out here, don't be. They're withholding judgment."

A phrase came back to me that seemed appropriate at this moment. I took a deep breath and said, "Dant."

"What?

"D-damn it!"

Abram smiled, a new off-center smile. "Now I know you're on the road back."

▾ ▴ ▾

LIKE a circle widening in water, my catastrophe didn't end with me, but reached to Abram. During the Vietnam war they had a term for what happened to those seemingly unscathed—"the walking wounded."

Being Abram, he turned to books. He didn't exactly read them. Where once he had argued, now he fought them. At the same time they were his hope. I saw him as wrestling on the edge of a precipice. For his faith. For his reason. With Abram it was the same thing. "God help me," he called out once. "All this wisdom is inscrutable. It reads like the Book of Revelations."

I wished I had words to help. I wished I could bring him a hot cup of cocoa.

My father phoned. He and Abram had a long conversation about me, my state of mind, and how to proceed with what they referred to as my rehabilitation. The weekly calls continued. Once they discussed finances. I heard Abram tell him that a trickle of royalties from my albums and a raise from the Wertheimers enabled us to get along. Nevertheless, he appreciated the offer.

My father wouldn't let it go at this. He sent gifts, a marvelous baby grand that took up a good part of the front room. And to show his belief in my recovery, a car was delivered, a Lincoln sedan fitted out to enable me to drive. That, I thought, was truly having faith in the future.

Abram immediately began to plan the drives he would take me on. "The bridges—you'll love the bridges. The Jacques Cartier has three connecting spans. It's an engineering marvel, stretching from Montreal to Montreal South, to Ile Ronde, and from Ile Ronde to St. Helen's Island. Then there's the Victoria, and the Canadian Pacific railroad bridge that connects with the United States. Also the Mercer Bridge . . ."

Yes, I thought my father was very generous—but although Abram invited him repeatedly, he did not come again.

One day when he called, Abram put the phone in my hands. He talked and I listened. I listened to my father's rich baritone, listened to the forced nuances of good cheer. While the cheerfulness was forced, the love and pain were quite palpable. I would have liked to reassure him, but I hadn't words.

My father spoke quickly. People in general did. It seemed to me they went at it like Ping-Pong, batting words back and forth. And I had to figure out what it all added up to. The conversation with my father was a ferocious challenge. I didn't know what he expected from me.

There were long silences while I tried to figure out what the words coming my way meant. Then how to reply? What should I say? How should I say it? I could pronounce words of one syllable and sometimes hook them up to make a sentence. To get them into a line and bring them out in the right order was tough. Sometimes the last word came out first. I tried to tell him I was glad he called. When I got to the second word I'd forgotten the rest. I substituted a noncommittal "Um-hm," which was not appropriate, and gave up.

Abram took the phone back, saying it had done me a world of good hearing my father's voice. It did bring back vividly the moment we had rushed into each other's arms—been father and daughter.

After the conversation I was exhausted and took a nap.

I dreamed I had a daughter. At some level it wasn't a dream. I knew I had a daughter and that I was dead to her. If those facts didn't destroy me, how could a little thing like being trampled in a riot?

My mind was beginning to take in my situation.

There were two things I wanted to know. I knew that I could ask them, even with my limited vocabulary, but would I be able to disentangle a complicated answer?

The first question was, "Will Pam always be here?" I didn't know to whom this should be addressed.

I was afraid of the answer. Or it may be that I had answered it myself. I knew Pam's motive. But I doubt that she did. In fact I was sure she did not. She really was a good person. She had a good and noble reason for being here, as good and noble as herself.

Abram, of course, was a man. Not a typical man, but a man. Men quite uncritically take adoration for granted.

My main motive for getting well was to be rid of kind, obliging, ever-present Pam. While not a high-minded objective, it was perhaps more effective than most. I would get that good, pious, selfless young woman out of my house, and the quicker the better.

So I strained to understand the torrent of words directed at me daily and picked a fight with the unsuspecting Pam, on whom my rancor and frustration had settled. It was over nothing, of course. I dropped my napkin and was about to retrieve it with my picking-up stick, a kind of tongs to grasp dropped items. It was quite efficient, and I was capable of managing, but before I could, Pam gracefully scooped up the napkin.

Did she have to do that? Couldn't she let me do one of the few things I could do? She wants to show me up, show Abram how helpless I am, and how good she is at picking up napkins. How I hate you, I hate you for standing up and walking around, for being able to talk straight, for picking up things, for doing everything I can't. God, how I hate you!

In my rage at not being able to communicate this, big tears rolled down my face. Pam knelt solicitously and wiped them away. She knew I had worked myself up, but from the emotional grunts and syllables had no idea that the fury was directed at her, that she was the object of my venom.

She continued soothingly with pious platitudes. "It's good for you to let off steam once in a while," she was telling me. "You've been so patient, I marvel at you, really I do."

I made a lunge in her direction, hoping to strangle her. The chair I was in knocked her stool over, and we both went down under splintering wood, spinning metal wheels, and leather cushions. A tablecloth floated on top of us as silverware clattered and a china bowl rolled along the linoleum floor.

Abram, hearing the commotion, left a customer looking for a mid-Victorian mystery novel and, dashing in, lifted the chair off us, and me off Pam.

"What in the world?!"

Pam was breathing hard and looking at me as though she'd never seen me before—and I don't believe she had.

Then she pulled herself together and said in her demure voice, "Kathy reached for something and the chair tipped over."

"Kathy, is that what happened?"

I was laughing too hard to set him straight, even if I'd been able to.

Question number two was another matter.

Question number two was better unasked.

As long as I didn't know the answer there was hope.

▼ ▲ ▼

REPLACING the shattered wheelchair was not in our budget. Abram hesitated to approach the Wertheimers; they had given us so much. But there didn't seem to be any other option.

At that point Providence unexpectedly came to our rescue, as if to settle the argument the church elders had debated so strenuously in our parlor—do God's gifts come by grace or for merit? Abram was opening the semiannual statement from the distributors of my old recordings. He called out from the shop through the connecting door we always kept open.

"They fouled up the accounting again." He laughed. "This time in our favor. Instead of six hundred dollars, it's twenty-six thousand."

He was about to return it with a note correcting their arithmetic, but I hammered violently on my bedpan. Abram rushed in, and I was able to convince him with garbled sounds and signs and pointing to the phone that it was worth a long-distance call before rejecting twenty-six thousand dollars.

The check was good. The company had been taken over by a group that specialized in reissuing old hits with new promotion.

That day Abram bought me a chair. It was the Cadillac of wheelchairs. Electric, of course. With the press of a button it raised or lowered, tilted forward or reclined. Its custom leather back, seat, and arms were not only comfortable but handsome. I had the handsomest wheelchair any girl ever had, the best that money could buy.

Abram explained to me in detail about my money. "Praise the Lord, we've got enough now to pay our bills and get you well. But we can't count on this happening again. We've got to stick with the old maxim: Waste not, want not." He smiled, knowing I hated and despised such prudent sayings.

I smiled back. I had a more important agenda. "Pam," I managed to articulate, and indicated with a wave of my hand that she was free to go, now that we could afford a practical nurse.

Abram shook his head. "No," he said. "You need someone who loves you. We'll make it up to Pam later. Help out with college, maybe."

A few days later he explained our financial situation to me all over again. He didn't know how much of what he said I could take in. I didn't either. Sometimes, when I wasn't tired, I thought I understood it all. Abram believed our windfall was due to a fluke, a passing craze for my cassettes among teens. That made sense to me most of the time. At other times it was a jumble and all I could do was smile up at him.

Two facts did stay with me. I had the best wheelchair in Quebec, and Pam would be here for the rest of my life.

▼ ▲ ▼

ONE day a flash of retrograde violence overwhelmed me.

I thought I had put that behind me.

Apparently not.

I squeezed my eyes together in an effort to make the memory go away.

I was able now to take my life right up to the benefit I didn't finish. People told me what had happened. They didn't need to tell me about boots and shoes—seen from the perspective of the floor. Looking up, I watched them descend. They blacked out the world.

I didn't know how to keep out these sudden flashes—What if the episode kept recurring?

I saw I couldn't handle it by myself. Abram had to help me. I trundled into the bookshop looking for him. He was checking a new catalogue, but he left it.

"The concert . . ." I managed to get out. "I see it."

Abram sat down on an unopened crate of books. I could see he took this seriously. "You know what I think, Kathy? I think you buried all that too fast. You didn't give yourself time to digest what happened. That isn't always the best way to get rid of something."

"What?" I asked, implying, "what is the best way?"

You could feel the tumblers drop in his mind. "How much do you know about benefit concerts?"

I shrugged. That was the easiest answer.

Abram was still thinking his way through the problem. "If you understood what your singing might have accomplished, you will see why you were perceived as a threat. To make it all clear to you, tomorrow you'll accompany me to my favorite hangout, the central library. You know the one, on Sherbrooke Street, East."

Since I hadn't been able to banish the flashbacks on my own, Abram's prescription was worth trying.

It was a big adventure for me, especially as I left Abram in the Philosophy stack and went by myself into the periodical section, where I tried out a new skill: bringing up microfilm articles. I stared at a gray tinged screen and scrolled down to Benefit. I was surprised and pleased to find it.

The modern benefit concert was born in New York City in the summer of 1971, in Madison Square Garden. Two shows were given, at three-thirty and again at eight o'clock. They were gotten together by George Harrison to provide aid to the desparate people of Bangladesh.

I read that in an effort to control its former province, the Pakistani government drove ten million people over the border into India and murdered a million more. Those left were among the poorest people on the planet. Harrison had come to know of the plight of this pathetic remnant through the Indian master of the sitar, Ravi Shankar. Harrison studied sitar with him and the two became friends.

Shankar, recently returned from the area, was devastated by what he saw. He talked about it with different people, some in the UN, but mainly musicians. If only something could be done to focus attention on the distress and need, if only the world did not turn away from Bangladesh.

"Music moves people," they told each other. "It unifies them. And song speaks directly to the heart; it speaks what words alone cannot." People, they felt, by and large, have a natural innate desire to help one another, to alleviate want and starvation, especially where it affects children.

If they got together, pooled their talent, performed gratis, they could bring out a large number of people and money could be raised, a great deal of money.

They got to work, contacted Jackson Browne's scholarship fund for Native American students and Pete Seeger's sloop plying the Hudson River, a floating classroom in environmental protection.

I looked up. I could see that wherever there was a cause—civil rights, antiwar movements, human rights, antinuclear crusades—there was now a new way to rally people.

Artists from all over answered. Ringo was in Spain making a film. Bob Dylan, who didn't perform much since his motorcycle accident, performed. Eric Clapton came out of retirement, the entire Badfinger band played, and other musicans, good, professional . . . and courageous, because gigs were lost and contracts abrogated.

As I read, I realized that the breakup of our own benefit, my subsequent hearing, and the way they had seized on the oversight of not having my green card updated, were some of the consequences those who protest injustice must expect.

I experienced a warm sense of pride and kinship that fellow musicians felt so strongly, that they had gotten together and through song drawn people of goodwill together.

They made a difference . . . as I almost had. Thanks to Gentle, I had joined in. My motive was simply to get my songs heard. That the concert was organized to restore Indian lands pleased me. But it was not the main factor.

Some of the idealism must have rubbed off on me, however, because one way or another, I was part of this courageous group. I even began to think of myself as a casualty in the on-going battle between the makers and the takers.

I clicked off the viewer. There were different images that could come now when I thought of our benefit concert. I rejoined Abram in Philosophy, my heart singing, and for the first time there was music in my head.

Once again Abram had known what to do and how to help me. Now I had to help myself, and to do this I had to think a few things through.

Chapter Eighteen

April 1982, almost three years since my accident, but in my mind it was both yesterday and forever. I couldn't walk. That question seemed to have answered itself.

Aside from a rest in the afternoon I no longer spent time in bed. In the morning I got up, washed my face, and brushed my teeth. I soaped, scrubbed, and rinsed myself in the shower chair. Applying makeup gave me a positive lift. I looked exactly like Kathy Little Bird, the famous singer. Twice a week Pam shampooed my hair, but soon I planned to take that over. Just as someday I would drive the Lincoln, which Pam thoughtfully kept limber by taking it into town.

A more urgent problem hovered in my mind. Nature helped me formulate it by devising a test. Not the winter that closed the port for months, whose thirty-below weather packed snowdrifts to fifteen feet, sweeping traffic, pedestrian and vehicular, from sidewalk and streets, and livestock into heated barns. I was Canadian, I knew these winters.

The test reserved for me was more cruel; it showed me that walking was the least of my problems. Later in the week I was bundled into the car. I watched Abram and imagined my hands on the wheel. Getting back a semblance of health was a career, a job that took all available time and energy. But it was lovely to be out of doors. On this crisp snowy day the sun shone brightly and I forgot I was on my way to the doctor's office.

I enjoyed the trees, whose leaves cried clear tears of ice. The smell of outdoors held the promise of spring. I inhaled it like a glass of cold water. I like water. I like the world.

I don't like doctors' offices or the way they smell—suspiciously clean. What disease or ailment lay on this sterile examination table before I did? For they had transferred me to a small partitioned space. Dye was injected into my spinal cord, which was then X-rayed for comparison with earlier pictures. Then small probes like needles under my skin to measure muscle potential. "A nerve conduction test," they told me.

Have fun, guys. It's my body, but what the hell, I don't feel anything anyway. They did a Babinski, scratching the soles of my feet with a silver metal pen.

Abram explained that they also needed a psychological evaluation. I was asked to repeat seven digits forward and four in reverse order, to spell backward, to remember three unrelated words. Later, when I thought we were all through, they asked for the words. Traps, one after the other. Now as a last trial I was required to darken boxes, while the doctor spoke to Abram.

I listened instead.

"Two major areas associated with language deficit are Broca's in the third frontal convolution and Wernicke's in the posterior third of the upper temporal convolution. In a right-handed person this is relatively easy to identify. Unfortunately, I suspect your wife to have originally been left-handed, and in such cases opinions differ."

He too blamed me for my left-handedness. Later when he spoke to me directly, I wouldn't answer.

On the drive back, Pam chatted about a quilt the ladies of the church were making. Yes, Pam was with us. Pam was always with us.

Abram concentrated on driving. I remembered reading that in the old days to get a brain like mine functioning, they'd blister the skull, bleed you with leeches, and suck up the skin by applying heated bottles. So it could have been worse.

This time I didn't notice trees or sky. I didn't notice anything. A gray membrane drew itself over my thoughts. I overload easily, can't take in too much, don't want to.

▼ ▲ ▼

I WAS grateful to Abram, who carried me upstairs and put me to bed. He'd done this before, countless times. This was different. He touched me in a different way, a way I seemed to remember. I responded to his fingers, which ran lightly over my hair, my throat and breasts. It had been so long, I had almost forgotten I was a woman. He leaned over me and I felt his body warmth, his body that had lent me pulses of pleasure and charged me with life. With expectant eagerness I reached out my arms and pulled him close. Oh yes, this is the way it is between us, the way it has always been.

His lips pressed mine gently open. The prickling sensations of pleasure started in my veins. The throbbing, the desire . . . desire that was anguish barely in abatement. Abram bore down and I waited for the ultimate, the incredible moment that had always been there for us.

Nothing.

I didn't feel anything. I was an inert mass, a stone.

When Mum died, Jas tried to shake her alive. Couldn't someone do that for me? Shake me alive?

I started to cry. Once I started, I couldn't stop. I lay there and sobbed.

Abram froze, then pulled himself up and stumbled to his feet. A moment later he sank to his knees and whispered, "Give it time, Kathy. It will be all right, just give it time."

I'd given it time. My mind was functioning again in fits and starts. My speech center could be brought back. My internal organs had resettled, I thought, in their normal places. Only it wasn't true of my woman's parts. The rush of wanting was there, but the excruciating pleasure that I strained for did not come. If I couldn't be a wife to Abram, if I couldn't be a woman, I wanted to be dead.

Pam, who slept over most nights, heard my uncontrollable weeping. She knocked timidly on the door and, receiving no answer, opened it and came in. "Abram, what is it? Is Kathy all right?" Pam took Abram's place at the side of the bed, stroking me into quietness, and then kissed me on the eyelids.

I heard Abram say, "She had a nightmare, that's all."

Speaking over my head, Pam replied, "She probably knows."

Knows? Knows what?

There followed a term I was becoming familiar with—"catastrophic neurological event," my condition, which made it impossible to concentrate, remember, spell, conceptualize, even *think*. This "deficit" of mine apparently had determined that I could no longer physically know the love of a man. It didn't matter how much or how hard I tried—it wasn't there.

Had Pam's moment come? Her piousness and prissiness were always more pronounced when Abram was present. Had she exaggerated those qualities to appeal to him?

Was that her strategy? Holier than thou, demure, always a pious saying on her lips. Abram approved of Pam, so helpful, so willing. Had she been willing? How willing? Was she willing now?

Still speaking over my head, Pam said, "You're going to tell her, aren't you?"

"Hush, Pam." He knows, or at least suspects that I understand.

Not Pam, she has no such sensibilities. "It's only a question of time, Abram, until she discovers for herself."

Discovers? Discovers?

I craned up, staring from one to the other. It was as though I weren't here. It had been so long since I was here that they had gotten used to discounting my presence.

Pam went over to him. She was wearing a proper flannel nightgown, but underneath she was naked. He knew this.

Her hair, so neatly pulled back during the day, was lying fluffy and soft on her shoulders. And her breasts, usually buttoned in, now spread out full and womanly.

"Abram," she said in a breathy whisper, "I haven't said anything all this while. But now, the tests confirm that nerve conduction may not regenerate for years. Maybe never."

"Pam, that's enough."

"Why? She doesn't understand."

"She does."

—Oh Abram, it could be never. And here is Pam, very much a woman. A woman who can feel and react to you. A woman who could be roused and return your passion. That's what you deserve, a woman, not a stone. Reach out a hand to her. I wouldn't mind that much. I might not even mind at all.

▾ ▴ ▾

I HUNG out bird feeders and gardened at large tubs that Abram rolled into the backyard. Since making a new start I did everything with my left hand. It's completely irrational, I know, but from the moment I gave in to the impulse to reach out with my left hand, to grasp, turn, twist, use my left hand exclusively—from that moment my speech began to return. Something in me seemed to have been freed, and the difficulty of getting my mouth and tongue around sounds disappeared. It still took a great deal of concentration, but I started to place telephone calls myself. I called my father and I called Jas. I laughed to hear how incredulous they were. "It's me," I answered them, "it's me!"

"Isn't it marvelous," we said to each other. Then, within days, I received a phone call that changed my life.

"Kathy," Jas was at the other end, "you won't believe this—I've just talked to your daughter. Kathy Mason was right here in the pub."

"Oh, Jas." I almost dropped the phone.

"She knows I'm her uncle. Elk Woman told her. She's a great kid; with that red hair of hers she's a knockout."

"Jas—" A horrible possibility occurred to me. I reverted to a month ago. I couldn't get the words out. My tongue almost quit on me, and my brain was ready to quit too. But I focused hard on Kathy. I'd never run out on her again. "Jas, you didn't say anything? You didn't tell her about me?"

"Of course I didn't, but I sure was tempted to. She came up here looking for her roots; you know how kids are. Asked all about you and her father. It seems a shame, her wanting to know about you, and you wanting her. Couldn't you—?"

"No! I couldn't. Jas, you promised me."

"I haven't said a word, and I wouldn't without your say-so. But if you ask me it's a rotten shame."

"Yes, it is, Jas. I agree with you. But it's the only way. . . . I still can't take it in. You met Kathy? You talked with her? What's she like, Jas?"

"Like I said, she's a great little gal. You'd be proud of her."

"Who does she look like? Mum? Does she resemble Mum at all?"

"Gosh Kathy, she's a looker, that's all I can say. She's got your eyes, dark, flashy ones. And when she smiles she reminds me of you."

"What did you talk about? Tell me everything."

"Well, she wanted to know why there was no record of you anywhere, so I explained how Jellet was, that us kids didn't attend school even, but lived like recluses. Oh, and she wanted to know what the J stood for."

"The J?"

"Yeah, on her birth certificate her father is listed as J. Sullivan. She laughed when I told her it was Jack."

I had a thousand questions. Most I thought of after we'd hung up, so I called back, spoke carefully, and the words said what I wanted them to.

Abram came in quietly and sat by the window smiling. He was happy that I had such recent news of my girl. I told Jas to be sure and tell Kathy the family stories, especially about Katherine Mary Flannigan, so she would understand about her name. To tell her all about Mum and about Erich. And he wasn't to leave out Crazy Dancer. Or me, the me he remembered as a girl—if there was anything good he could think of to say about me.

I told Jas that every time he saw Kathy Mason he was to call me. My picture of her was filling in. The insubstantial musings were more vivid, more real.

I remembered when I had thought myself so alone, so friendless. But the return of speech was due, I recognized, to Abram, and to friends, good friends like John and Lucinda, and yes, my father, Jas, and Elk Woman. I'd had an extraordinary amount of help. Following Lucinda's example, the ladies of the choir, followed by the ladies of the congregation, gradually filtered back to us.

The elders had made their statement. They had prayed about it, and that fulfilled any obligation they had toward us. The women no longer stole in the back door, washed the kitchen floor, changed the sheets on my bed, and left soup simmering on the stove. Now they came as neighbors, as friends. They came to sit a while, as they took out knitting and chatted.

This made a deep impression on Abram. "You know, Kathy, I dig into my books these days in the hope of finding answers. The Greeks believed wisdom was to be found at the bottom of a well. Philosophers look for it in the end notes of weighty tomes. The Buddha's enlightenment came only after profound meditation. These good women answered in another way. When our need was urgent, they answered by doing, caring, thoughtfulness, and devotion. . . . Just knowing these qualities are in the world gives meaning, don't you think?"

"I do. Oh yes, Abram, I do." And I performed one of the tasks I had taught myself. I made cocoa in the kitchen, getting down the cups with my handy picker-upper.

Abram's lonely search for answers was alleviated by John's company. Many evenings now John sat and debated with him, toasting stockinged feet at our hearth. I brought them pots of cocoa.

▼ ▲ ▼

LIKE the ladies of the congregation, Abram gave and gave and asked for nothing, which was lucky because I had nothing to give.

He, on the other hand, invented a world for me. I was broken and he put me together. I couldn't think, and he unscrambled my brain and made a life for me.

This one.

With infinite patience he taught me to drive the car my father had bought me, the Lincoln with leather seats. The car was a soft blue-gray, and I loved the way it smelled. Still, it was difficult for me to drive. It took concentrated effort because the controls were managed from the steering wheel. Mostly it was Pam who took it for spins.

Abram had the kitchen remodeled with new cabinets and easy-glide drawers. I began somewhat tentatively to do a little cooking. But Pam was so much quicker that she was soon doing the majority of the meals.

For a while Abram and I teamed up to prepare gourmet Sunday dinners. I was a great salad tosser and expert at arranging food to look appetizing. Abram did the serious cooking. He was a master of aromas. He claimed that sixty percent of what you think you taste, you really smell. Then one day I had a headache and Pam took over. And for some reason that's the way it seemed to fall out from then on: Pam freeing me of one more task.

One day a half-grown, forlorn Siamese cat found us. We fed her, petted her, and she took over. In no time she became a sleek beauty we called Ming-Ling. A favorite pastime for both Ming-Ling and me was to watch Abram shave. When he left the Believing Church the beard had come off. For him it was symbolic; for Ming-Ling and me the daily process of scraping off stubble was fascinating. I couldn't say why—except that Abram did it. So a small custom was initiated. But Pam didn't think it was hygienic to allow the cat on the counter.

I was thinking about this as I sat drowsing in the last of the sun. The warm June day was cooling off and I was glad of the throw Abram had tucked around me. Or was I? I didn't like the picture it generated—blanket, wheelchair, cripple. My mind jumped to the First Nation people of the Arctic Circle. They have a custom that when a member of the family is too old or too sick to contribute, they are set on an ice floe with a few days' provisions to gradually fall into frozen sleep. Cruel? No, it is the natural way. The proof is that it is the person herself who makes the decision and pushes off on the ice.

The Cree always begin stories by saying, "This is a true thing I tell you." So I suppose it's true about the ice floe and I wonder about the story Pam read me this morning. It was a Bible story. Genesis, I think, Abraham and Sarah. Sarah had an Egyptain slave girl whose name was Hagar. Sarah told Abraham to go in to her slave girl. And Abraham listened to the voice of Sarah, his wife.

I could hear Pam bustling about. She was very much at

home in my kitchen; she knew where everything was. Abram had gone in to lift out the roast. I could hear them laughing.

Abram came out. "The sun is almost gone. Let me bring you in."

I smiled at him.

"You were sitting here so quietly," he said, "I thought you'd fallen asleep."

"I was thinking of Bible stories. Do you have a favorite?"

"I hadn't thought about it."

"I do, the one about Abraham and his wife."

"Where Sarah conceives at the age of . . . "

"No, the part about Hagar."

Abram didn't answer, but released the brake on my chair. "What about Hagar?" he asked.

"Nothing much. Just that I like the story."

Pam called from the kitchen; he brought me into the living room and went to help her. He wouldn't attach importance to it now. Later he'd remember.

I didn't want to traumatize him further. I hoped he'd attribute it to my music. He'd think, "She couldn't live without her music." The truth is, Abram . . . I'm not in pain. I don't lack for anything. Everyone is kind to me. And from the beginning you've been Abram, which is my highest praise. But I can't live any longer without living.

People will say, "She knew success, fame, fortune. . . ." But I was what they made me: Mac, the agency men, producers, sound mixers, all those years. In that time of tinsel and glamour, there'd been no more than an occasional glimpse of me. So now there was not much to hold to. Too late I'd married Abram. Too late the Cree songs. Too late I became left-handed. The time of the benefit—I think I was meant to go then; it would have been a fitting climax.

Abram returned to wheel me to the table. Recently he seemed light of heart. The haggard look he'd worn had lifted. Just when had this happened? I tried to think back. My mind came to the night I made that discovery about my inability—about my body. And there it stalled. Perhaps he hadn't waited for my tacit complicity. Perhaps he had no need of Bible stories. Was it from that time that Pam had begun bustling about in my home so efficiently?

Abram sat beside me and took my hands. I think he wanted to talk about Abraham and Sarah and Hagar, but Pam came in with the roast on a platter.

It was a lovely dinner. I particularly enjoyed the cucumber salad.

Perhaps the simplest method would be to take the Lincoln for a spin. But what if I survived? I had a surer way. In my medicine cabinet were forty yellow-jacketed sleeping pills. Knowing they were there had made it possible to go on.

No more. Today it was over.

Why today?

Because it was like every other day—that's why.

After dinner I drifted off into a kind of dream state, in which I took off my clothes, discarding them one by one. Indians believe that disrobing in a dream is a sign of approaching death, a shucking off of the body.

A careful assessment would leave no doubt.

I'll begin with Mum. I ran out on her when I ran out on my brothers.

I went off with the first man who promised to take me to the bright lights.

But I wasn't good even for Jack. He was getting by just fine selling ponies and winning bar bets. I dragged him into showbiz, where he was outclassed. Gambler and drinker he was, but he had a wonderful gift for enjoying life. Until I came along.

I didn't treat Mac much better. It must have taken a lot for a man of his pride to keep begging me to marry him. I considered it a joke. But he thought of it as a fitting climax to a successful partnership, with me in the spotlight and him pulling the strings. The denouement was the appearance of Abram. He figured I'd marry Abram and he'd be left in the lurch, so he took another way. He figured he'd earned it. Consequently, instead of the wheeling and dealing he thrived on, he's stuck in some Caribbean hideout, shacked up with a local belle, paying off the *policia,* and bored, bored, bored to death—thanks to Kathy Little Bird.

Jim's case was next. I really let him down. Jim Gentle. A perfect name for him. A gentle, sweet person in this rough, uncaring, dog-eat-dog world. I let him teach me music and songwriting, I let him teach me lovemaking. Then, the moment I learned he had problems, I was gone. That it finally turned around, that he'd made it, in no way absolves me. It was one of those lucky breaks that happen.

Abram I saved for last. I'm ruining Abram's life by my dependence on him. He seemed ready, willing, and able to shoulder all the grief I brought with me. But what of the night he broke down and cried? It's not right to load it all on him. Mum used to say, "The weak eat up the strong." I hadn't known what that meant then, but I am doing that to Abram. Besides, how long can I go on playing the part of a housewife who doesn't keep her own house? Of a lover unable to feel or respond to sex?

Anything else?

Oh yes. Kathy Little Bird as mother. Leaving the main indictment out of the list was signficant. I can't bear thinking of my redhaired daughter.

So what does it add up to? I'm not a mother, not a lover, not a wife. I'll never walk again. I'll never sing again. The answer is forty gelatin capsules.

▾ ▴ ▾

PAM was humming as she stacked the dishwasher, and Abram, complaining that he'd been doing too much reading, went to check on a new shipment. I wheeled myself into the bathroom and poured out the yellow-jacketed pills. I knew how many there were. Forty. I counted them to make sure. I didn't want to do things halfway, make a mess for Abram.

I put all forty into an empty aspirin bottle, which I took to my bedside table. It wouldn't look suspicious there if anyone should see it. I had decided on tonight. I would go to sleep and not be a bother or make trouble, or stand in the way of Abram having a wife. Or anything, anymore.

I wandered out into the living room and, going to the piano, picked out my Cree Shadow Song with one finger. I thought Abram was still in the shop, but he came in through the house. I was struck by the way he stood there in the doorway looking at me.

"What would you think," he asked, "of a world of becoming?" I waited, knowing he had more to tell me. "You, me, the earth, the universe, God himself, all in the process of evolving." He advanced farther into the room. "And what would you think of a God that needed our help as much as we need his?"

"Hmm," I said.

If this solution lifted the burden he lived with, I liked it. I was glad that God, after years of banishment, was back in his life. I knew Abram would be happier with God.

"Thomas Aquinas says that God gave human beings two paths to understanding: the way of faith and the way of reason. But since there is only one truth, the two paths must arrive at the same conclusion."

"Are you there yet, Abram?"

"No. And I may never be. But it's enough to know that even though the two paths diverge sharply at the outset, they will join at the end, resolving all theological dissension, and produce pure thanksgiving."

He knelt beside my chair. "Once again you have brought light to my life."

"How?" I asked, because I really couldn't see how.

"By sitting there patiently listening to me even when you couldn't talk. By every once in a while wheeling yourself into the kitchen and fixing me a cup of hot chocolate. Kathy, I feel now what I was unable to as a boy—a call. Remember, you asked once how the call was heard. And I said it was felt through your entire body. That was right, Kathy. That's how it is."

I was glad for Abram, glad that the agony of doubt was lifted from him. It had been good for him to reason it all out with John. I was glad too that I had a part in it. But in case he would think I wasn't acting normally, I told him he was hopeless, the same dreamer he had always been.

He cheerfully agreed. "You're absolutely right, Kathy. But everything in the world got here by way of an idea—in God's mind or ours."

I laughed and threw the rest of the evening paper at him. He divided it, keeping the sports pages, carefully avoiding the entertainment section, and tossing me the editorials. I scanned it. Nothing of interest. I don't ordinarily read letters to the editor, but something caught my attention—a signature.

One of the letters was signed Kathy Mason.

A sharp quiver ran through me. Partly it was pain, but with it an inordinate alertness. I read with a concentration I hadn't been able to summon till that moment.

Kathy Mason wrote on behalf of a young man, a First Nation person. Lone Walker. That name had been in the papers recently. Wasn't that the Indian they were looking for in the murder of a Mountie?

The letter from Kathy Mason was written to say she was with Lone Walker at the time of the shooting. She asked for amnesty so he could come in and give himself up. He was, she wrote, an innocent man. . . .

The print blurred.

Kathy. It was my Kathy. And it seemed she was in love with Sam Lone Walker, wanted for murder. Jas hadn't said a thing about this, and Elk Woman, if she knew, decided I was in no condition to handle it.

If I had put this together correctly, then this was a girl in trouble.

This was a girl who needed her mother.

"When she needs you," Abram had said.

I remembered asking, "How will I know?" And his reply, typical Abram: "Have faith, you'll know."

I read the letter through again.

My poor child, what had she gotten herself mixed up with, and who? Why hadn't the Masons taken better care of her? Why had she been traipsing around Alberta on her own?

"Abram," I said, handing him the section. "Read this."

He ran his finger down to URANIUM STRIKE.

"No, no. Letters to the editor. The first one."

He read carefully and looked at me with a troubled expression. "You think it's her?"

"It's got to be."

"Call Jas before you jump to conclusions."

My fingers were trembling so that Abram took the phone and dialed for me.

"Look, Kathy," Jas said when he heard my voice, "I know I should have called you, but I didn't realize at first that she was involved with Lone Walker, who at best is a maverick and at worst a killer. How was I supposed to break something like this to you?"

"Oh my God."

"I guess I was wrong not to call, and I'm sorry, but . . ."

"I'm not angry, Jas. I can see how you felt. But what do we do now? That's my question."

"Well, she's determined to clear Lone Walker."

"And he won't give himself up?"

"No, they've thrown a bunch of new charges at him. He's convinced he'll be railroaded."

"And will he be?"

"In my opinion, he'll get a fair trial and then they'll hang him."

"If things change, Jas, phone me immediately. And this time do it." I hung up and looked at Abram.

"What next?" he asked. "Will you write her?"

"Write her and see her."

"Not without a plan. We need a plan if we're really going to help."

I clutched his arm. "Oh Abram, she needs me, just as you said she would. For the first time in my life Kathy needs me."

"What will you do?" Abram asked again.

"Spend the money my records are making. I'll write Kathy that I'm interested in the cause of indigenous people." I laughed shakily. "I'll say I read her letter in the *Standard,* her account of Lone Walker. I was touched by it and am offering financial support. They'll need a good lawyer."

"Go slow, Kathy. I don't want you hurt."

"It's Kathy Mason we've got to be thinking of. Can I count on you, Abram?"

He smiled at the question. I squeezed his hand.

Immediately my schizoid mind veered to the forty sleeping pills in the aspirin bottle. How could I have ever contemplated such a thing? Who would have been here for Kathy?

I wheeled myself into my room to retrieve them. . . .

They weren't there. I looked frantically on the floor, and felt behind the table in case the bottle had fallen down. This was one of those cases where you know before you look that it's not there, but you look anyway.

Frantically I opened the drawer in the table. My fingers searched to the very end of it. Of course there was no aspirin bottle; I had never put it there. Storm burst around me, while I at the center was untouched, able to think calmly.

Abram had found the pills. That was the only explanation. I thought back to my decision, back to the cucumber salad. He mentioned that he'd been doing too much reading, implying that he had a headache. He worked in the shop a short time, then must have gone to get an aspirin from the medicine cabinet. Finding them gone, he thought of my bedside table.

Instead of aspirin he found forty sleeping pills.

What had his reaction been? To talk to me of his return of faith. Knowing what I intended, he told me I had been a light to him. In Abramese that meant—I love you, I need you . . . Why couldn't Abram say things directly? Why was it so hard sometimes to figure him out?

I went back to the living room.

"I'm going to write her this minute," I said, and asked him to hand my stationery down to me. When he bent to place it in my lap, my arms went around him.

I wrote Kathy Mason care of the *Standard,* going over the letter several times to keep it businesslike.

I enclosed our number, and for days wouldn't answer the phone for fear I couldn't handle hearing my daughter's voice.

Finally she called.

Abram picked up, and motioned that it was Kathy.

I was at his elbow in a moment; the next the phone was in my hand and I heard her as though she were in the room. Voices are important to me. Hers was low, resonant, a good voice. She spoke decisively, asking if we could set up a meeting. "Of course," I agreed, I hope not too eagerly. *Keep it businesslike,* I reminded myself.

While thinking this, I was making the offer Abram and I had agreed on, of sending her a round-trip ticket to Montreal to initiate a Justice for Lone Walker campaign.

I could tell she was amazed, but she managed a casual tone, and we arranged to meet at the Mirabel airport.

Friday afternoon, two o'clock, at the baggage claim, I would see my daughter.

Abram wrote it all down and handed me the slip of paper.

I lifted my face to his. "She has a wonderfully warm voice."

Smiling, Abram completed the litany. "And beautiful red hair."

It was one of the few things I had known about her. Now I was to see for myself. Kathy Mason and I would know each other. The named and the namer.

Chapter Nineteen

No performance had ever put me on edge as the thought of the coming meeting. I couldn't settle to anything and was so nervous I was almost ill.

On the drive to the airport I reminded Abram once again that Kathy wasn't to know who I was. "I'm a wealthy eccentric, interested in—in causes. That's all she needs to know."

"It's the truth, isn't it?"

I had to laugh at his dry comment. "I guess it is at that. Oh Abram, do you think she'll like me?"

"I think you will get on very well. . . . Some time in the future I think you should tell her."

"Yes. Some time. If this goes well. Imagine, Abram, we'll be face to face. I never had the courage before. Who do you think she takes after? Me? Jack? My mum? I hope it's my mum. She was a wonderful woman, a strong woman."

"Well, Kathy Mason has certainly gone all out for that young man."

"She has, hasn't she? Lone Walker. Accused of murder." My laugh was a bit tremulous. ". . . You don't think he did it, do you?"

▾ ▴ ▾

Two hundred yards away I recognized her, trim figure and glorious red hair that cascaded to her shoulders. She gave the impression of being beautiful, except for the von Kerll nose, which is slightly crooked. If this was a defect, it added to her charm.

She came toward us holding out a slim hand.

I took it in mine and couldn't say a word.

"Mrs. Willems. I knew it had to be you."

It was Abram who answered, introducing himself and inquiring about her trip. I was content just taking her in. Eyes like Mum's, and that meant like mine too . . . black on black.

Abram drove us to a busy restaurant off the main thoroughfare. This quiet man, bless him, did most of the talking. We were lucky to find a table. I sat down across from my daughter.

I liked this girl. I liked everything about her.

I loved this girl! I loved everything about her!

It was Abram who drew out the story of Sam Lone Walker. His father had been an activist for self-rule by First

Nation people, whose dream had been to lay the case before the UN. But he had died as a result of the confrontation with U.S. marshals at Wounded Knee. His twelve-year-old son had witnessed it.

Kathy Mason's glance compelled us to see what this would mean for a boy of that age. When she went on she had herself under control. "He took on his father's crusade. He's in hiding now because there was an oil strike on Cree property. That's what this is all about. The oil companies on one side trying to buy up Indian land, and the Cree on the other, protesting. It's a holy site, where they hold their vision quests. Sam Lone Walker organized a demonstration. That's when the Mountie was killed. But I was there. I was with him—just as I said in my open letter. He didn't do it. He didn't even have a gun. I can testify to this."

Abram ordered for us. Neither Kathy Mason or I had looked at the menu.

Abram waited for the waitress to leave, leaned across the table, and asked, "Why did he run?"

"He knew they'd blame him. They consider him a troublemaker. This was their chance. There's unbelievable money at stake for the oil companies, billions of dollars, Mr. Willems."

I barely heard "oil companies, environmental damage, vision site"—I heard my daughter saying, *I love this man*. Saying, *help me save him*.

I saw my daughter's pain, felt her anxiety. I don't think she was as certain as she said that he would give himself up. But the conviction with which she spoke made it plain that her life was vested in him.

Abram was explaining the business end of our proposal to her. "What's needed is first-class legal help. Mrs. Willems has authorized me to write a check in the amount of twenty-five thousand dollars as a retainer."

Kathy Mason looked stunned. "I guess I don't quite understand. You represent a foundation that is concerned with aboriginal rights?"

She didn't pause for an answer. She was peering at me intently. "I know you," she exclaimed, interrupting herself and almost upsetting her water glass. "Aren't you—? Why, you're that famous singer. You're Kathy Little Bird."

"Shh," I said nervously, and glanced around at nearby tables. But the din was such that no one heard.

"I'm sorry," she said, realizing that the woman in the wheelchair might not want to be identified. "It came over me all at once who you are. I had the feeling from the beginning that you were someone I knew, or should know. No wonder—I have your albums. I'm a big fan. I think you're wonderful."

"Well," I said, to stem the tide, "that was a long time ago."

"Not really. Was it two or three years ago that you—?" She broke off, confused and embarrassed. How sweet, that she was embarrassed. It showed what a nice person she was, sensitive to another's misfortune.

"Yes." I spoke casually, trying to put her at ease. "It was a case of being in the wrong place at the wrong time."

"I remember . . . it was a concert some place . . . a riot. You were injured. It was in all the papers. But you're well now."

"Praise the Lord," Abram said, "that's the truth."

If she recalled the vituperative press, the hearing and deportation, she didn't let on. "Do you sing any more?" she asked. "Professionally, I mean?"

I tried to keep it light, and at the same time dismiss the subject. But Kathy Mason was on a crusade. She had a gleam in her eye. "Kathy Little Bird!" she said. "I can't believe I'm sitting here having lunch with you."

I smiled. She was so young. And she bought my albums. My voice had been in her room, part of her growing up. I wish I had known that.

"With a voice like yours," my daughter continued, "singing the way you do, I don't see how you could give it up."

"It gave me up," I said with a laugh.

"I'm afraid I don't believe you. It must be so difficult to do without music."

"Music wasn't always kind to me," I said.

"But you touched so many people, made such a difference."

"I never thought of it that way. It was just something I liked to do."

"You didn't realize the effect you had on people?"

"Not really."

"But you did. And you haven't changed. I mean, you're as beautiful as ever. And you did that benefit of ethnic music in . . . was it South Dakota? That's right, isn't it?" She rushed on, completely caught up in enthusiasm, "How marvelous it would be if we could organize a benefit for Lone Walker and the vision site, and you'd sing that same repertoire."

My mind jumped to the fatal benefit, as I heard my daughter say: "You would come out of retirement. If I could persuade you to do that—it would mean everything. More important even than a lawyer, your singing would bring everyone to the cause. They wouldn't dare railroad Sam then. And the oil company would be beaten once everyone knew what they were up to. Is there a chance you could be persuaded to sing again?"

"It's a totally impossible idea. I haven't sung in three years, not a note."

Kathy Mason shrank back against the leather of the booth. "I'm sorry," she said. "It's just that it came over me how wonderful it would be. Not that I don't appreciate what you're doing, it's unbelievably generous. And as you say, it will get us a first-rate lawyer. But the other side will have lawyers too, a battery of them. I'm sure it will come right in the end because we have the truth on our side. Sam Lone Walker is innocent. Still, who knows? They could fabricate evidence, bribe witnesses, all the things they do."

I had not expected Abram to enter this conversation. He did. "I think young Kathy Mason has the idea of a lifetime. Come out of retirement, sing for Lone Walker, sing for the environment." He was so carried away that I almost thought he would say, "Sing for your daughter—" but he caught himself and finished rather tamely, "You'd be a sensation."

"I've *been* a sensation," I said wearily, "and look what it got me."

Then I saw the disappointment in my daughter's eyes. It was the only thing she had ever asked of me.

I berated Abram all the way home. "You took her side. Why? Why? Why did you do that? Why did you let me agree? I've got myself in too deep. I can't do it. I don't have any voice left. I can't possibly go through with a wild, hare-brained scheme like this. I have to get out of it. You know I haven't sung in years. It would be a fiasco. I'd be pathetic. . . . They strike up the music, I come out in a wheelchair, I open my mouth, and out comes a croak. Besides . . . I'm too old."

"Old? Who's old? You're thirty-six and you look twenty-six. Sitting across from you I couldn't tell which was the daughter."

"Stop it, Abram. It's your fault. I can't go through with it . . . and I can't disappoint her. Oh Abram, isn't she lovely! A lovely girl. And did you notice?"

"Of course. She's left-handed, just like her mum."

I allowed myself only a moment before answering, then started in again, marshaling the myriad reasons why a benefit featuring Kathy Little Bird was out of the question. I argued, I yelled, just as I used to. I carried on and convinced myself all over again of the impossibility of it.

I kept it up even after we arrived home and ended locking myself in the bathroom, this time not to count pills. Now I had something to live for. At the deepest level, at the Sargasso Sea level, I wanted to disprove everything I'd concluded.

Tentatively I let out a single note, cautiously, more spoken than sung, more breathed than spoken. I tried a scale, also barely more than a whisper. The line was almost inaudible, but it was true. It was on pitch. It had timbre. The Little Bird sound was there, waiting to be coaxed out.

I tried broken chords, a third, a fifth, an octave jump. I added words, snatches of songs. Elk Woman's Cree melodies, the Wind Song, the Shadow Song. I heard them in the bones of my head, I heard them flung back at me from the four walls.

Abram, on the other side of the door, expelled his breath in relief.

The music that I had disavowed, that I had kept resolutely choked down, reemerged.

I unlocked the bathroom, once more my rehearsal hall, threw it wide open, and came wheeling out singing at the top of my lungs.

Abram was transfixed.

Before he could speak, I asked, "What about the wheelchair?"

"Your voice is back. The chair? That's irrelevant."

▾ ▴ ▾

ABRAM was right, and he was wrong. My voice was back, but it was far from my old sound. I had been so amazed and excited to hear a musical note issue from my lips that I jumped to the conclusion I was myself again. And Abram elevated a phenomenon into a miracle. He kept repeating "Praise the Lord" under his breath and, when I asked him for constructive criticism, shook his head as if perfection could not be improved.

The truth, as I discovered next morning when I tried to rehearse, was that my voice, although there were flashes of the old brillance, was creaky, cranky, and undependable. It would break in unexpected places, vanish completely at others, and become reedy on a high note.

It needed work, work, work. I remembered how Jim Gentle's activist sentiments had wakened a tardy sense of myself as Indian. When I was a kid, I'd figured out I was forty percent Cree. That was as far as it went; my ethnicity had never played a part in my life. With Jim's passion for causes, my own sense of identity awoke, and for the first time I'd followed the treatment of Indians on both sides of the border. But I turned from this when I turned away from him. Now, though, the prospect of reviving the program I'd worked out and almost sung gave me a spiritual high. It was more intense than even the songs themselves. I felt like the prodigal son. I had returned. I felt myself to be part of the First Nation people.

This benefit I would sing through to the end.

It gave me a nostalgic pleasure to get in touch with Jim Gentle.

"Kathy!" he said at the sound of my voice. "My God, you sound like yourself."

"I've come a long way. I don't walk and probably never will. But I sing."

"You sing?"

"Yes, I do. I'm calling because I need you to organize another benefit. Can you do it? You'd have to drop everything. Will you?"

"Upside down, inside out, standing on my head and yodeling. What guts, Kathy. I'm proud of you, proud that you call on me. Whatever you want, it's done."

"What I want is to do the concert we tried for, and this time finish it. Incidentally, I'm not doing it as a way to return to show business. It would just be this once."

"If it's not a comeback, what is behind it?"

"Would you believe—I'm doing it to feel good about myself."

"That's the best reason."

His laugh made me remember. I remembered our jam sessions, our work sessions. I remembered the good stuff.

▼ ▲ ▼

GENTLE flew in.

It didn't hit me the way it once had. I was able to look at him and know I was happy just to see him, that he was a good friend. One who didn't come around at all seasons—only when music was concerned. That was the part of me he loved, and I was glad to have figured it out.

We set our sights on late August. It would be tight but we could do it. Besides getting myself and my voice in shape, there were a million things to attend to. I rented a studio downtown and Jim managed to drop by every day to hammer out repertoire. Sometimes he just listened. Jim hadn't changed. He lived life in a major key, throwing himself totally into the moment. He planned the build of the program, without in any way neglecting the smallest nuance. He pounced on my failure to hold a note, and criticized my diction. He was meticulous. He listened with his pores. His truth was music.

Gentle didn't waste time on regrets. He never alluded to old involvements, never pitied me, but accepted that this was a new moment in time and this was the way I was. He didn't think of me as a cripple or even handicapped, but imposed hellishly long hours on us both.

During one of our quick lunch breaks I told him that my

CDs were now being distributed by a new firm, Doric. "They bought out the old company."

"Yeah," Jim grinned, "I know." He stood up, drew himself to his full height of six foot five, and said, "Meet Doric Recording Company."

"You? You're Doric?"

"I knew way back, the minute I heard you, you were something special. You have what I call . . . *floyt.* If you don't have it, you can sing like an angel and it means nothing. But when you got it . . . well! . . . So I raised money and made an investment. I bought up all your singles, albums, everything. I got you cheap because of the lousy publicity, being booted out of the country and all. Then I waited. Let it die down, until all anyone remembered is your sound.

"And now we're starting to make it big-time, releasing your stuff slowly, feeding it into the market. You were always good for me, Kathy. And I'm glad, really glad that I have a chance to be good for you."

He allowed only for a warm exchange of smiles before we were at it again. We worked at top speed, battling out our differences.

Gentle carried off a marvelous coup. I was still prevented from entering the U.S., but he got around that by recalling that in the fabulous fifties Paul Robeson, the great black baritone, had also been at odds with the INS, and told if he left the United States he would not be allowed back. His advance people scoured possible concert sites and hit on a great spot. A Peace Arch erected in an international park where Blaine, Washington borders on Canada. The arch is constructed of dazzling white concrete and the marine park where it's located is a neutral area spanning the boundary of the two countries, commemorating their friendship. Citizens of both countries come together without border passes. There is an outdoor amphitheater and awesome views of Point Roberts, Vancouver Island, and the San Juans. So Robeson gave a memorable concert under the arch. "And," Gentle finished up, "so will you."

▼ ▲ ▼

I STOLE time to have coffee with my daughter. Just to look at her was a tonic. The Wertheimers gave her their attic room, but I never saw her. She'd been sitting in on the planning of Lone Walker's defense, and it took all her time. As a result she was flushed with excitement one minute, pale and nervous the next. Though she tried to present a calm exterior, I sensed that she was near panic. I think she believed Lone Walker, who had eluded capture, might show up at the concert, might even turn himself in.

"He's really a wonderful person, Mrs. Willems, full of ideals, in a world that doesn't work that way. By now, he must know I'm working to help him. And yet he isn't in touch."

"Perhaps he's afraid of a trap."

"You mean, that the concert is a set-up? He'll see that for himself . . . police everywhere. It would be easy to take him."

"Don't worry. He'll give himself up when he's ready, not before." I leaned across the table. "You love him."

"Yes, I do. And it's going to be hard to explain to Mom

and Dad Mason. They're the wonderful people who brought me up. But they won't understand any of this: the benefit . . . you, the famous singer . . . and, on top of it, a wanted man. They'll think I'm crazy. I know that."

My voice was almost inaudible. "What about your biological family, the ones you came to find?"

"Actually, I found my uncle Jas. He's a great guy, owns a pub on the outskirts of St. Alban's."

"Was he the only relative?"

"There was a brother, who's dead."

At this unexpected reference to Morrie I was jarred into a different reality, but Kathy's voice brought me back. "I also met my father, but I don't want to talk about him."

My God—Jack. Something else Jas didn't tell me. It's a wonder it hadn't all come out. Of course Jack was still on the payroll and too sharp to kick a good thing. I had Mac to thank for that. But I wondered if he'd been tempted.

When I told him about it, Abram put a bookmark in the volume he was reading. "You know, you can't hide things forever."

"I know. But I need this time to become friends."

Abram knows when not to talk, when to put his arms around me.

My father came. I had invited him, but never expected him to actually come. He flew in the day before the benefit. I dropped by his hotel after Gentle and I finished for the day.

It couldn't be casual between us. And I could see he had steeled himself against seeing me after two years still in a chair.

I thanked him again for coming. "It means a lot to me."

He responded with the gallantry natural to him. "It means a great deal to me to be here, to see you take hold like this. Overcoming the odds. It reminds me of—of the circumstances I had to deal with. I refer to the amputation. I was in a chair for quite a while, and then crutches. If it hadn't been for your mother . . ."

"I know from Mum that you handled it extremely well. I didn't. For instance, this concert . . . I didn't take the initiative. It's for my daughter. I've met her, Erich, and gotten to know her a bit. She's just as I imagined." And I told him how it had come about. Taking my father's hand, I said, "She doesn't know. She has no idea who I am. Right now she's grateful to me. I can't jeopardize this. It's more than I deserve, much more."

He patted my hand and nodded.

"You'll meet her after the performance, in my dressing room. You'll love her instantly, as I did. There's a spirited quality about her, and . . .

"And her name is Kathy," he finished for me.

"I must have your word that you'll say nothing."

"But of course." And then, "Are you sure that's the way you want it?"

An emphatic "Yes" left no doubt. "There's something else, even more difficult to carry out. So difficult that I'll need your help."

His look was an unformulated question.

I blurted out the decision I had forced myself to make. "After the concert I'm not going back to Abram."

I could see his shock. "Not going back? Did I hear you?"

"Yes. Yes you did. I'm damaged, even more than you can tell by looking at me. I'm not able to be a wife to Abram. The only thing I can do is try to be fair."

This time the pause was protracted.

"Does he know about this?"

"I need to get the concert out of the way. Then I'll tell him."

"I can't believe this is right, Kathy . . . for either of you."

"Only because I won't let him go. But there is a young woman who is devoted to him."

"And he? I don't hear you saying he is devoted to her."

"That's because, oh you know how Abram is. He wouldn't let himself even think . . . But if I weren't around . . . Don't you see, he could have a life."

My father shook his head, unconvinced.

▼ ▲ ▼

It was thrilling to hold our event at Peace Arch, simply to know there was such a place in the world dedicated to people, to peace, and to music. They wheeled me on stage in the dark, a roving spot found me, and the combined audience of Canadians and Americans exploded in applause. It was only minutes since I'd screamed at Abram that I couldn't possibly do it.

Then this blinding applause. Blinding because tears got in the way of sight. Abram was right, the wheelchair was invisible. A hundred thousand people were telling me they were glad I was back.

They were glad I was here, glad I was going to sing to

them. As I faced this blur of humanity, another spot came on, and its rose gelatin wiped out the world.

I had dug out my old wind-band and tied it across my forehead. I was singing for my daughter tonight. And for the Grandmothers who had guided her to me. I sang music drawn from the earth itself, intoned by Elk Woman as she baked bread, soaked hides, and drew stick figures on soft bark.

I began the first number with its low, throbbing notes, a song of shadows, elongated, flickering as though in firelight, but a staccato beat stole in and out of related time. Sung neither in English or in Cree, it was a boy and girl trading shadows. It was the moon, a shimmering resonance, showing its scarred face. It was Mother Earth weeping to her children, rehearsing her wounds—mineshafts and oil wells. The forests laid bare their old growth, dismantled and dead. No one can express betrayal like the Indian.

My voice thundered, cried, laughed, beguiled. Past the endless drift of possibilities I sang the years, I sang death, I sang rebirth, I sang it all. And in singing the spiritual values and the striving of the Indian, I sang my Mum as she'd be today. I sang my grandfather, who was dying even when he came to me. I sang my father, who had claimed me. I sang the AIM warrior, Sam Lone Walker, who I didn't know, but who my daughter loved. The one person I couldn't sing was Abram. The nearest I came was to sing the love that my mind felt and my body was denied—a plaintive, half-frenzied lament.

The audience was startled. They had never heard such weird juxtapositions of chords.

Silence hung over the arch, over the crowd. I couldn't see them and now I couldn't hear them. I only knew the audience was absolutely silent.

Spellbound? Captivated? Traumatized?

Was it a silence of resentment?

Then . . . a rush!

A roar!

I was wrapped in the thunder of a hundred thousand clapping hands, of calls, of shouts. Warriors in ancient lands, in ancient times, ate the heart of a brave enemy to make those qualities their own. The audience did that to me. They took my heart. It was too fierce to be love. And yet it was. They made me theirs.

I was pelted with flowers, bouquets tossed in my lap.

They surged onto the stage. They overwhelmed me. Jim, watching from the wings, saw my panic, as I thought *shoes*—patent leather, wingtips, loafers, workman's boots.

He hustled me off stage and into the dressing room. He shut the door, but not on everyone. Somehow there were promoters, agents, producers, old friends, and acquaintances all talking at once.

Abram, excited as I've ever seen him, swept me into his arms. "You've done it, Kathy!"

For an iridescent, soap bubble moment I gloried in it. Gentle too, was quivering, triumphant, on fire. "The music," he gasped out. "You and the audience hyped each other in some miraculous way. I've never heard you sing like this, Kathy. Do you realize it puts you back on top? It's as though none of that stuff that happened, happened. You're bigger than ever, and in the way you want. You did it on your own terms. Not many do it that way."

"Oh Gentle, I still hear it in my head. You were the one who told me a singer doesn't hear herself the way other people do but through the bones in her head. Well, the bones in my head are still ringing."

But it was my daughter's praise I was tuned to. My mum's eyes shone through Kathy's, shone with gratitude.

The moment was right.

If I was going to tell her, this was the time. I had, as I told my father, very good reasons against it. But suppose I came out with it . . . or would it be better to lead up to it? If I did it carefully, cautiously, taking cues from her reaction—I'd lose my courage. "Grit your teeth," I told myself, "and simply say, 'I'm your mother, Kathy.'"

Then what? What did I expect? That she would hug me with newfound joy? That she would thank me for claiming her at last? At last, after eighteen years? More likely she'd look at me, and a stunned, strained silence would set in. "It took you almost twenty years to make me part of your life? You say you're my mother. I *have* a mother. All I know of you is your albums. . . ."

I was conscious of Abram looking at me with concern. He spoke to Kathy, who came over to say good-bye and thank me once more.

She hugged me, and kissed me.

Kathy was hugging me, kissing me. I was holding my girl. I never dared dream this; I'd been afraid to imagine it. It was only for a moment, but my entire life was in that moment.

I was her friend.

"Lone Walker was too smart to come in. I was right about the police being everywhere," she whispered.

I squeezed her hand. I had her confidence. This was more than I ever thought to have of Kathy. My daughter was part of my life—if I was careful, if I didn't mess up. If I didn't tell her.

Abram still watched me. I put on a smile and introduced her to Erich von Kerll.

"Your father?" She turned to Erich. "You must be so proud."

He bowed over Kathy's hand, very European. She was charmed. There was a strong resemblance between grandfather and granddaughter. I was charmed.

The next moment I was also saying good-bye to her.

Goodbye, wonderful redhaired Kathy Mason of Oakdale Street. I promised myself to tell her. I would soon. But not tonight.

Abram escorted her out, arranging to send an accounting of the proceeds of the benefit and meet with the attorney who had undertaken Lone Walker's case. Good-byes, even happy ones, are hard. What about the other kind? Could I face up to that?

My father was pressing my hand. "That was she? That lovely young lady? You are to be congratulated she is back in your life."

"Yes, I believe she is."

"What a marvelous success tonight. And the offers that I hear discussed at every hand . . ."

"Stay close to me," I whispered to my father. I would have liked to rest, but contracts were thrust at me, deals proposed, percentages suggested. Jim Gentle looked at everything, talked to everyone. He was in his element.

Abram looked bewildered.

As for me? I found myself listening.

This was a last chance, one that wouldn't come again. The offer that appealed to me, that I felt I could make work, that I felt I had the strength for, was a recording deal to do the program I'd sung tonight. It was open-ended, leaving it to me how many I would do. I'd be singing my own songs, songs of the Alberta prairie and of a people that didn't die and didn't go away. Their music had been accepted here tonight, received in a spirit of openness. The audience had become part of the dream that Cree music is made of. If I did an album my strange, ethnic music would be another thread in the multihued tapestry of musical America.

As Little Bird I had finally learned how to soar. Now, when my body was broken, when I couldn't even love my love, I'd soared, my motorized vehicle and I.

Abram had come back in and withdrawn to a corner of the room.

Show time!

I maneuvered my chair past an MCA packager and Gentle, who were tallying percentages. Gentle caught my sleeve. "This is it, Kathy. You sang your stuff and made them listen. You've found your audience, and they've found you—they are the global young in tune with the earth." He bent down to my ear. "This is for you, Kathy, something you'll be able to handle. You cut as many or as few CDs as you want. It's up to you."

"Sounds good," I said and wheeled past him.

I joined Abram; I had revved myself to follow through. Not with yellow-jacketed pills, not with death—but with life.

I was conscious of my father standing by as I'd asked. Going up to Abram, I took his hand. "Thank you, Abram. Once again you pulled me through. This concert proved that I can survive on my own. And that's the way it's got to be, Abram."

Always quick to sense my mood, he looked worried, but not unduly so.

"You tried hard, Abram. But the things I want to be for you, I can't be."

He was beginning to understand. "How do you know what I want?" he asked, almost harshly.

I lashed out with it. "You're a man, Abram. And I'm no longer a woman."

"The concert was a miracle, Kathy, a miracle from the Lord. What makes you think he doesn't have more in his pocket?"

I allowed myself to touch his cheek, to run my hand over the shock of thick blond hair. "I'm leaving you."

"Kathy, don't you think we may need each other?"

"I don't need you. Isn't that wonderful?"

He didn't reply to that, at least not directly. When he finally spoke, it was to say in a low, husky voice, "What's wonderful is that we traded shadows."

That was not fair of him.

My good intentions teetered, ready to crash, so much rubble. "Abram, for God's sake, run. This is your chance. Take it. Be free."

"Free? Free for what? I asked that a long time ago. And it comes down to this: I can't get a good shave without you and Ming-Ling cheering me on, or study without an occasional cup of hot chocolate."

I made an effort to marshal my forces, to follow through, to continue, to do the magnanimous thing. It's curious—you're always learning about yourself. I could kill myself, but I couldn't wheel myself out of his life. As for being magnanimous, it just isn't part of my nature.

I gave up. It was good to be defeated.

Abram bent over me and our shadows blended.

My father kissed me as though bestowing a blessing and left. I looked up at Abram. Like two schoolkids, it felt as though we were just starting out. Later, when we were alone, I told him about the recording deal.

Immediately he figured out how we could do it. "I'll fit up the storeroom as a studio." Why had I agonized about Abram not fitting in? He fit in, with a saw and a chisel and a paintbrush. In other words, in his own distinctively Abram way.

▾ ▴ ▾

WHEN we got back home, Pam was gone.

"Pam?" he said, as though he had trouble recalling her name. "We don't need her any more."

"No," I said, "we don't."

That same night—I don't know how it came about—I don't even know who initiated what—when Abram held me my heart gave a kind of caper, because I felt for the first time, certain stirrings. Like what had happened to my mind and my speech, sensation was returning. I had no doubt that soon we would be like any old married people.

A cadence filled my head. I still couldn't sing Abram. I had a good start though: the boy and girl of the Shadow Song. Then a strong tonic chord indicated that, although I couldn't manage to get the different parts of him into a single song, maybe when we'd been together a few years longer . . . like maybe fifty.

Lucinda and John come over many evenings. John and Abram sit before the fire, and Abram continues to expound the many turnings and twistings of his search for faith.

John listens and nods, and puts an occasional question.

"God relies on us, John. It's a wonder."

The two of them put their feet on the grating and wonder together.

Lucinda worried about the unorthodox discussions taking place before the fire. But I told her that Abram's mind was peaceful, and no matter in what form it appeared, peace was from God. That settled her down. Later that evening she helped me prepare cocoa in the kitchen. "I never noticed before. You're left-handed."

"Praise the Lord," was my answer.